"HIS VISIONS AND IMAGINATION ARE
STRONGER THAN EVER . . . WHETHER ONE
READS THE BOOK AS A PARABLE OF MODERN
CIVILIZATION AND ITS DISCONTENTS OR AS
AN UNADULTERATED FANTASY, ONE IS
INDELIBLY TRANSFIXED."
—*Library Journal*

"The writing—terse, colloquial, evocative—makes
this ambitious history lesson seem an enchanting
evening around the fireside."
—*Time*

"THE WRITING, LIKE A POLISHED DIAMOND,
IS PERFECTLY HEWED . . . MR. SINGER'S
CHARACTERS ARE AS WITTY AND FUNNY AS
EVER, OFFERING GENEROUS AND ODD
INSIGHTS INTO LIFE."
—*Atlanta Journal and Constitution*

ISAAC BASHEVIS SINGER has been awarded both
the Nobel Prize for Literature and the Pulitzer Prize,
as well as the National Book Award. He has written
nine novels, ten collections of short stories, and
many books for children. *The Death of Methuselah and
Other Stories* is available in a Plume edition.

NOVELS

The Manor [*I. The Manor* • *II. The Estate*]
The Family Moskat • *The Magician of Lublin*
Satan in Goray • *The Slave* • *Enemies, A Love Story*
Shosha • *The Penitent* • *The King of the Fields*

STORIES

Gimpel the Fool • *A Friend of Kafka* • *Short Friday*
The Séance • *The Spinoza of Market Street* • *Passions*
A Crown of Feathers • *Old Love* • *The Image*
The Death of Methuselah

MEMOIRS

In My Father's Court

FOR CHILDREN

A Day of Pleasure • *The Fools of Chelm*
Mazel and Shlimazel or The Milk of a Lioness
When Shlemiel Went to Warsaw
A Tale of Three Wishes • *Elijah the Slave*
Joseph and Koza or The Sacrifice to the Vistula
Alone in the Wild Forest • *The Wicked City*
Naftali the Storyteller and His Horse, Sus
Why Noah Chose the Dove
The Power of Light
The Golem

COLLECTIONS

The Collected Stories
Stories for Children
An Isaac Bashevis Singer Reader

Isaac Bashevis Singer

THE KING
OF
THE FIELDS

A PLUME BOOK

NEW AMERICAN LIBRARY

A DIVISION OF PENGUIN BOOKS USA INC., NEW YORK
PUBLISHED IN CANADA BY
PENGUIN BOOKS CANADA LIMITED, MARKHAM, ONTARIO

Copyright © 1988 by Isaac Bashevis Singer

All rights reserved. For information address Farrar, Straus,
Giroux, Inc., 19 Union Square West, New York, NY 10003.

Translated from the Yiddish, *Der Kenig vun di Felder,* by the author.

This is an authorized reprint of a hardcover edition published by
Farrar, Straus, Giroux, Inc., and published simultaneously in
Canada by Collins Publishers.

Original hardcover designed by Constance Fogler

 PLUME TRADEMARK REG. U.S. PAT. OFF. AND FOREIGN COUNTRIES
REGISTERED TRADEMARK—MARCA REGISTRADA
HECHO EN BRATTLEBORO, VT., U.S.A.

SIGNET, SIGNET CLASSIC, MENTOR, ONYX, PLUME,
MERIDIAN and NAL BOOKS are published *in the United States*
by New American Library, a division of Penguin Books USA Inc.,
1633 Broadway, New York, New York 10019, and *in Canada* by
Penguin Books Canada Limited, 2801 John Street, Markham,
Ontario L3R 1B4

LIBRARY OF CONGRESS CATALOGING-IN-PUBLICATION DATA
Singer, Isaac Bashevis, 1904-
　　[Kenig fun di felder.　English]
　　The king of fields / Isaac Bashevis Singer.
　　　　p.　cm.
　　Translation of: Der kenig fun di felder.
　　ISBN 0-452-26312-3
　　I. Title.
PJ5129.S49K413　　　1989
839'.0933—dc20　　　　　　　　　　　　　　　　89-12287
　　　　　　　　　　　　　　　　　　　　　　　　CIP

First Plume Printing, November, 1989

1　2　3　4　5　6　7　8　9

PRINTED IN THE UNITED STATES OF AMERICA

Contents

PART ONE

1

Krol Rudy, the Red King

THE story begins—when? The calendar of the Romans was not yet known in the land called Poland. The country was divided into many regions, with small settlements of pagans serving various gods. Agriculture was known but not widely practiced. The men hunted and fished, and the women dug roots and with little effort picked berries and fruits which the earth lavished on them in season. There was talk that, while people increased, the animals in the forest and the fish in the rivers and lakes were growing scarce. There were rumors that in faraway places, somewhere along the Vistula, many people were cultivating fields, plowing, sowing, reaping, thrashing. They called themselves Poles because in their language *pola* meant field.

These people were not one nation. They were ruled by kings called *krols*, who often fought one another. Some Poles forged iron swords and spears, attacked tribes of hunters, subjugated them, and forced them to work the fields. This is what happened to a small tribe of forest dwellers called Lesniks, not far from the Zakopane mountains. A krol had come riding through with his band of fighters, called *woyaks*. They killed off most of the young Lesnik men and ordered the survivors to clear the trees from a tract of land, plow it, then sow it with seeds they had brought along—wheat, rye, barley, oats. There the krol settled down with his men and waited for the crops to ripen. The survivors, mostly women and old men, muttered among themselves: "Who has the patience to wait so long?" But still they were forced to plow and to sow. The smallest hint of rebellion was severely punished. The krol with his *pans*, or *kniezes*—nobles or knights —could communicate with the Lesniks because they shared the same language, although they spoke it with certain variations.

The krol was a tall man. His eyes were blue and he had a thick mane of red hair and a fiery red beard. His men called him Krol Rudy, the red king. Krol Rudy could have had his pick of the many young and pretty maidens captured by the woyaks, but he had vowed not to marry until the green shoots came up in the fields. Krol Rudy wore a short fur vest, trousers made of animal hides, and leather boots. He and his kniezes had come into the camp on horseback, but the woyaks had arrived on foot, without shoes. Krol Rudy himself had shown the Lesniks how to work the wooden plows.

The old Lesnik men and women predicted that the seeds Krol Rudy planted would rot, be eaten by birds, or freeze in the winter. They warned that those who plowed the soil desecrated Mother Earth, and that the goddess Baba Yaga, who flew about on a broomstick as long as a spruce tree,

in her wrath would spread darkness over the world and cause
a pestilence to destroy man and beast. But the young women
admired Krol Rudy; when he was not shouting at them, he
smiled at them. He rode about on a white horse with a fancy
bridle and reins. While the Lesniks lived in tents, Krol Rudy
and his kniezes had cabins built for themselves, with roofs
which kept out the rain and chimneys which let out the
smoke. Krol Rudy supervised their construction, making sure
that the beams fitted snugly, without holes or gaps.

The young women, as they are wont to do, quickly adapted
themselves to the new rulers. They lay with them and soon
bore their offspring. The old men and women, on the other
hand, complained that the Poles were a band of savage murderers who did not serve the gods properly, abolished old
and venerated customs, and disrupted the life of the camp.
The old people had one consolation—death. Many of them
died that winter, not only of disease, but of distress over the
strange new ways.

The winter months dragged on, cold and bitter. Even the
Polish conquerors went hungry and had to slaughter some
of their horses and eat them. A few women miscarried; many
infants died. The woyaks tried to hunt in the forests, but
unlike the Lesniks, they were ignorant of the animals' habits
and hiding places. Most of the woyaks had been raised by
parents who tilled the soil, and they knew little of trapping
animals and fishing. Some of them plotted to desert Krol
Rudy and return to their homes. But Krol Rudy had his
informers, and he had the chief conspirators beheaded. Besides, other krols were ruling where the woyaks had come
from. Once warriors left their homes and took to the road
to loot and kill, the way back was closed for them.

Before the cold had set in, the Poles sent the girls and women to pick baskets of blackberries, blueberries, gooseberries, currants, cherries, apples, plums, and whatever fruit generous Mother Earth had produced during the warm months. The women took a portion of the produce to their families, and brought the rest as a tax to the rulers. Krol Rudy had warned that those who took too much for themselves and left not enough for his men would have their hands chopped off. But instead of eating the fruits and the berries, the woyaks used them to make an intoxicating beverage, called vodka. After they drank it, they staggered about half naked, bellowed bawdy songs, shrieked abuses. Later they returned to their huts and beat up their new wives. Some girls who were serving the kniezes also tried the intoxicating drink, and were soon giggling, hiccupping, shrieking, and falling into each other's arms. The old people grumbled that the krol and his men were undoubtedly possessed by demons. In the mountains there lived a spirit the people called a *smok*. The smok was part man, part snake, part devil. He played all sorts of tricks on people, dazzled their eyes, confused their senses. At his command was a host of gnomes, witches, bloodsuckers, all of whom carried out his nasty errands. Some old women muttered that Krol Rudy himself was a smok in disguise, and a sorcerer.

So many woyaks had died during the cold days and long nights that it almost seemed no one would live to see spring. But all at once the sun broke through the clouds and the days became warm and bright. And all over the fields which the Lesniks had sown, the grain began to sprout—later to be baked into bread, or *chleb*. The trees blossomed. Starlings, swallows, storks returned from distant places and hastened to build nests or repair old ones. Krol Rudy sent a drummer around to address the people. He called the Lesniks brothers. He told them that enemies were lurking and waiting to lay waste their camp and to set fire to their fields. But he, Krol Rudy, would protect them and foil their plans. He also announced that he had chosen a maiden from among them to wed on the day of the first moon. He wanted to establish a blood bond between himself and the Lesniks. He said the girl he had chosen was named Laska. A cry of joy erupted in the crowd. There was singing, dancing, clapping. The mighty krol had chosen a girl of their stock for his bride.

Everyone in the camp knew Laska, whose mother and two sisters and brothers had perished in the massacre. Laska herself had been raped. Her grandmother Mala, who had hidden in the bushes during the raid, feared that Laska might carry her attacker's child, but fortunately the girl's menstrual period had come on time. Together with the other girls, Laska picked fruit and berries for the woyaks that summer, and that was when Krol Rudy had seen her. He asked for her name, and sent her a gift. Now when he announced that she was to be his krolowa, his queen, the women looked around, and only then realized that Laska and her grandmother were not among them.

Laska, it was quickly learned, was ill. She lay on a pile of hides in her grandmother's tent, her body hot. Mala prepared a potion from a mixture of herbs, but the girl did not respond. When the women came with the good tidings, Mala said, "Laska is going to die. She refuses to eat." After a while Krol Rudy arrived, surrounded by some of his men. The girl's eyes were closed, her blond hair disheveled, her face pale. Krol Rudy shook his head. He asked Mala if she had other relatives, and the old woman answered, "Her father is hiding in the mountains. Your woyaks killed everyone else."

"What is her father's name?"

"Cybula."

"I want him to come back. I promise not to harm him."

"No one has heard from him. He may be dead," the old woman said. "And to what should he return? Our lives here have been uprooted like trees in a windstorm."

"When a tree is uprooted, another grows in its place," Krol Rudy answered. "If Laska does not die, she will be my wife and bear my children. When the wheat ripens in the fields, there will be bread enough for everyone."

"Soon she will be dead."

"Give her plenty of water to drink."

"Tomorrow she will be with her mother and the other spirits in the hollows of the earth. Soon I shall be with them, too."

Krol Rudy cast a last glance at the ailing girl and left. He wore his sword in a leather sheath. In the land from which he came, near the Vistula, blacksmiths hammered out iron swords, spears, horseshoes. Ships arrived from regions where the Germans lived—Niemcies they were called, mute ones, because they babbled in a language no one understood. Most of the men in Krol Rudy's tribe tilled the soil and raised crops. The Germans supplied them with scythes and spades, as well as saws, hammers, nails, axes. In exchange the Poles gave them honey, flax, barley, fruits, skins, and wood for lumber. All these transactions were conducted in sign language. Unfortunately, the Poles always warred among themselves. Every few years some new krol or another chieftain would rise up and lead his men on a rampage. They killed, looted, raped, set fire to homes and crops, drove off herds of cattle. Krol Rudy himself had barely escaped with his life during one such attack. Later he assembled a band of woyaks, and together they set off in search of regions where people subsisted by hunting and gathering. It was easy to subdue such people. Bows and arrows were their only weapons. With a sword and a spear the world was open to men who did not hesitate to spill blood or to perish in battle.

Now Krol Rudy and his kniezes left the tent and returned to their cabins. Laska seemed to him almost lifeless. It grieved Krol Rudy that he had not been informed of her illness, but it was his own fault. He seldom confided to his men what he was preparing to do. They were drunk much of the time and could not be trusted to hold their tongues. Each of them sought only what he could gain for himself, whereas he, Krol Rudy, took care of them all. The truth was, he had had his fill of the roaming, the looting, the fighting. He wanted to settle in one place, have wives, children, and rule over a people which had plenty to eat. He was hoping for a good harvest. Those who lived off the fields had to acquire the forethought and the patience not to devour every last bit of grain, and to put aside a portion for sowing.

But harvest time was still a long way off. Krol Rudy regretted having permitted his woyaks to kill so many men. There was no one left to do the hunting. Also, several of his spies informed him that the Lesniks who had escaped to the mountains were preparing a surprise attack. They were waiting for hunger to weaken the camp and then, in the dark of night, they would set fire to the fields and sneak up on the sleeping woyaks.

Who will be my krolowa if Laska should die, Krol Rudy
wondered. Other than Laska, there was not one girl in the
camp who appealed to him. The young ones were all pregnant, and Krol Rudy had no wish to sow in soil where
others had left their seeds. As he walked along and pondered
these things, a young girl—barefoot, wearing a skirt made
of animal skins—came walking up the path. She could not
have been older than twelve. She carried a basket of turnips.
Although the sun was shining, the air was cold. A wind
blew from the mountains, disheveling her dark hair. Krol
Rudy stopped her.

"What's your name?"

The girl did not answer. She kept looking back, ready at
any moment to run.

"Don't be afraid. I'm not going to eat you. What is your
name?"

"Yagoda."

"Yagoda, huh? Come with me."

The kniezes all burst out laughing. The girl began to
stammer. "I have to bring the turnips to my mother, to the
tent."

"Your mother can wait."

Krol Rudy held her by her neck. "Don't try to run away.
If you do, I'll twist off your pretty little head."

"My mother is hungry."

"Your mother will eat later. I will give you some bread
for her."

The girl still resisted, but Krol Rudy pressed her throat
with his thumb and index finger. With his left hand he
grabbed her basket and handed it to one of his companions.
He led the girl to his cabin—a large room, floorless, the

walls constructed of unhewn beams. A square opening in one wall served as a window, and was covered with an animal's bladder, which let in light. On a table lay swords, spears. Dried meat bulged out of sacks—sides of calves, sheep, hares. The room smelled of mildew, rancid fat, and rotting fruit. The kniez put down the girl's basket and disappeared. Krol Rudy said, "Don't be afraid, Yagoda. This is the room of a man, not a bear's cave."

"Mother ..."

But this was all the girl managed to utter. Krol Rudy threw her down on a pile of hides and raped her. She cried out, but he clamped her mouth with the palm of his hand. Then he stood up on his bloodied legs and called out the name of a woyak. The man opened the door.

"Take the wench away. Give her a pretzel," he ordered.

(2)

When the Lesniks escaped to the mountains, they took their bows and arrows with them. There were fewer animals in the mountains than in the valley below, but the men hunted enough to keep them from starving. The mountains abounded in caves that gave them shelter. Their leader was Laska's father, Cybula. A short man, all skin and bones, he was almost bald—except for a few scraggly hairs. He became their leader because he was skillful and clever. He had the name of a marksman. His arrows penetrated deep into an animal's flesh. He had a knack for weaving and casting fishnets and setting traps. He cracked jokes about idlers, cowards, and fools in the camp. He even dared to poke fun at Baba Yaga, the smoks, and the other spirits and gods.

He knew how to keep up the camp's spirits. He was short and nimble, could scamper up the tallest tree, turn somersaults, imitate the howls of wolves, the snorts of boars, the calls of birds. Sometimes he entertained the camp by mimicking old women's talk, their moans and groans, the curses and blessings they heaped on one another, their laments and complaints against men. Even the death of his wife and his children in the last massacre could not defeat him.

However, when there was talk of hitching men to plows and coaxing the earth to bring forth wheat, barley, and other such grains, Cybula would turn serious. He argued that as long as men hunted and fished they were free to move from one place to another, to live as they wished, and to leave to women the tasks of keeping the home fires burning and raising children. Men who tilled the soil grew attached to it like trees. They stayed in their tents as women did, and begged the earth to yield up those accursed grains. There were rumors, moreover, that in some regions the kniezes and the pans had divided the land among themselves and made those who worked the land their slaves. Why can't we live as our fathers and grandfathers lived? Cybula would ask. It was not necessary to tickle and scratch Mother Earth to make her produce. That which she had to give, she gave of her own accord every summer.

Long before Krol Rudy invaded the camp, the Lesniks were debating the merits and shortcomings of tilling the soil. True, in the last few years food was growing scarce. Old people remembered times when there were many more animals and fish. But was this really so? Old people often invented stories, and often their memories were not reliable.

Every winter they swore that the cold was never as severe as this year, and every summer they said the same about the heat. True, more people were starving these days. But could barley and wheat eradicate famine? Death took whomever it wanted. Were it not for death, the world would be crammed full of people clear up to the sky.

Most of the Lesniks agreed with Cybula, and together they plotted to destroy Krol Rudy and his men. They agreed that a man would be sent down to spy on the valley, while the others readied themselves for the war to follow. But meanwhile, spring arrived, and the Lesniks took time to welcome it with prayers and chants. In years gone by, spring had been welcomed with gifts to the spirits and gods. A young virgin was chosen to be sacrificed on a stone altar, and later the men dipped their fingers in her blood. The women were never permitted to witness the ceremony. But since there were no virgins among those who had escaped to the mountains, hymns and incantations were offered instead.

At this time Cybula learned that Laska, his daughter, had survived the attack and now lay ill in her grandmother's tent. He immediately insisted on going down as a spy, but the Lesniks refused to listen. If he should be discovered and killed, who among them could take his place? Another man was sent instead; he brought back the news that Laska had recovered, and that she was to marry Krol Rudy on the day of the new moon.

One dark moonless night, while Laska lay sleeping in her grandmother's tent, she imagined she felt someone touching her lightly. She woke up with a start, ready to scream; then she heard her father's hushed voice: "Don't be afraid, daughter. It is your father."

Old Mala was also awakened, and when she learned who their visitor was, she said, "Leave her alone, Cybula. If the woyaks find you here, they will tear us to pieces. Laska is going to marry Krol Rudy. You know I have lost everything, and she is all I have left."

"Who is this you are marrying, daughter? A man who has killed your sisters, your brothers, your mother?"

"What do you want?" answered Laska. "I was sick. They had already prepared a grave for me. I can't go with you to the mountains, I am too weak. Besides, I can't leave Grandmother alone. He will take his revenge on her."

"Come with me, both of you. The cold days are over, it is warm in the mountains. Come and live in my cave. My brothers, the hunters, are preparing to come here and wipe out Krol Rudy and his men."

"When will they be coming?" asked Mala.

"Anytime. Maybe even tomorrow."

"What should I do, Grandmother?" Laska asked.

Mala sighed. "You are too weak to climb up the mountains. You will stumble along the way and fall, and the vultures will peck your eyes. Laska, marry Krol Rudy and let him fatten you up with his pretzels and his smoked meats. When you recover your strength, you will be yourself. I myself will soon be dead, and you won't have an old woman to drag across the mountains."

"Grandmother, you may be right," Cybula said, "but meanwhile, the krol will lie with her and make her belly swell up."

"Others have already lain with her," said Mala. "She was

raped on the night of the raid. It's a wonder that she is not carrying someone's child."

Laska was silent for a long time.

"Does Krol Rudy know this?" Cybula asked.

"No, he doesn't," Mala answered.

"When he finds out that I am not a virgin, he will instantly kill me. Better death than this life we live," Laska said.

Cybula waited a while, and then he said, "I'll be back. We'll all be back." And he left as quietly as he had arrived. He walked along the ground, watching and listening. His ears picked up the faintest rustle. His eyes pierced through the darkness like a wolf's. He suddenly spotted a small girl emerging from a tent. She had come out to relieve herself. Cybula waited. When she stood up, he pounced on her, quickly covered her mouth with his hand, and began to drag her with him. The girl struggled and gasped for air. He half carried, half dragged her, and soon they were outside the camp. In a sack he was carrying some rope, the hide of an animal, as well as a bow and arrows and a roasted bird. He removed his hand from the girl's mouth and said, "Try not to scream, or I'll strangle you on the spot."

"Mother . . ."

"Who is your mother? Who are you?"

"My mother is Kora and I am Yagoda."

"Kora is alive? I am Cybula."

"Let me go. My mother . . ."

"You must come with me. If you don't come willingly, I will tie you up and drag you by force. I am not your enemy. My brothers, the hunters, and I will soon be coming to kill all the Poles. We will set Krol Rudy on a stake and pierce him all the way to his head. Your father, Kostek, and I were like brothers. We used to hunt together. On the day you were born we planted a branch from a cherry tree near his tent. It was I who persuaded him to name you Yagoda."

"My mother won't know what's become of me. She'll sob and wail and tear her hair."

"She'll know. We have our spies and we'll let her know."

"Let me go."

"No."

Cybula took the rope from his bag and tied it around Yagoda's waist. Whenever she started to whine, he slapped her mouth and she fell silent. When they were far away from the camp, he set her down, tore a chunk from the bird, and gave it to her. When they had finished eating, he threw her to the ground and raped her. Later he asked, "Who did this to you before me, the woyaks?"

"No," she answered. "Krol Rudy himself."

(3)

The Lesniks, the Poles, and the other tribes who spoke more or less the same language had various customs for contracting a marriage. In some tribes the men bought their wives, in others they kidnapped them. If the young couple belonged to separate tribes, the groom lived with the bride's parents after the wedding and only years later moved his family back with his wife to his own native tribe. Sometimes the marriage was arranged strictly by the parents, and the young couple first met on the day of their wedding. An animal was sacrificed to Baba Yaga, or some other goddess, and then the groom showed off to the bride's father his skills as hunter and marksman. Brides had to be guarded by young maidens, day and night, against any intrusion of evil spirits. In former times a bride could be burned at the stake for losing her virginity before her marriage. With the rise of fieldwork and the rule of kniezes and pans, a bride often was forced to submit to a pan before submitting to her husband. Sometimes the marriage ceremony itself was bound up with rites for invoking rain and for expelling the demons who hid in fields and in bundles of wheat. One tribe even staged a mock funeral—bride and groom were led to their graves accompanied by hymns and laments—in order to fool witches and sorcerers who robbed grooms of their vigor and gave brides long bleedings. On the day before her wedding, the bride wove sprays of flowers into her hair, then circled the camp from tent to tent to invite the people to the ceremony. In every tent she knelt before the invited guests and kissed their feet. The groom was meanwhile regaled by his friends with jokes, teased with advice, and challenged to duels. Some hunting tribes had a custom of putting the young couple to bed but not allowing the groom to touch his bride until the stargazer signaled the arrival of the proper moment.

Because Krol Rudy and his kniezes and pans stemmed from diverse regions, and because so many young Lesnik men were dead or in hiding and the women pregnant with their enemies' offspring, Krol Rudy decided to marry Laska without fanfare or ceremony. The pans simply accompanied him to Mala's tent, and there Mala turned Laska over to her husband's care. The old grandmother murmured a few silent words under her breath, and no one could tell whether she blessed the union or cursed it. The Poles were by this time entirely intoxicated. They waved their swords at Krol Rudy, and for a while it seemed that they meant to prevent his marriage. But Krol Rudy overcame them, and they moved aside and let him pass through.

Krol Rudy's house was still not finished. During the summer the stench had grown even more overpowering, and through the four-cornered opening in the wall all sorts of flies, butterflies, moths, and bees had flown in. In the corners cobwebs were hanging. Because he stored food supplies in his house, field mice scurried across the floor. His woyaks were growing drunker and louder. The last of their horses had died, and they were skinning it, preparing to eat it. Krol Rudy could suppress his yen for the bitter drop, but he could not repress his bitter feelings. That one of the mountain men had managed to steal into the camp and carry Yagoda off meant that the woyaks he had assigned to watch the camp were sleeping.

The Lesniks in the mountains could easily trample the fields or set them on fire or do any manner of damage. Several of his pans had told the krol that it was senseless to dally and wait for the harvest. The woyaks were fit for smashing heads, burning homes, raping women, but when it came to work, they were lazy. They were accustomed to roam and to plunder, not to settle down and toil. Some of them had already been insolent to the kniezes, even to Krol Rudy. There were many woyaks and only a handful of kniezes. Several of his most powerful kniezes had died during the winter. Some of the woyaks had gone partly or completely insane. They stopped using human language and grunted or roared like animals, laughed, wept, attacked old women, and were unfit for hunting or plowing. Several of them should have been flogged to death or hanged, to set an example for the others. But the kniezes knew that any punishment could set off an uprising among the hungry woyaks.

Krol Rudy had pinned all his hopes on the harvest. But there was not much rain during the spring. It was foolish to be taking a wife and thinking of children when so many perils confronted him. However, Krol Rudy refused to give up. Should he wander still farther? Attack still more small camps and destroy them? He, Krol Rudy, had wanted to bring bread to those people who spoke a language similar to his own. He had wanted to make of them one nation—a nation of Poles. Often he awakened at night and lay on his bed, unable to sleep. His own bodyguards could have entered and finished him off. Quite a few chieftains and krols had come to such an end. He had heard of a land where krols were crowned for a single year, after which they were put to death. He had heard of a place where the krol married for only a year or two. As soon as the queen gave birth to a child, she was declared a goddess and beheaded by the krol himself, so that when her body died, her spirit either soared up to the gods and prayed for her people or else plunged into the depths where the dead rule and became a queen of the underworld.

When now Krol Rudy brought Laska to his cabin—in keeping with custom, he carried her over the threshold—the room's stench made her grimace and ask for some water. Her illness had left Laska weak and pale. Krol Rudy brought out meat and a pretzel, but she could not eat. Every now and then a kniez or a woyak stuck his head through the opening in the wall to see whether the krol was lying with his bride. Krol Rudy covered the hole with a pelt, carried

Laska to his bed, and lowered himself down on her. But he found he was entering through an open door. He struck her face, and she confessed that on the night of the raid two woyaks had raped her.

"Who are they? What are their names?" Krol Rudy demanded.

"How should I know? It was dark, and my mother was lying near me in a pool of blood. They hurt me and left."

"They never returned?"

"Never."

"Why didn't you tell me this earlier?"

"You didn't ask."

Krol Rudy gave her a shove, pushing her off his bed. He said, "You may not know who they are, but *they* know who *you* are. And tonight they are laughing at me. Everyone knows my shame by now, but I don't know whom to punish."

"How could they know you'd choose me to be your wife? They slaughtered and raped in the dark of night."

"You are making excuses for them?"

"No."

Krol Rudy would have liked to stand up and strangle Laska, or to plunge a sword into her breast. But he restrained himself. It was not her fault, and it would cause an uproar in the camp. He should have chosen Yagoda, not Laska. Yagoda was a virgin. But Cybula had carried her off into the mountains. Krol Rudy asked, "Are you pregnant?"

"No, my period came."

He helped her to her feet and carried her back to his bed. The thought that a woyak might chance by and kill him did not frighten him. How could one fear death and the grave when out of the earth sprang so much life? An odd thought began to take shape in his mind: when he died, he would like to be buried and to have a field planted over his bones. Perhaps man would stop shedding the blood of animals and nourish himself on the bounties of soil, sun, rain.

(4)

Cybula had been following the tracks of an animal. By its footprints, he knew it was a large beast, probably a "he." But what sort of beast it was, Cybula could not decide. What was more, its tracks led consistently down the mountain, all the way to the valley. That made Cybula suspicious, because the mountain animals did not travel so deep into the valley. It must be an animal he had never encountered before. He did not bring Yagoda along this time, because she was having her period. Cybula followed the footprints, spear and bow at hand, ready to aim for the animal's rump the moment he saw it. But then a bizarre thing happened: the tracks suddenly vanished, as if the animal had grown a pair of wings and flown away, or else the earth had swallowed it up. Cybula was tired and sat down, and he took out a chunk of smoked meat. His meal made him drowsy, and soon he was fast asleep. The light of the full moon woke him up. A breeze carried the animal's scent to his nostrils—a scent he had never smelled before—and he rose and followed it, not so much to capture the animal as to see what sort of creature it was. The hunters often told tales of animals that outwitted men with magic or with tricks.

Suddenly Cybula stopped short, as if thunderstruck. Before him stretched a vast field of wheat, its spikes already high, and the stalks packed close to one another. The moon showered its silver beams on the field. Some who had escaped from the camp had told him that Krol Rudy's crop had failed, that the soil was too rocky, the wheat grew sparse and short, the husks were empty. But it seemed they had lied to him, or else what his eyes were seeing was a dream. With the tips of his fingers Cybula crushed a husk of wheat and tasted the kernels. They had an unusual flavor. A longing to plunge into the field took hold of him, a yearning to lose himself in the lush growth. He was often told by the older hunters that those who plowed the earth bruised it, and the grains that it brought forth were poisoned. But over this field hovered something godly and blessed. A bright light shone from the moon, as if day and night had intermingled and become one. To Cybula it seemed that the sky had never been so crowded with stars as on that night, as if it were a field itself, strewn with sparkling crops.

It was not in Cybula's nature to bow down and worship either men or gods. But he fell to his knees and paid homage to the field as one would to a god. He inhaled deeply, taking its aroma into himself. He murmured a prayer to the hidden power which brought so much wonder out of the womb of the earth.

Cybula stood up and began to move deeper into the valley. He wanted to see the hut (or perhaps by now a big cabin) where Laska lived with Krol Rudy, but he thought that a guard was sure to be stationed there. It pained Cybula to think that his only daughter lay with her mother's murderer, kissing and fondling him. A bitter taste filled his mouth. Men made wombs for their enemies. In a way the same was also true of sons. The very best that man possessed was given away to strangers. Cybula continued to walk. The night turned colder, the moon hid behind an elongated cloud with scales resembling those of a fish or a snake. Suddenly Cybula found himself standing before Kostek's scorched hut. Kora was there, Yagoda's mother. It was then that Cybula knew why that strange vanishing animal—a night spirit probably —had led him to his home of old: to bring Kora to Yagoda. He had no time to lose. Everything had to be done with haste. He threw himself at the door and pushed it open. The moon illuminated the room, and Cybula could see Kora's half-clad body asleep. She lay on a pile of hides. The air smelled of rotting meat, garlic, urine. With one hand he grabbed Kora's throat, and with the other he covered her mouth. "I am Cybula," he hissed. "Come with me."

He tried to drag her along, but she resisted, trembling and choking. In her terror she could not grasp who he was and what he wanted. A terrible cry broke from her throat. She clung to his leg, pulled him down, fighting with him. She tore at his face with her nails. He wrestled himself free, and with his fist he struck her forehead, her nose, her skull. He was terrified that the woyaks might come by and tear him limb from limb. He realized he had lost his spear and his bow. He dropped Kora and ran outside. He crouched on the ground and searched for his weapons. The sweat blinded his eyes. He heard a ringing in his ears. A sweet-sour fluid flooded his mouth. "I must not weaken!" he resolved. At that moment it was as if a flash went through his brain, and he collapsed.

When he came to, someone was bending over him, trying to revive him. It was Kora. She helped him to his feet. She held tightly to his hand and tried to pull him after her. He remembered the weapons he had lost, but it would be madness to turn back. A great shame overcame him for his weakness. Together he and Kora passed by the field once again, and he caught a glimpse of it. The moon had disappeared.

The field seemed to lie in a deep, restful sleep. Only now did Cybula notice that Kora was stark naked. He took out a pelt from the sack that hung on his hip and wrapped it around her shoulders. They stood facing each other in the chill of the night. He was so agitated he could hardly speak. "It is I, Cybula," he said. "I am your friend, not your enemy. I came to take you to Yagoda."

"Cybula! My Cybula!"

Kora trembled with excitement, as if she only now realized who he was. She flung her arms around him, nearly throwing him off his feet. She kissed him, embraced him, wet his face with hers. Her body exuded a female kind of fever. She pressed him to her with such force that he could hear his ribs crack. She wailed. "They killed everyone: Kostek, our brothers, our sisters. Children's heads were rolling on the ground! The wrath of the gods came pouring down on us! Baba Yaga . . ." And Kora began to tear her hair and sway to the left and the right. Cybula snapped, "Be quiet! They'll hear you and . . ."

"Why did this happen to us? It was a punishment, a punishment! The earth was red with our blood. A curse and a shame! And where were our men? They scattered like mice and left us alone."

"Kora, no one expected them. They came in the night like wolves. I opened my eyes and the whole camp was on fire..."

"Brother of mine, father, friend! Every night I lay in my bed and spoke to you—to you and to Yagoda. She had awak-

ened and gone outside. I waited, and she did not return. I
looked everywhere but could not find her. I was sure the
woyaks had killed her and thrown her body away. Only later
did one of your men come to tell me that she was with you.
My savior, my god!"

"Come, Kora, let us go!"

"I fell asleep and dreamed about you. Every night you
came to me in my dreams. You and Kostek, Kostek and you.
Then I would open my eyes and find somebody pulling my
arms, my legs, my hair. They defiled all of us, they enjoyed
our suffering. They ripped open fat Yonda's belly and put a
rat inside. She writhed in pain, and they spit on her face . . ."

"Kora, enough . . ."

"Where are you taking me? Master of mine, son-in-law.
I have always loved you—since we were children. You were
supposed to be my husband, you belonged to me. But your
Yasna came running and took you away. Came like a she-
wolf, dug in her claws, and dragged you to her lair. She left
me with an ache and an empty heart. But you remembered,
you did not forget. And now Yagoda will carry your seed.
Your child will suck at her breast. It is a miracle, an omen
from the gods that our love did not die."

"It is true, Kora, I longed for you."

Cybula shivered. His teeth chattered. Was it from the cold
or from desire? His stomach tightened. He bent his head
down low. In the midst of all his trials and pains, old desires
of his were being rekindled. More than once he had imagined
Kostek dead, Kora a widow, Yagoda an orphan. In his lust
he had lain with both mother and daughter. But those had
been just dreams. Gods or elves listened to every worthless
trifle, every whim and wish, and sometimes fulfilled his

desires. Kora took his arm and pressed it to her breast. She kissed him and her hair tickled his cheek. She asked, "Is there no cave somewhere near here?"

"Yes, a little farther."

"Looks as if dawn is breaking."

"Yes."

Cybula raised his eyes to the sky. Stars were going out one by one. Birds awakened, each with its own call. In the east a cloud reddened, like a sore about to burst. In the west the edge of a cloud began to glow. The great and mighty gods took care of heaven. It was the minor godlings who looked after every drop of dew, every pebble on the ground. He, Cybula, had lost a spear and a bow, but he had regained a woman. Now, with everything in ruins, women no longer required wedding ceremonies; men no longer had to send gifts to brides—the old customs had crumbled. All they needed was a cave. He had longed for her when they were still children playing husband-and-wife. He used to pretend to go hunting and bring her a fox, a marten, a rabbit. She would pretend to roast a bird for him. Together they crawled into the bushes, tickled each other, and murmured words whose meanings they did not understand. Now Kora's daughter was his wife, Kostek was dead, and Kora, his mother-in-law, was looking for a cave after all these years of hidden passion.

All at once the sky was splashed with crimson. The sun arrived shining and wet, fresh from bathing in the sea. A flock of birds flew up to meet it, squawking a birdish good morning. Cybula glanced at Kora: she was only a bit shorter than he was, her loose brown hair now sprinkled with crimson, her face thin, her cheeks hollow, her long neck lined with wrinkles and veins. He observed her belly, her hips, the calves of her legs. The pelt covered only her shoulders. A submissiveness looked at him out of her large dark eyes, a willingness to surrender to him with a love whose fire was never extinguished.

(5)

When Cybula had set out the morning before with his bow and his spear, Yagoda had asked him how long he would be, and he had shrugged his shoulders. Now, as day ended and Cybula had not come back, Yagoda grew worried. A daughter of hunters, she knew that animals were not hunted at night. Yagoda lit a fire in the cave and roasted a piece of meat, but she had no desire to eat it. Shadows danced on the rock walls. Outside, the air was cool, but inside the cave reigned a wintry chill. Had a wild beast attacked him, or a woyak? There was talk in the mountains that the woyaks were planning to climb up and slaughter them all. Sitting by the fire, wrapped in a pelt, Yagoda made up her mind that if Cybula did not return by morning, she would put an end to her life. True, she could let the other Lesniks know that Cybula had not come back, but their caves were too far from hers and she was sure to lose her way in the mountains. It also seemed to her that some of these men had been looking at her with hungry eyes. Every one of these witless men repeated the same tasteless joke: "Yagoda, I'd like to eat you up." (Yagoda, in the language of the Lesniks, meant berry.)

Most of the Lesniks were light-haired and blue-eyed; she, Yagoda, had dark skin and brown eyes. The tribe's jesters said she resembled a porcupine, a mouse, a squirrel. The few

women who managed to run away from the Poles were blab-
bers, backbiters. They poked fun at each other, whispered in
each other's ears, gossiped that this one did not keep herself
clean, the other could not cook or roast, the third was un-
faithful to her husband, the fourth was too thin, too fat, too
foolish, too sly. When they dug roots or picked fruits, they
struggled to outdo one another in speed, dexterity, in extract-
ing the best from the earth or the tree. But Yagoda did not
try to join in with them. They envied her because Cybula
had chosen her to be his wife. "What did he see in you?"
they would ask her. "What is it that you have there between
your legs?" And they would wink, and hint, and give each
other knowing looks.

She, Yagoda, was so different from them all. She was, at
the same time, both childish and too earnest. She was almost
thirteen years old, but she played like a girl of five or six:
she gathered pinecones—not to burn them for heat, but to
use them as toys. For no reason at all she picked thistles,
poisonous berries, mushrooms, colored pebbles, tiny eggs of
unknown birds, butterflies, feathers, plumes, and other such
childish things. She made believe that a tree was her dead
father, Kostek, and she spoke to it and even kissed its bark.
She had similar fantasies about her mother, Kora, who
remained in the camp. Sometimes Yagoda pretended that her
long-dead brothers and sisters were still living, and she spoke
to them, danced with them, played hide-and-seek with them.

Since the woyak raid, and after what Krol Rudy had done
to her, Yagoda's life was like one long dream. Her mother,
Kora, believed in a spirit called a *domowik*. She often said
that a domowik lived with her, hiding out among the trees,
the bushes, the pelts. He brought her wood from the forest,

found food, carried water from the spring for her. Mother
Kora allegedly inherited him from her father, Chmielnik,
and her mother, Trawka. Kora swore that once, when she
had some ailment in her eyes and could not see, a domowik
had climbed into her bed and with his tongue licked her
eyes all through the night. In the morning, when she opened
them, she saw clearly again. Yagoda often searched for this
domowik, wanted to make him her own spirit as well, but
he eluded her. Only from time to time did he make his
presence known, when he rustled through the logs that her
father had chopped, or splashed the water in the barrel. Sometimes, when Yagoda went out to relieve herself behind the
hut, he tickled her buttocks. Sometimes he blew a whisper
in her ear, but what he said she did not know. When Yagoda
complained to her mother that the domowik avoided her,
Kora promised that he would disclose himself to Yagoda after
her, Kora's, death. Or else in a time of danger.

On this night, when Cybula did not return, Yagoda spoke
to the domowik. She told him all that had befallen her and
begged him to help find Cybula. She spoke out loud, asking, "Is he still among the living? Or is he already in the
hollows of the earth, where it is always dark? Is he together
with father Kostek and my grandfathers and grandmothers?
I miss him, domowik. Without Cybula I don't want to live,"
Yagoda said. "Make me as I was before I was born—nothing.
I don't want to remember that Krol Rudy raped me. I don't
want Cybula to know that it really happened. I want to
become nothing, I want to cease to be . . ."

So drowsy did Yagoda become that she slipped off the log
on which she was sitting and remained lying on the bare
stone floor. Sleep overcame her, and she did cease to be. But

something remained alive—a bubble, a hair, a cobweb from which she hung like a spider. She was too heavy for the web, but she did not dare to let go, because below her yawned a bottomless pit: if she let go, she would fall and sink into the abyss.

When Yagoda opened her eyes, daylight was streaming in through the opening of the cave. The fire had gone out and only ashes remained. Her feet felt numb and she could not stand up. She forgot where she was. She could not at first remember her name. Suddenly she remembered—Yagoda. Cybula had not come home last night; he was dead. Yagoda could not even cry. I'll never leave this cave again, she thought to herself; here is where I'll die. She usually arose hungry, but this time her tongue was coated and her throat constricted, and she could not even swallow her own saliva. She closed her eyes once again, and immediately began to dream. She was no longer in the mountains but in another camp, where a massacre apparently had taken place. Men were lying everywhere, their throats slit, and she could see women with their bellies ripped open. How odd: one of them seemed to be giving birth and a calf's head protruded from her thighs . . .

Yagoda slept for a long time. Whenever she started to awaken she remembered that Cybula had not returned, and again she went off to sleep. Her head, pressing down on her shoulders, felt as if it were a heavy rock. One instant she was awake, the next asleep. Again her wanderings began: strange camps, unfamiliar faces. Yagoda was searching for her cave, and people were showing her paths, trails, crevices in the earth which would lead her back. But she knew that instead of drawing nearer, she was drifting farther away . . .

Yagoda opened her eyes, and by the reddish light outside, she knew it was dusk. She sat up and shuffled toward the opening. The sun had set behind the mountain. Birds were sitting on the branches of trees. Yagoda walked out naked and went to the stream to bathe. Though the water was ice cold, Yagoda immersed herself in the rushing current. Cybula had told her that the stream flowed into a larger river, and the river into the sea. Two-headed giants, with long tails and four arms, lived there. Every time Yagoda plunged into the water, she opened her eyes to look for Topiel, the spirit said to dwell at the river bottom with his wives. When she raised her head from the water for the fifth time, she heard someone calling her name. The voice seemed familiar, but she was not certain to whom it belonged. Soon another voice joined the first. Two half-naked people jumped into the stream. Cybula grabbed Yagoda in his arms and someone else—Kora, her mother—hugged her with a wild cry.

(6)

That evening the news spread among the Lesniks in the mountains that Cybula had returned with Kora, Yagoda's mother and Kostek's widow. They hastily gathered outside Cybula's cave, bringing with them food and drinks squeezed from fruits. The night was warm and they sat outside on the ground. Cybula told them how the tracks of an unseen animal had led him down to the valley, and how he had rescued Kora. He spoke about the field, the blessing that the gods had bestowed upon the land. Cybula had brought with him a few stalks of wheat, which he showed to the Lesniks against the light of the moon. Every Lesnik took a stalk and examined it. Some dug out a kernel and tasted it. Several of their spies had brought back the news that the wheat grew poorly, and that nothing would remain of the crop but empty shells and chaff that the wind would blow away. But the wheat which Cybula brought back was good to the taste. Cybula said that yes, the Poles were murderers, but the grain they brought with them was not at fault. It held in it seeds that would grow and multiply in years to come. The work in the fields was not done by the woyaks, Cybula said, but by the old men and the young women who remained alive in the camp. He mentioned something else: most of the young women in the camp were carrying the offspring of these woyaks and it would be an injustice for the unborn children to be made orphans before they came into the world.

The Lesniks listened silently. One of them blurted out, "You are defending the murderers because they made your daughter their queen."

"No, not true," Cybula answered. "For my sake you can go ahead and kill Krol Rudy, but don't forget the woyaks have iron swords and spears, which we do not. They are not going to sit with folded arms and wait for you to kill them. A new slaughter will start and the first victims will be our sisters and daughters."

"What is your advice?" asked another.

Cybula did not answer immediately. "My advice is that we make peace."

The talk went on for a long time. Several of the Lesniks were whispering quietly into each other's ears. Cybula caught the word "traitor."

2

Cybula and Nosek

IN the valley the summer turned out to be blessed. The days were bright. Once in a while the sky clouded over and some rain fell. Then the clouds dispersed and again the sun was shining. Flocks of birds flew over the fields trying to taste the grain, but Krol Rudy, who had been raised by parents who worked the land, had several corpses dug up, the flesh peeled from their bones, and the skeletons set up on poles. The terrified birds shrieked and flew away. Old women grumbled that Krol Rudy was sinning, because what the earth covered up should not be uncovered. They warned of famine and plague. But Krol Rudy was determined that the seeds he and his woyaks had carried in bags on their backs would not be devoured by birds.

That night, as on all other nights, Krol Rudy went to bed drunk. He could stifle neither his craving for strong drink nor his sadness. Things were not turning out the way he had planned. The house which was being built for him was still not ready. The women were too busy in the fields. The woyaks could not or would not pitch in and help with the building. They were all lazy, fit neither for hunting nor for working the land. Several among them became half crazy. They ran around at night howling, making frightful noises. They wanted to kill the old and crippled Lesniks, set fire to the fields, and move on. Where? They themselves did not know; perhaps over the mountains. Krol Rudy held this to be ill-advised. The number of woyaks was small—perhaps no more than forty. The number of men who had escaped to the mountains was at least one hundred. To bring back these runaways and allow them to live—wouldn't this turn victory into defeat?

Krol Rudy glanced at the bed where Laska lay sleeping. Her mood was even darker than his. She still grieved for her mother. She longed for her father. The few times that Krol Rudy had approached her, she remained cold. She lay so still in the night that he never knew whether she was asleep or awake. Now he stretched out his hand and touched her. "You are sleeping, what?"

Laska awakened immediately. "Yes. No. What is it?"

"What do you do all night? You think?"

"Yes, sometimes."

"What do you think about? Tell me!"

Laska did not answer. Krol Rudy was ready to give her an embrace, but at that moment he heard her say, "Ah, all sorts of things. You should not have killed so many men in the camp."

"I should not, eh? If you don't kill an enemy, he kills you."

"Not everyone. Others might have given in and made peace."

"Nonsense!" Krol Rudy said to Laska and himself. "Maybe this is what happens among women, but not among men. A man, if you grab the least of his possessions, immediately thinks of revenge. They are plotting something up there in the mountains, preparing to war against us. Your own father is their leader. I know everything. I have spies."

"My father wants to harm no one," Laska said, amazed at her courage to speak in this manner to her husband and master. Krol Rudy scolded her: "You are his daughter, that is why you take his side. He is an enemy like all the others. He dragged Yagoda to his cave like a wolf. He stole her mother also. They plan to attack us with their bows and arrows and their spears, but we will behead every one of them. If the women go over to their side, we will tear them to pieces."

"All the women want is peace."

"Who is going to make peace, you?"

Krol Rudy was shaking. For a moment he wanted to stand up and choke Laska, but he restrained himself. With whom would he replace her? He closed his eyes and soon began to snore. A while later he woke up. "If you want, I'll send you to your father to arrange for peace. But real peace, with no lies. No one can deceive me."

Laska sat up. "You mean this?"

"I am not one for making jokes."

"I won't know what to say."

"I'll send Nosek with you. If they harm him or threaten you, we'll come up and there will be a bloodbath in the

mountains. Swear to me that you'll return. I'll hold your
grandmother Mala as a hostage."

"I'll return."

"Tell them to come to the valley as brothers, not as foes—
without weapons."

"Yes."

"I need them for the harvest. If there is bread, everyone
will eat."

The two of them fell silent. Laska could no longer hold
back tears.

"What are you crying for? No one has died yet."

(2)

All day long the Lesniks were busy in the mountains. The
weather was hot even at that elevation. From sunrise to sunset Kora and Yagoda picked cherries, gooseberries, currants,
immature fruit which the women later let ripen in the sun.
Several of the women had brought clay pots with them from
the valley, and they cooked some unripe fruit as well as roots
which were too tough to be eaten raw. Meat was also plentiful. The woods swarmed with animals and birds, and the
men either caught them in traps or shot them with arrows.
Cybula and some other hunters killed several stags and does,
and as was their custom, the whole camp ate them together.
Some of the older hunters argued again and again that to
plow the body of Mother Earth and sow seeds in her womb
would bring nothing but grief. The spirits of the earth would
be furious with those who tore up her flesh, and they would
seek revenge. Men who nourished themselves only on plants

would become like dumb cattle, begin to eat grass, bellow like oxen, and be eaten by beasts of prey. Sooner or later the kniezes, pans, or whatever the Poles called themselves, would take the fields for themselves, and those who plowed and sowed and reaped would become their slaves—as had already happened in many faraway places. Cybula tried to argue with the Lesniks, but they shouted him down. There could be no peace between hunters and growers. The Lesniks should arm themselves as well as they could, go down to the valley, kill off the remaining woyaks, and return to the old ways.

Well, but returning to the old way of life was also impossible. In olden times the Lesniks never settled down in one spot but wandered from place to place in search of animals and fish. They usually lived in tents and they knew nothing of cooking, pots, or domestic animals. Some of the neighboring settlements were herding sheep and goats, but for the Lesniks this was a sin and an abomination. They had even heard of camps that had domesticated cows, and even horses, and exchanged them for fruit, honey, and furs, but the Lesniks never had the need or skill for all this. They never even learned to keep dogs. What for? Dogs were unclean. The Lesniks never tasted milk, except from their mothers as infants. But the last few generations of Lesniks had settled down. They stopped walking barefoot in winter and wore shoes of fur hide with soles of bark. The winters had become colder. More furs were needed for protection against the cold. Cybula often reminded the Lesniks how difficult the last winter had been in the mountains, how many of them had become ill and died. The old folks were perhaps right: the people were becoming weaker, the cold stronger, the woods

sparser. Demands for comfort had grown not only among
women but also among men, and this kindled the wrath of
the gods.

Now, in the summer, it was warm in the mountains. There
was plenty of food. Everyone ate meat, fruit, roots, till their
stomachs were full. In the evening they lit fires and talked,
told stories, jokes. The number of women was small—there
were at least four men for each woman. But they believed
more women would manage to steal out of the valley and
join them in the mountains. The Poles had destroyed the
Lesniks' former family life. Hot-blooded women could do
whatever they pleased. Old people warned of bitter punish-
ments, but belief in the gods had declined. Where was Baba
Yaga, with her celestial broom? Where was Swiatawid, the
four-faced god, who could see from one end of the world to
the other? Where was the three-faced god hiding? Where
was Pirnon, the god of thunder and lightning and storms?
Where were the spirits Yedza and Nocnica and all the others
when the Poles attacked the camp and spilled so much innocent blood? If there was no justice among the gods, why
should the people obey their commands? Cybula had spoken
openly: All beliefs were lies. As long as men lived, they
should enjoy themselves as much as they could. A dead man
was no better than a dead frog. No one ever came back from
the hollows of the earth to tell what was going on there.

When Cybula brought back Yagoda and her mother, Kora,
he aroused the men's envy and the women's resentment. It
was clear that he had relations with both. But he was, and he
remained, the Lesniks' leader. He had a great store of knowledge, a clear mind, and was skilled in many crafts. As Cybula

spoke, people listened to his words, even if they thought him wrong. A few of the young men argued that, who knows, perhaps the Lesniks should not act hastily and set fire to the fields. If the gods did not want the earth juices to be tapped, why did they bestow power on the murderous Poles and provide them with iron swords and spears?

The old and the weak went to sleep early that evening, as they did every evening, while the young and healthy stayed up late into the night. They sang, they danced, they made jokes and asked questions of each other. They raised their eyes to the night sky—so many stars and so many different colors. Were the stars gods? Were they fires lit by the gods to brighten up the night? The same stars could be seen in the valley and in the mountains. Wherever one went, the stars came along. When one ran, they ran, too. Sometimes it seemed that they were laughing with a heavenly laughter. They looked down on earth like sparkling puzzles, and winked so that men might solve them. The old people swore that these same stars were shining when they, the old people, were children. The stars might be as old as the world. But how far back did the chain go? They would all live out their lives, die, and fade from memory—just like the animals which they had killed and eaten. It was terrifying to think about these things. The young women begged the men to stop talking about these mysteries, which caused a chill to go up and down the spine, and also a craving to kiss, to embrace, to come close, and become as one.

That evening Cybula, Kora, and Yagoda went to sleep early. Cybula stretched out on the pelt between the two women, and he lay first with one and then with the other.

Mother and daughter discarded all feelings of shame, because this was what Cybula had asked for. Both treated Cybula as if he were a god whose every word was a sacred command. He taught Yagoda not to be jealous. It was not a stranger whom he had taken but her beloved mother. Kora's happiness was also Yagoda's happiness. Cybula taught them how to tease him, but Kora needed no teaching, she knew everything. She said things which kindled his desire, aroused Yagoda's envy, and made her want both to laugh and to vomit. Kora had names for the limbs of the body which Yagoda had never heard before. She taught her daughter as a mother bear teaches her cub. She confessed that the woyaks had come to her in the night, and although she cursed them in her heart, she had submitted. There were times when Yagoda hated her mother and wanted to shout: "Get out of the cave! I am not your daughter anymore, and you are not my mother!" But Kora would quickly apologize, call herself nasty names, and regret her behavior. Sometimes she would say to Cybula, "This is the truth. If you want, kill me. It's better for me to die by your hand than to be caressed by the hands of others. Yes, kill me and eat me up. Drink my blood!"

Sometimes when her mother and Cybula spoke and played with each other, Yagoda pretended to sleep. She even snored from time to time. Her mother still treated her like a child, but she understood everything. Her mother had not been faithful to her father, Kostek. She had lain with him and thought of Cybula. Kostek could not satisfy her, he only whetted her appetite. Kora admitted that she was sinning against the gods with her hunger for men. Demons appeared to her in her dreams and warned her that she would turn into a *vikalak,* a she-wolf. She would wallow in swamps, be bitten by snakes, strangled by smoks. But her body was consumed with desire. She had hated the woyaks, had prayed to the gods for their death, but when they came to her she fell into their arms.

That evening Yagoda heard Cybula say, "The gods are not gods and the people are not people anymore."

"What are they, then?" Kora asked. And Cybula answered, "Rats, spiders, lice."

"You, Cybula, are a god," Kora blurted.

"If I am a god, the gods are nothing."

(3)

It was a hot day. Kora and Yagoda left at dawn to dig roots and gather fruit. Cybula had carved a new bow and ten arrows for himself and went hunting, but he seemed to have lost the lust for pursuing an animal. Why did a stag or even a hare deserve to be killed? More than once it happened that his arrow entered an animal but instead of dying, the animal trotted away, leaving behind a long trail of blood. Some wounded animals waded into a river or lake and drowned there. Did they do this because they wanted to die? Or did they think the water would heal them? The animals that fell into traps suffered even more than those that were shot. Often they were impaled on sharp poles and days would pass before they died. "What is happening to me? Am I becoming soft-hearted, like an old woman?" Cybula asked himself. His thoughts carried him again and again back to the field. Those who plowed and sowed harmed no one. On the contrary, they provided food to birds who could manage to steal a few grains of wheat.

After hunting a while, Cybula knew he would have to go home empty-handed. There was enough meat in the cave for a few days. Often the other hunters asked him and his women to eat from their catch. The sun had already reached the west, the sky was glowing a purplish blue, tomorrow promised to be another bright day. Cybula walked slowly, whistling to himself an old Lesnik tune. As he approached his cave, Kora came to meet him. Something had happened. She was not smiling her usual smile but looked at him intently, like a bearer of bad news. Yagoda might have fallen off a tree and died, Cybula thought. He quickly made up his mind that, if this was true, he would put an end to his own life. He had enough of killing and death, both of animals and of people. He believed only in one god—the god of death, the healer of all pain, the liberator of all burdens. Cybula nodded his head at Kora, but she did not respond. He said, "I know, I know."

"What do you know?"

"Nothing. Tell me what happened!"

"Your daughter is here," Kora answered in a low voice.

"My daughter, Laska? Has she run away from Krol Rudy?"

"No, Krol Rudy sent her. He wants to make peace. She arrived stealthily. She looks pregnant." Cybula could not believe his ears. "How can this be?" he asked.

"It's true. He sent one of his kniezes along—Nosek. He is waiting for you by the four linden trees near the stream. Everything must remain a secret."

"This must be a trap, to have me killed."

"Your daughter would not take part in such a crime," Kora said. "Not many Poles survived the winter. They may not be able to do the harvesting. They are lazy and drunk. Laska told me it's not a trap to deceive you—they need us."

"Where is Laska?" Cybula asked.

"With Yagoda in the cave."

"If our people hear of this, they may kill us all," Cybula said. "They already call me traitor."

"Wait until dark. I'll go with you. You take a spear and I'll take a knife. Nosek is not a murderer. He is the only Pole who did not kill and did not rape. Everyone in the camp knows this. He came here unarmed."

"We'll see."

"You must be hungry. Your sack is empty," Kora said.

"I could not hunt today."

"We prepared a meal for you."

Cybula slid nimbly into the cave. That Krol Rudy should ask for peace and send Laska and one of his kniezes seemed like a miracle. "Maybe it is not my time to die yet," Cybula murmured. The cave smelled of roasting meat, the smoke of pine branches, the juices of cherries and strawberries. Some time passed, as always, before his eyes grew accustomed to the darkness. Yagoda ran to him, threw her arms around his waist, and clung to him. Laska, who sat by the fire, stood up. Cybula hardly recognized her. She looked years older. Her stomach was swollen. She gave him a kiss on the forehead. This was no longer his little girl whom he used to bounce on his knees while she covered his face with kisses. This was a grown woman, pregnant, the wife of a krol. She wore a sort of wreath on her head, like all women who had husbands. To Cybula it seemed that even her breath was different. Could it be that she drank the vodka? he asked himself.

Kora and Yagoda brought meat, fruit, vegetables to Cybula while Laska sat and spoke to him. Her husband, Krol Rudy, was not the murderer everyone thought he was. True, he had attacked the Lesniks. He was a warrior, not a lamb. However, he had seen enough bloodshed. Now he wanted peace between the Lesniks and the Poles. What was gained by all these wars? The gods had showered their blessings on the fields, and men were needed for harvesting and thrashing.

Cybula listened to her and gaped. Laska spoke to him as if she were older and wiser than he was. In some ways she reminded him of his mother, his grandmother. He wanted to ask his daughter about her life with Krol Rudy, how she could tolerate a man who had ordered her mother killed. But he could not ask this in the presence of Kora and Yagoda. Where did she learn to speak so seriously, Cybula wondered.

"How are things at the camp? How do you live there?" Cybula asked.

"Ah, Father, you know yourself. Everyone has lost someone dear. It is not good for us to be separated from each other. I miss you. Not a day goes by when I do not pray to the gods for your health."

Who taught her to speak like this? Cybula asked himself. Not her mother and not I. He fell silent, and Laska also spoke no more. Slowly night fell. Laska said, "We can go now, Father."

"I'll go with you," Kora said. "I'll wait nearby. One can never know what this Pole might want to do. I'll take my cleaver. You, Yagoda, stay in the cave and watch the fire."

"Yes, Mother."

"We'll go out one by one," Cybula said. "You, Laska, go first."

Laska kissed Yagoda and crawled through the opening. Cybula took his spear and followed her out. "Whatever happens," he said, "they will not take me alive."

The sun had set behind the mountains, but a brightness remained in the sky. The stars lit up one after the other. Crickets chirped, frogs croaked. The birds had all settled down on branches of trees, except for two, which flew about squawking at each other—a couple that could not find a fitting branch on which to bed down. But why? There were so many trees and so many branches! Cybula understood these creatures' behavior no better than he could understand the behavior of men. Some songbirds ceased singing, while others warbled and trilled. They slept in pairs close to each other, kissed each other with their little beaks, groomed each other's feathers and plucked out vermin. Yet he saw other males attack the females, even peck them to death.

After a while Cybula caught up with Laska, and they walked beside the stream, which spattered and splashed in the night. Water always flowed swiftly downhill, Cybula thought; the steeper the slope, the swifter the current. But why? When he was young he always had one question: *Dlatshego*—why? And his parents' answer was always the same: *Tak yest*—this is how it is, this is what the gods want. In later years he gave the same answer to his own children, even the ones who had been massacred. In fact, Laska herself used to ask her father, *"Tatele,* why is the summer hot? Why is the winter cold? Why does a cow moo while a goat bleats? Why should a duck swim and a hen be afraid of

water? Why does wood burn but not stone?" And Cybula
would say, "This is how things were created. Now leave me
alone!" But afterward he was troubled by these questions.

(4)

Father and daughter approached the linden trees, and by
the light of the stars Cybula could see the form of a man: he
was slightly built, with neither hair nor beard, and a pale
face. The two men bowed to each other. Then the other said,
"My name is Nosek. My krol sent me here to greet you and to
urge the Lesniks to return to the valley. My krol will punish
no one. He is ready to forget the wrongs you did us and those
we did to you. We won the war, but we cannot fight forever
and shed each other's blood. My krol wants you Lesniks to be
our brothers and the camp to be a Polish camp. The gods have
blessed our fields and we need your help. We cannot and do
not want to eat all the bread the fields will grow. We want
your daughters to become our wives, as some have already
done, and may the new Polish land increase and multiply.
This is the wish of our krol, his kniezes, and his woyaks. Come
down to us, all of you, and we'll face you as brothers. The krol
also sent to you, Pan Cybula, this gift." And saying these
words, Nosek handed Cybula a pretzel made of wheat flour.

Cybula took the pretzel, thanked Nosek, and then began
to speak the words he had previously prepared. "Worthy
kniez, I greet you and your krol in my name and in the name
of the Lesniks who fled when the woyaks fell upon us. We
Lesniks never wanted war. We lived in peace for a long
time. But you attacked us and killed our men and women,

and you did not even spare our children. Those of us who fled to the mountains suffered through a cruel winter; many lost their lives to the cold and to hunger. We who survived would like to come home to the valley where our mothers, sisters, wives, and children still live. But what assurance have we that your peace offering is not a trap to kill us all? Without such a pledge not one of us will return, even if we do miss our homes, and even if we are ready to help you with your tasks and share in the blessing with which the gods have favored us . . ."

For a long time the two men conversed, while Laska stood silent. Nosek explained to Cybula that Krol Rudy and his woyaks had nothing to gain from killing the Lesniks. Besides, the Poles were few in number, and if it was violence that Cybula feared, they were more likely to lose than the Lesniks. Peace between the two former enemies would have to be based on trust. After some time, the two men agreed that Cybula would gather his people the next day and convey Krol Rudy's proposal to them. Meanwhile, Cybula suggested to Nosek that he spend the night in a hideout known only to Cybula himself, while Laska returned to her father's cave. Laska would serve as proof that Krol Rudy truly meant peace, because no krol would send his queen as bait to lure an enemy into a trap.

It struck Cybula that Nosek behaved better than the other kniezes and pans. His language was clear and honest. He mentioned rivers, cities, and names of krols and leaders of whom Cybula had never heard. How did it happen that a man like this was traveling in the company of a band of Polish robbers and murderers? He told Nosek what hiding place he had in mind: it was a hut which Cybula used for building animal traps and where he kept the necessary tools. There was a pile of pelts there which Nosek could use to cover himself. The hut was quite far and Cybula offered to escort Nosek to it. But Nosek replied that if he could not find the hut he would spend the night under the stars. At that, Laska spoke up for the first time: "Your worthiness could catch a chill by sleeping under the stars. Nights in the mountains are cold."

"Thank you, but men like me do not chill so easily. I like to take a stroll at night and think my thoughts."

What sort of thoughts? Cybula wanted to ask, but he felt he was not addressing the kniez correctly. He wished to use more fitting words, but he could not find any. Instead Cybula asked, "Was it your plan to bring peace to the Lesniks and the Poles?"

"Yes, mine, but not mine alone. Krol Rudy thought of it first. He even spoke about it with your gracious daughter, the krolowa."

Cybula felt embarrassed. This learned man called his daughter gracious and krolowa. Cybula had never before heard the word "gracious" about a child of his. It would have been better had she been Nosek's wife instead of Krol Rudy's. He began to explain to Nosek how to reach the hut. The moon would soon appear and the night would become brighter. The two men parted, and Cybula said, "I have full trust in you, your worthiness."

"And I in you, your worthiness. Under your leadership we shall have peace."

Then Nosek took leave of Laska. Again he uttered words

which were unfamiliar to Cybula but whose meanings he could guess. Cybula had always had a liking for the female sex, but it occurred to him that this was the first time a man had so appealed to him.

As soon as Nosek was gone, Kora jumped out of a clump of bushes and cried, "I heard everything, every word."

"Yes, you would have made a good spy."

"Everything you said is true. Every word of yours was worth kissing."

"Was this not true also of Nosek's words?"

"He is false," Kora answered. "They all are. They make pretty speeches, with flattery, but all they want is to make maidservants and slaves of us. With their smooth tongues they make our daughters surrender themselves, but when the girls' bellies begin to swell, the sly foxes pretend they know nothing. Nosek is no better than they are. And what's more, he is not even a man."

"What is he, then?" Cybula asked.

"They say he is fond of men."

"You, Kora, have seen this with your own eyes?" Laska asked.

"Ah, I know. There is no concealing things from me. I see everything and know everything."

"Kora, we cannot remain here another winter," Cybula said. "We will all die."

"Yes, I know. Wherever you go, we, Yagoda and I, will also go. We'll wash your feet and drink the water!"

The three of them returned to the cave. It was now clear to Cybula that Kora and Laska disliked one another. But why? Yagoda was asleep by the fire. Only a few coals were still glowing. That night Cybula did not lie down between Kora and Yagoda but prepared for himself a separate place to sleep. Laska went to her own bed without a word.

Cybula was tired, but he was unable to sleep. Nosek had insisted that the Lesniks come down to the valley unarmed. They could take their bows but no arrows. But how could he be sure that armed woyaks would not attack and kill them? Even if Nosek was trustworthy—which he seemed to be—how could a bandit like Krol Rudy be trusted? Cybula could foresee that when he assembled the Lesniks and reported Nosek's words, they would charge him with being a traitor. They might even want to kill him and Laska. Perhaps it would be better for him to flee now. Cybula had often heard about forest dwellers, people who left their camps and went deep into the woods to live out their years alone, without wives, without children, without huts or tents. All they possessed were bows and arrows. Cybula had toyed with the idea of doing the same. There was no need to share one's bed with a female. No one ever died from living alone. Cybula had never liked the mindless talk of men and women, their chatter about the gods, the rumors they spread about one another, their gossip. He did not enjoy being a leader of men, but he surely had no desire to be a follower. Yes, this is what I must do, he said to himself. I'll live alone and die alone. I'll turn my back on the whole breed of men. Perhaps I should set out right now? Neither Kora nor Laska needs me. Laska has a husband, a krol. And Kora likes all men. She would give herself to a stallion if she could. Cybula felt pity only for Yagoda. Perhaps he should take her along? She would follow him anywhere. Finally, he fell asleep.

When he woke, the sun was shining outside. A fire was

burning between the stones which served as an oven and Kora was roasting meat. She tore the pretzel which Nosek had brought into four chunks—one for each of them. Cybula and the women ate silently. The coming day would tell their fate. The pretzel was stale, but Cybula chewed it slowly and felt he was tasting the flavor of the field, the stalks of wheat. Compared to the meat, he thought, the pretzel was easier to digest. No beast had to be killed in order for him to eat and enjoy his food. After the meal Cybula left the cave to convoke a meeting of the Lesniks. Kora and Yagoda went out to gather roots and fruit. Laska remained alone in the cave. It was dangerous for her to be seen before Cybula could explain to the people that she had come to make peace.

Laska had not slept well during the night, and when the others left the cave, she returned to her bed. But she could not sleep. In her dreams she saw Krol Rudy dead, Nosek the new krol and she his krolowa, her father a kniez. There was peace between the Lesniks and the Poles. She and Krol Nosek lived in a big house. He took her with him wherever he went, and talked over with her all the events of the camp: whom to reward and whom to punish. She bore him ten children, five boys and five girls. Her father married Yagoda and sent Kora away. Kora committed some sin against him and was put to death. Laska imagined Kora bound with rope to a tree, and a woyak standing beside her waving a sharp sword over her head. For a short time Laska delighted in this dream, but then she began to ask herself, What is it that I have against her? True, she took my mother's place. But so did Yagoda. No, it is not this. It is that I cannot bear her falsehood, her gossip, her flattery, her looseness. She lies with her daughter's husband. All the woyaks have had her. How can my father lie with such a whore? Laska fell asleep, and the sound of voices woke her up. Cybula had gathered the Lesniks outside his cave. He came to bring Laska to them, so she could talk to them of Nosek's offer of peace, and of the answer he had given Nosek.

3

The Lesniks Return to the Valley

EVERYTHING happened quickly. On the first day the Lesniks discussed the offer among themselves, shouting their suspicions and grudges against Krol Rudy, Nosek, Kora, Laska; calling Cybula traitor, spy, threatening him with hanging, beheading. The next day Nosek appeared among them unarmed, repeating everything Cybula had said the day before. And on the third day most of the Lesniks were ready to go down to the valley. They refused Nosek's plea that they leave their arms behind, but they swore by the gods that if the woyaks did not attack them, they would not attack the woyaks.

The men walked along, carrying their weapons. The women carried baskets and rolled-up mats in which they had packed household things. Several women were leading goats. A group of Lesniks remained in the mountains. Some of them predicted that those who went down to the valley would descend even farther—to the hollows of the earth in death. Others had decided to wait and see how the first Lesniks fared.

It was a warm day. The farther down they got, the warmer it became. Since they had not taken any children when they escaped into the mountains, they were all adults, except for one child born in the mountains, which the young mother carried in a basket on her back.

Before they set out on their way, Cybula had chosen a tall, long-legged youth, Wysoki, to run ahead to tell those in the valley that their brothers and sisters were coming home. Wysoki's mother, a widow, had wrung her hands, crying that her son had been sent to a certain death. But Nosek assured her that no harm would come to him. The woyaks all knew that Krol Rudy had offered peace to the Lesniks. Also, it was a law in all Polish lands that messengers were not to be harmed. Wysoki carried a flag—a pole with three notches and a small hide whitened with chalk.

The men walked in silence. One man tried to sing, but when no one joined him, he soon fell still. Some of the women were crying. Cybula had told them that they were coming home as winners, not losers. But still their hearts were heavy. They might have made the way down in one day, but they all walked slowly. Besides, Cybula and Nosek thought it better to arrive in the daytime and not at night. Therefore, it was agreed to spend the night en route and arrive in the morning. They would stop by a wood stream where they could rest, eat, wash the dust from their feet, and refresh themselves with cold drinks.

The night passed. In the morning the Lesniks bathed in the stream, each ate what he had brought along, and together they set on their way. They could scarcely believe their eyes when they saw Krol Rudy, his kniezes, his woyaks, the whole camp, coming out to greet them. The woyaks were singing a song of welcome. The Lesniks who had remained in the camp were crying and laughing, hugging and kissing their returning brothers and sisters. Beverages, pretzels, roasted meat, and fruit were brought out. Krol Rudy had ordered the drummers to drum and the buglers to sound their horns. Children came carrying baskets of flowers.

Krol Rudy had put on his robe and his sword, and on his head he had a pumpkin with wax candles. He was already intoxicated, but still he addressed the crowd. He promised to treat the mountain Lesniks with love, as brothers and sisters, as Poles. He also announced that their leader, Cybula, would henceforth be promoted to kniez. Then Krol Rudy and the kniezes and woyaks drew their swords from their sheaths and swore an oath of loyalty to the men of the fields, the Polish nation. Krol Rudy reminded the camp that soon the harvest would start and everyone's help would be needed. He also said that huts would have to be built, since the winters were cold and tents were suited only to the warm summer months. He finished his address with a prayer to the gods, and with the promise of a sacrifice—once the harvest was over—to the god of rain, dew, sunshine, and bountiful crops, Chlebodawca.

The Lesniks had never heard of him, but Nosek had told Cybula that this god lived both in the rivers and on land. When he became enraged he called forth a flood, a cloudburst, even hailstones as large as goose eggs from the sky. He could also send out locusts to devour every grain of wheat in the fields. Those who lived near large rivers such as the Vistula, Warta, Bug, Wieprz, could sometimes see him—a giant, his hair and beard curled and the color of straw. When he laughed, thunder rumbled and lightning shot out of his eyes. The clouds were his horses. He flew like a bird and swam like a fish. Sometimes in the morning one could see him bathing nude in the river, and with him all the young maidens who were sacrificed to him—stark naked, with hair that reached down to their hips, with breasts and bellies so beautiful that they blinded all who gazed upon them. Nosek confessed to Cybula, "I myself never saw him." And he winked and shrugged his shoulders.

Krol Rudy and the woyaks invited all the Lesniks—both those who had stayed in the valley and those who returned from the mountains—to a festive meal. Tables made of tree trunks and benches of hewn wood were quickly set up outside. Women brought meat, vegetables, and fruit from their huts and tents. Krol Rudy ordered that the food be shared, because all Poles were like the children of one father and one mother. Krol Rudy declared the day a *swieto*, a holiday, and ordered pitchers of vodka and mead served at each table. Those Lesniks who had stayed in the valley had grown accustomed to indulging in these beverages, but the mountain people had not. The drinks raised their spirits, helped them forget their cares, made them sing, dance, kiss, laugh. The men told funny stories, the women giggled and clasped each other's arms, naked children joined hands in a circle, hopped and danced and stamped their little feet. After the feast a choir of woyaks sang a song to the gods, to the fields, to the orchards. Then they began to dance.

Cybula had never seen such dancing before. First the woyaks half squatted; then they leaped like frogs, turned somersaults, stood on their heads, walked on their hands. The sun's rays alighted on Krol Rudy's beard, and it seemed to be on fire. He yelled, "*Niech zye Polska!*—Long live Poland!"

And everyone answered, "*Niech zye!*"

"*Niech zye Krol Rudy! Niech zye Krolowa Laska!*"

"*Niech zye Kniez Cybula!*"

They had placed Laska between her husband, Krol Rudy, and her father, Kniez Cybula. They placed a pumpkin with candles on her head, also. Next to Cybula sat Nosek, while Kora and Yagoda were put at the far end of the table. Krol Rudy once again was addressing the crowd. His face was strangely red, and he was shouting, "Kniez Cybula, since you are Laska's father, you are my father also. It was she who persuaded me to make peace. She was lying in bed with me, and she pulled at my beard and said, 'Krol of mine, I want peace.' And I said, 'If you, my krolowa, want peace, then go to the mountains and make peace.' She thought I was joking, but a word from Krol Rudy is like a word from the gods. Our enemies accuse us of tearing open the earth's skin and un-covering her when we plow. But we Poles say, 'The earth is like a virgin: if she is to be seeded and fertilized, she has to be torn open. The earth, like a woman, wants to bear fruit and to be opened.' Is this not true, Kniez Nosek, my great and learned friend?"

"Yes, true," Nosek murmured.

"And you, Kniez Cybula, do you agree with me? Speak the truth, don't be afraid."

"In this I do agree with you," Cybula said.

"From this day on, you are a Pole, a Polish kniez. And I am a Polish krol. Our kingdom here is small, but it will spread and expand and become large. A day will come when we will belong to one nation, the greatest and strongest in the world. And all the other nations will serve us and worship our gods, and our fields will cover the earth. Is this not true?"

"True! True!"

"And one more thing . . ."

As he said these words, Krol Rudy suddenly stopped speaking. He shivered and fell facedown on the table. Cybula was frightened. He thought that his protector had been struck dead. But the other kniezes burst out laughing. They knew that this happened whenever the krol was drunk. "Put him down on the grass," Nosek ordered some woyaks who stood nearby. "And pour cold water on his face."

(2)

When Cybula saw the field the first time, it had seemed immense to him, stretching far into the distance. But now, when he saw it in daylight, it became clear that the field could never feed the entire camp. At best it would provide a snack of bread to be eaten with the meat. The other Lesniks knew this, too, and even kidded Cybula for being a victim of Polish claptrap. One of them asked, "Was this, then, worth shedding so much blood?" Another said that to feed the whole camp a lot of forest would have to be cleared. The gifts of the forest would be lost forever—blackberries, blueberries, strawberries, mushrooms, logs for building, wood for heating and cooking. Also, if the forest was cut down, the birds and animals would run away. There would be no more meat, no pelts. But all this was useless talk. Meanwhile, Krol Rudy ordered every man, woman, and child to cut wheat, tie it in bundles, thresh it, grind it. Only small children, those who were ill, and women about to give birth were not required to work. Even the kniezes and Krol Rudy himself worked during the days of the harvest.

Krol Rudy ordered that the skeletons that were used as scarecrows be taken away so that women with child should not see them and bear monsters or dead children. The Lesniks who had stayed in the valley had labored for a long time: they plowed, sowed, weeded. And now everything had to be done to ensure a plentiful crop. Prayers were chanted to the gods, the sun-god was called upon to shine and the clouds not to make rain. During the woyak attack, many of the gods had been smashed or set on fire. But Lesniks who had the necessary skill made new gods from clay or carved them from wood: male and female gods, shapes of birds, oxen, deer, even wild boars. In the beginning the woyaks tried to force their Polish gods upon the Lesniks, but Nosek persuaded Krol Rudy to let the Lesniks worship their own. Besides, the woyaks themselves were not of one mind. Each came from his own neighborhood and worshipped his own gods.

Besides their own local gods, the Lesniks shared a few gods in common. One was a huge ancient oak. Its trunk was so thick that five men surrounding it with their arms outstretched could barely touch fingers. Its roots spread out in all directions, its branches were large. There was a deep hollow in the oak, burned out by lightning. It was the custom of young maidens to gather around the oak on warm summer evenings, pour holy water on its roots, and sing songs. Old folks would tell how, long ago, a giant with three heads and a tail fell down from the sky. No sooner did he see the oak than he made up his mind to uproot it. But the oak did not budge. For three days and three nights the giant struggled, but he could not overcome it. On the third night he let out a

dreadful roar and fell down dead. Flocks of scavenger birds
came flying from all corners, and it took from one new moon
until the next before they could devour the giant's body. From
that time on, the oak became a god. Its acorns were placed in
children's cribs to give them vigor and health. There were old
women in the camp who believed that the opening in its
trunk led to where the dead dwell. There was also a clump of
holy lime trees not far from the camp. On a stone altar in
their midst, every autumn a child was sacrificed to Baba Yaga.

Yes, the Lesniks did not forget their gods. There were
several old women who spoke the gods' tongue, and people
sought their advice in matchmaking, healing the sick, fighting
an enemy. One wrinkled old witch could bring up spirits of
the dead and make them foretell what is to be.

On the night before the harvest, the young maidens assembled around the holy oak, chanted a lengthy prayer,
sprinkled water on its roots, rubbed their hands and faces
with its bark. Short prayers were also said at the clump of
lime trees. The next day the camp was awakened with the
beating of drums and sounding of horns. This was to be the
camp's first harvest.

Krol Rudy and the kniezes allotted the work: men would
reap with scythes, women with sickles. The woyaks warned
the reapers to cut the wheat straight, not to spoil the straw,
which would later be used for making thatched roofs. That
day the gods were with the Poles. The sky was clear, with not
even a puff of white. Krol Rudy himself grabbed a scythe and
reaped. With his strong voice he sang as he worked, and the
others, picking up the tune, sang and worked with him.
Cybula was given a sickle, not a scythe, since he was short
and not young anymore. Nosek taught Cybula to work slowly

or he would soon tire. The reapers reaped and the balers tied up the wheat in large bundles. Flocks of birds soared up from the field, then flew back and around it. They screeched and squawked with voices that sounded almost human.

Cybula worked briskly, eager to show that he was as skillful a reaper as he had once been a hunter. But he was growing very tired. He was beginning to see that chasing an animal in the woods—shielded by shade-giving trees—was one thing, while working in an open field was something else. He had not brought a hat with him, and he had no hair to cover his head. The closer it came to midday, the hotter the sun blazed. The joints in his arms were aching, his legs could barely hold his body. "What is this? Am I getting old?" Cybula asked himself. From time to time he lost his breath. He sweated profusely and was so drowsy that he could keep his head from nodding only with the greatest of effort. Kora and Yagoda, who worked nearby, were throwing him curious glances. Large drops fell from his forehead. His throat was dry and his knees buckled under him. Kora came over and said, "My kniez, rest a while."

"Don't call me kniez. My name is Cybula, and it will stay my name until I die."

"Your head is as red as a beet—all sunburnt. Don't you have a hat?"

"All I have is this bald pate."

"You are also hoarse. Wait, I'll bring you some water."

"Where are you off to? Why did you stop reaping?" a woyak shouted at Kora, waving a whip over her head.

"I am going to get water for Kniez Cybula. His head was burned by the sun."

"Go back to work! An old woman will be by shortly to

bring water to those who are thirsty." And the woyak gave Kora a lash on the bare calves of her legs.

Some of the reaping women laughed, others gaped. Kora had many enemies among them. Yagoda ran up and shouted at the woyak, "Why are you hitting my mother?" Cybula knew that he should confront the woyak, defend Kora. But all his courage had left him. With one arm he tried to shield his head from the broiling sun; he felt its rays were scorching his scalp, his forehead, his neck. The light blinded him and whirled dizzyingly in front of his eyes. A nauseous fluid flooded his mouth. He knew that if he provoked that mean woyak, he would taste the sting of his whip also. He, Cybula, was ashamed. He had been singled out and disgraced. Cybula searched for Laska among the reaping women, but apparently she worked far from where he stood. Some of the men had taken off all their clothes and were working naked; many urinated in public; even women crouched to defecate without any shame. Then someone brought him a drink of water in a wooden ladle. Cybula looked for shade, but as far as his eye could see, there was not a tree or a tent in which he could hide from the god of the heavens. Of what worth was a speck of life to the sun-god, who lived forever, but he, Cybula, was already on the brink of death. "Death, the redeemer of all futile hopes, you are my true god! I will serve you until my last breath!" a voice in Cybula cried out.

(3)

Krol Rudy had promised Cybula a house, but the building had not yet begun. Meanwhile, he lived with Yagoda in Kora's fire-ravaged hut. Since he had sunstroke and could

not work, he lay on a pelt in deep sleep. The sun had set
by the time Kora and Yagoda came to wake him. The men
and women who did the harvesting lit a fire near the field,
then gathered around it, sang, danced, roasted meat on the
coals as well as ears of wheat. The young women danced in a
circle, and the old ones told stories about little red people who
lived under the earth, about mermaids who were half women
and half fish, about children born with hair and teeth who
returned to earth after death to play evil pranks on the living.
One old woman told about a man who went out to urinate
one night and the earth swallowed him up; days later, his
voice was heard calling from the depths, but no one could
reach him. Another woman told about a wench who was
digging for roots one hot summer day, when suddenly a
whirlwind picked her up and carried her off forever. Another
told the story of a starving young mother who was no longer
able to suckle her infant. The distraught woman went into a
tent where she kept a *bagini*, a goddess, knelt before her, and
prayed for help. Suddenly warm milk began to flow from the
goddess's clay breasts, and the child was nourished until it
was weaned.

In the camp there lived an old man, Rybak. It was said
that he was a hundred years old and that he could remember
a time when the Lesniks had neighboring camps. Rybak
had belonged to a tribe which called itself Rybaki, the fisher-
men. They had a lake full of fish. During one of the wars,
Rybak was taken prisoner and for years served the Lesniks as a
slave—a woodchopper, a water carrier. One day his master
chose him to be his daughter's husband, and Rybak was a free
man. He remembered a summer when the sky was overcast for
three months straight. The days were as dark as the nights.

The sun never showed itself, and people began to believe that a jealous god had extinguished it. In the months when usually it was hot, that year it snowed. The trees never bloomed and their branches remained bare. There was no grass, and oxen, cows, horses, sheep, and pigs all died of hunger. The vines produced no fruit and the earth no vegetables. Entire tribes starved to death. Even the fish in the rivers perished, since they, too, needed the earth's plants. A sorceress foresaw that the end of the world was coming. But suddenly the sky cleared and the sun shone. One day it was winter, and the next, summer came. That night old women saw a brightly lit ship in the sky, with shimmering sails.

One old woman remembered a summer when it never rained. Men and animals died of thirst. Bits of fire dropped from the sky. There was lightning, but no thunder. Hot winds blew up from the south and set trees on fire. So hot was the earth that people who walked on it barefoot scorched their soles. A huge serpent fell down from the sky not far from the camp. The stench from its carcass brought sickness, and an epidemic spread throughout the camp.

Even though Cybula was still somewhat ill from the sunstroke, as well as the disgrace he had suffered that day, he came out in the evening to join the merrymaking. He expected to be mocked with laughter and catcalls, but everyone asked about his health and wished him a speedy recovery. Some women smeared his skin with ointment. Nosek came to see him, and the two men sat late into the night talking about the plight of the camp. No, there was not nearly enough wheat to feed the people. They would need more fruit, berries, mushrooms, and meat. Without hunting and hunters, people would starve during the winter months. Cybula tried to apologize for not having been able to finish his work in the field, but Nosek comforted him by saying, "We had enough harvesters. All we need is more wheat to harvest!" It was already past midnight when Cybula returned to the hut, to Yagoda and Kora. He had sworn to serve the god of death, but the desires of the living still burned in him.

(4)

Nosek, speaking for Krol Rudy, reached an understanding with Cybula. All matters pertaining to fields—when to plow, sow, harvest, how much wheat and roots to set aside for beer and vodka—were under the kniezes' control. In matters relating to the Lesniks only, Cybula was in charge. Cybula thus became what he was before: the elder of the Lesnik camp. New huts were needed before the rains and snow began. Old huts needed repair. The time for every man to do as he pleased was over. Hunters needed some kind of payment for sharing their catch with others. Guards had to be posted against woyaks who continued to steal and to rape. Children were born and no one knew who fathered whom. Most of the women had been raped by more than one woyak. If the camp was to become truly Polish and live on the fruits of the land, large tracts of forestland would have to be cleared, roots of trees pulled out or burned, rocks carried away. But who would take on this work of his own free will? A way had to be found to provide for those who worked. And finally, it was not only woyaks who were guilty of misdeeds. Thieves, robbers, rapists arose among the Lesniks as well—evil always bred more evil. Someone in the camp would have to serve as judge and make sure that justice was done.

Since Cybula was the one Lesnik everyone trusted, most of this burden fell on his shoulders. He often remarked that were it not for Nosek, he would have collapsed under the weight. From morning until evening people assailed him with their demands and complaints. Some had received a smaller share of wheat or straw than others. One family was promised a new hut, while another had only a roof repaired. There were now more than twice as many women in the camp. Mothers and widows had neither the time nor the strength to dig holes, chop wood, carry logs, put up roofs, tasks which required men. To persuade men to build huts for families not their own meant that a new order had to be set up, one which would provide fairly and amply for everyone.

Cybula often had to laugh to himself. He had never foreseen what entanglements the fields would bring with them. He now appreciated how simple it had been in his former life, when a hunter, and his family, ate of his own catch, built his own hut or tent, set up his own traps, took care of his own beehives. The fields, and those who forced them on the Lesniks, brought with them a partnership which the people did not want and the gods perhaps did not approve of. Sometimes Cybula thought that the only way out of their plight would be to get rid of all the woyaks and return to the old ways. But that would bring on another bloodbath. Moreover, there were rumors that the Poles in different regions were growing steadily stronger and their kingdom was spreading far and wide.

It became known that not more than ten days' ride from the camp, the Poles had built what they called Miasto, a town. Fields, gardens, and orchards extended in every direction, as well as camps called *gospodas* which belonged to a kniez, a lord, a pan, or whatever the owner called himself. The owner had a large house—a gospoda—built for his family and servants. He had woyaks to guard him from his enemies. He owned herds of oxen, cows, horses, sheep, pigs. Dwelling in Miasto were artisans: shoemakers, tailors, furriers, hatters, coopers, blacksmiths, tinsmiths, carpenters, and others. There were also *kupiecs*, merchants, who traded one kind of merchandise for another, keeping a portion for themselves. They had stores in which they weighed goods on scales or measured them with sticks. From regions where the Vistula flowed into the sea, merchants came to buy wheat, honey, hides, horses, sheep, wool, even slaves, and paid for them with articles produced by the Niemcies, the Germans—the mute ones. They babbled in a language no one understood, but these foreigners could build ships, tan hides, spin threads, extract from the earth mineral stones or sand, which was later smelted in ovens and made into glass, mined lead, copper, tin.

Both Niemcy and Polish krols had foundries where coins were made of silver or gold. The coins were called *pieniadze* (money) or *zloto* (gold). Even though the Lesniks had nothing to sell, Nosek persuaded Cybula to ride with him to Miasto simply to see what it was like. Not all Poles were savages like Krol Rudy and his woyaks. There were many who could speak to the Germans, the Czechs, the Russians, and even with people who lived across the sea. Cybula could only listen to Nosek and gape.

Alone in their corner of the world, surrounded by forests, far from other tribes, the Lesniks—like a worm in horseradish —believed their burrow to be the whole world. But a new time was coming, with new ways. Men were no longer limited to hunting and fishing. They dug into the bowels of the earth and found treasures there. They sailed ships over the rivers, lakes, and seas. Wheelmakers made carts, wagons, *bryczkas*. In the winter some men traveled in sleds. Nosek told of soldiers who fought wars with chariots. He also told Cybula about writing: an animal's hide was tanned and made into parchment and then, with a quill, people drew marks on it which others could read. Nosek spoke of faraway places named Persia, Greece, Rome, Egypt. In the land of Africa black people lived. Some countries had strong fortresses with towers, and krols who wore crowns on their heads. Beautiful women wore garments of silk and satin, adorned themselves with chains, bracelets, earrings, necklaces, nose rings. There were wise men called astrologers who knew what happened high up in the heavens. Nosek uttered names which the tongue could not pronounce. Nosek also told Cybula that in his many wars, during his plundering days, Krol Rudy had amassed a large treasure of silver and gold which could be bartered for oxen, sheep, clothing, shoes, weapons, coaches, saddles, and whatever else the heart desired. Krol Rudy was prepared to entrust Nosek with part of his riches and send him to Miasto to exchange his gold for goods. Nosek was willing to take Cybula along. The journey would not be altogether safe, because bands of robbers lurked on the roads. Miasto itself swarmed with thieves and murderers, but a clever man could steer clear of these dangers.

Cybula chose to mull the trip over in his head before agreeing to go. It was not easy for him to leave the camp; he always missed Yagoda whenever he had to leave her alone. But Nosek told him that no woman could make this journey. Nosek also asked him to make up his mind before the rains and the snow began, because he found his way by the sun or the stars, as did the men who sailed on the seas. There was no topic Cybula could not discuss with Nosek, except the riddle of why men and animals suffered and died. Whenever Cybula asked about this, Nosek would reply, "Only the gods can answer."

4

❧

Journey to Miasto

WHEN Cybula told Kora and Yagoda that he planned to ride to Miasto with Nosek, to be gone almost four months, Yagoda burst out crying and wailed that she would never see him again. Kora warned him that bandits infested the roads, as well as vicious smoks, *babuks*, and other devils who dragged people over the mountains to dark pits at the end of the world. But Cybula was firm: he had given his consent to Nosek, who had passed it on to Krol Rudy. Besides, the camp needed horses, wagons, plowshares, scythes, sickles, hoes, saws, hammers, and many other tools for the fields and their new houses. He also promised to bring back gifts for Kora and Yagoda. Kora allowed herself to be placated after a while, but hard as he tried, Cybula could not convince Yagoda that the trip would bring something good to her, to himself, to the camp. It was close to dawn when the three finally fell asleep.

Soon after sunrise Nosek came to awaken Cybula. Everything was ready: two horses for the men, a third horse to carry their supplies as well as Krol Rudy's booty. For the first time in his life, Cybula carried a sword at his hip, and wore a hat with feathers, as well as the long cloak, a *zupan,* worn only by kniezes. He looked like one of the great heroes grandmothers told stories about on long winter nights. Krol Rudy and his kniezes took leave of the two emissaries. Cybula deftly climbed up on his horse. He kissed Yagoda, Kora, and the other women and girls, who came bearing baskets of flowers and fruit. Two rows of woyaks saluted the riders: they pulled out their swords, put them together to form an archway, and shouted words of praise. Nosek distributed to the children pretzels baked of the first harvest's flour. Krol Rudy came, accompanied by Laska, who, although the weather was warm, had put shoes on her bare feet, as befitted the wife of a king. She kissed her father, and Nosek kissed her forehead and knelt before her. Krol Rudy shouted out, "May the gods be with you!" and he signaled the riders to begin their journey. Yagoda had promised Cybula not to cry, but she wailed nevertheless, even as she accompanied him to the road outside the camp.

Cybula, who had never left the region in which he was born, knew nothing of the road he was taking. He relied completely on Nosek, who said they must find a stream which flowed down from the mountain and follow it all the way. It was Nosek who had wandered in many lands for years, fought wars, met all kinds of people. Nosek rode on one horse, leading the other along, and Cybula rode behind, his eyes and ears watchful for surprise attacks. One hand held the reins as the other rested on the handle of his sword. The road meandered

through a forest. It seemed to be more of a trail, too narrow
even for one man, and now disappearing under moss, fallen
pine needles, branches, cones. Previous travelers had carved
some markings on tree trunks, but Cybula could not understand how these markings indicated direction. It was odd to
have left the camp not as a man fleeing his enemies but as a
pan, a kniez. And on whose mission? That of his former
enemy, a king who had married his daughter and perhaps
killed his wife. Even though events happened one by one,
as one looked back on them they resembled a clever plan
arranged by some godly sage who wanted no one to guess
how it would end. If someone had told Cybula on the night of
the massacre that the murderers' leader would become his
son-in-law, and would send him to a distant place, entrusted
with his precious possessions, Cybula would have thought it
madness. Yet the powers had seen fit to decree it all.

So that the horses were not overtaxed, the two men rode
slowly and let them rest, graze, drink. They themselves
also rested and ate. On the road they became even closer to
each other than before. Each needed the other's help. When
one dozed off, the other stood guard. One evening, after the
two had eaten and prepared to spend the night in the forest,
off the road, but not too far away, Cybula said to Nosek, "All
troubles come from men. What would happen if there were
no men in the world? Women would never turn to robbing,
and no one would have to fear being attacked in the night.
Women are weak and are reluctant to leave their tents after
dark."

Nosek smiled. Cybula had such strange thoughts. Nosek
answered in his simple way, "If there were no men, there
would be no women, either."

"Somehow I can't imagine a woman with a sword or a spear, hurting another woman and stabbing her," Cybula said.

"Female animals are just as bloodthirsty as male animals," said Nosek. "A female wolf would tear apart a deer or a man as quickly as would a male wolf. Our own women kill small animals and fish. They don't kill each other because we men do it for them."

"Yes, true," Cybula agreed, "but men are different from animals."

"They are not so different. Women are lazy; they only appear to be softhearted. They send men out to face all the dangers, and they stay in their huts and warm themselves by the fire."

A long while passed before Cybula answered: "You, Nosek, don't like women."

Nosek smiled. "Not much."

"Why?"

"Ah, it's hard to speak to them. If you say something that displeases them, immediately they raise a hue and cry. And they always complain about men: men don't love them enough, don't pamper them enough. Women hate each other, but still they always fall into each other's arms and claim to be devoted. If one is ill, another comes immediately to fill her place in bed, next to the husband. It could be her own sister!"

"Are men any better?" Cybula asked.

"Men are more honest."

"People say that you don't want to marry. Is that true?" Cybula asked, and immediately regretted his words.

Nosek did not answer at once. Then he said, "I have become used to living without women. In the years when we

were a fighting band, months would go by when we never saw
them. Our woyaks would kill the old and ugly women, and the
young ones would be so terrified, they could only scream and
void. Some of them fought the men until they were covered
with blood. There's no pleasure in lying with a female who
spits on you, curses you, and tries to gouge out your eyes."

"Is it better to lie with a man?" Cybula asked.

"When two men do this, they are friends, not enemies,"
Nosek answered.

Night fell; the stars came out. Nosek said, "We have
ridden so far, and yet we see the very same stars."

"You recognize the stars?"

"Yes."

"How?"

"By their position, how they stand together. It's always
the same."

"What are they?" Cybula asked.

"Some sort of fires, I think. But they must be very large
and not as small as they seem. I once saw these very same
stars near the Vistula and in many other places. They move
away, but they come back every year. Some in summer, some
in winter." Both men fell silent. It was hard to know whether
Nosek was sleeping or awake. Cybula was already beginning
to dream, when something bit him. He sat up with a start.
Was it a snake? He was well aware that one could die from
a snake's bite. Even some mushrooms and berries had poison
which killed if you ate them. Every minute, man put his life
in danger. Cybula thought he heard a rustle, footsteps among
the trees. Was it a wolf? A bear? He kept grabbing the handle
of his sword, but of what use was a sword against a bear or a
wolf? Cybula longed to talk more to Nosek, but he did not

dare awaken him. Nosek, apparently, was not as attached to life as he was, or as gloomy as he, Cybula. Nosek did not burrow into the worries which gnawed at Cybula day and night.

(2)

They were lost. They could not find the stream which led to Miasto. They had ridden for hours and there was no one to ask. When they did chance on someone—a barefoot wanderer with a stick and a pack on his back—the fellow had never heard of Miasto. He did not quite understand the language in which they spoke to him. Now clouds gathered on the edge of the sky and darkened it. A cold wind blew. The horse carrying the supplies began to limp. Cybula looked for a cave to hide from the coming rain, but there were no caves in the valley. He blurted out, "The gods don't want us to reach Miasto."

"What does it have to do with the gods?" Nosek asked.

It started to rain, and the sprinkle quickly turned into a torrent. The two men and their horses rode deeper into the forest in search of cover. There was thunder and lightning. Wet animals rushed past them, frightened by the flooding waters. Cybula was too tired to pick up his bow and shoot at them. His mother had told him that thunder was caused by gods who quarreled and rolled stones at one another. But why should gods quarrel? And what was lightning? If it was fire, then why didn't rain put it out? Cybula was asking himself the same questions he had asked as a child. From time to time a deer sped by, or a hare, a fox. It was odd: animals had only one way out—to run. But at least they did not commit the follies that men did: they did not go off in search of some town, did not try to sell someone else's booty, did not set up kings, did not become kniezes. The horses, which were tied to two trees, also wanted to flee; they tugged at their straps trying to break free. Their large dark eyes—all pupil—looked at the two men with fear and wonder, but the men could ride no farther. Night was beginning to fall. Nosek said wryly, "If we die here, Krol Rudy will think we ran off with his gold." And wet and miserable as his face was, he still managed to smile.

Both men sat quietly, their backs against the trees. Nosek arose, walked toward the horses, and from a bag tied to one of the saddles took out a chunk of meat and tore it in two. The horses could have easily bent their heads and eaten their fill, but they showed no hunger. Although Cybula was a hunter, accustomed to kill animals or lure them to traps, he also felt pity for them. He knew that their suffering was the same as man's—the same helplessness, the same fear of ceasing to be and becoming carcasses. At that moment Cybula's lot was the same as theirs, perhaps even worse than theirs. The horses were not restless, but he, Cybula, was in a hurry; if he was meant to die, let it happen soon. He longed to speak to Nosek, but Nosek kept stubbornly silent and behaved as if he clearly knew what not to do.

Cybula felt that he would not sleep a wink, but soon he was fast asleep. He was walking in a green meadow where horses, oxen, cows and calves grazed. A stream gurgled near-by. He was searching for a field, but whenever he thought he found it, the field kept moving away. He saw some people harvesting, but instead of tying the wheat in small bundles, they let it dry in the sun, heaping wheat on top of wheat, until it rose high above the treetops—a mountain of wheat! Cybula opened his eyes. The rain had stopped. He was wet and cold, but something of the warmth of the dream remained in his body. He looked around and saw Nosek busying himself with the horses. Cybula arose with better spirits, eager to resume the journey. He could sense that the day would grow warmer. He threw off his wet zupan and strolled over to Nosek naked.

"Shiva had a thorn in her hoof," Nosek said. "No wonder she limped."

"Did you pull it out?"

"Yes. She tried to bite me, but I managed to get it out."

They dressed, mounted their horses, and soon after sunrise rode out of the forest.

(3)

Slowly the days became weeks; the full moon became a half-moon and the half-moon turned into a new moon. The trail they had followed now merged with a wider roadway, and soon they saw other riders, wagons, and carts. They had reached a region settled by people who spoke the Polish language in their own strange way, and no day passed without Cybula learning new words and expressions. He kept discovering things he had never seen before, passing fields, orchards, fish ponds, wells, stone mills to grind wheat and corn, stables for horses, pigsties, windmills, bridges to cross streams and even rivers. He saw huts with thatched roofs, and a few with wooden shingles. Soon he saw a high wall with large towers looming in the distance, and as he gaped and they approached, Nosek explained:

"This wall was built by the rulers of Miasto of stone and brick, and they have posted guards in the watchtowers to warn them of approaching enemies. The krols and kniezes are always fighting, invading each other's gospodas, looting, and capturing slaves. Every settlement like Miasto has to be protected, and strangers like us will be stopped at the gate. If they allow us to enter, we shall have to pay a toll."

Outside the walls, the fields stretched out, already harvested. Cattle, horses, and sheep grazed on the grassy plains. Even the smells were new to Cybula, a mixture of smoke, garbage, something rancid, and something good like fresh baked bread. Nosek explained that not everyone in Miasto was allowed to own an oven and that the baking was distributed among a number of town dwellers.

At the gate, Nosek told the guards their journey's aim and paid the toll. Nosek spoke Polish, but he used words that Cybula could barely understand. Soon they were walking their horses down a street with houses on both sides. There were stores among the houses where bins of merchandise were displayed such as Cybula had never seen before. The ground was still muddy from yesterday's rain and puddles dotted the street. The street teemed with people. Wagons, pulled by horses or oxen hitched to wooden yokes, passed by. Cybula had entered into a new world. Even the people seemed new to him: they were all busy, yet they did not seem to know one another. Nosek said, "I think this is their market day."

As they walked along, doors opened and women emptied out slop pails, peels of onions, radishes, cucumbers, other vegetables and fruit. A man came out of one door hobbling on crutches. A blind man sat on a step humming to himself. Outside a house Cybula saw a large block of wood, and a man wearing a bloodied apron chopping meat and bones with an ax. He was selling chunks of a slaughtered ox or pig. An unpleasant odor arose from the meat and Nosek explained, "Here people have no time to hunt. They buy their meat from a butcher."

"Why does the meat smell?"

"It takes time for an animal to be slaughtered and skinned and brought to the butcher. The butcher does not always sell the meat in one day, and what remains the next day or on days after that must still be sold."

Dogs gathered among the women, sniffing the air. When a sliver of meat or bone dropped to the ground, they pounced on it, grabbing and tearing it from each other's mouth. The butcher picked up a heavy stick and began to chase after the dogs, hitting those he could reach. Cybula noticed that the meat was weighed on a scale, and when a woman received her portion, she handed some coins to the butcher. Nosek told him that this was money, copper groschens.

Until now Cybula had believed he knew human nature, understood people's needs and conduct. But the people he saw here were different. They were pressed together in heaps as if the town were an anthill. He and Nosek could steer their horses through the crowds only with difficulty. Pedestrians and wagons were coming from all directions. A man balanced two buckets of water on a wooden yoke braced over his shoulders, shouting, "Let the water man through!" The houses were built one next to the other and had rooms for workers to practice their crafts. One made shoes, another sewed clothes, a third cut hides. Nosek and his two horses were already far ahead; the street was not wide enough for the men to walk side by side. Here in town the air was hot, heavy, and

stifling. Through four-cornered holes in the walls—windows
—and through open doors Cybula could glimpse half-naked
women and naked children. One woman was nursing a child
at her huge breast, another cooked by a fire which blazed not
in an oven but on top of it. Here and there a room had a
wooden floor, but in most rooms the ground was muddy and
filthy. How could people live like this, Cybula wondered. The
huts in the Lesnik camp were larger, roomier, and not as
cluttered as these with beds, cribs, tables, benches, barrels of
clean water, and vats with foul water and scum. Children
came out to the street to answer nature's calls.

They left the narrow street and entered a large open square
which Nosek called "the market." Here there was a well and
the houses were higher than before, stories piled one upon
the other. In open stalls and on the ground merchants spread
out and exhibited their wares: earthen jugs, pots, sheepskins,
fur hats, fringed shawls, kerchiefs, tubs of honey, baskets of
mushrooms, beans, peas, turnips, radishes, cucumbers. Nosek
explained that those who came to the market to shop were
not kniezes' slaves but *kmiecies,* small landowners. They paid
tithes to the noblemen, and they were free. Often they had
parobeks, servants who worked in the fields or helped with
the housework. Nosek stopped a passerby to ask where an inn
might be found, explaining to Cybula that one did not spend
the night out of doors but stayed in a guesthouse. The guesthouse pointed out to them was a wooden structure of two
stories, so tall that Cybula was certain that it was about ready
to collapse. Two people came out to greet the new guests,
and Nosek—estimating their stay at six to seven days—asked
for the price. While one of the innkeepers was conferring with
Nosek, the other led the horses away after the leather bags

which held Krol Rudy's valuables were removed by Cybula. After a great deal of talk, a bargain was struck and a price agreed on. They would receive a private room with a door they could lock and a window overlooking the market. They would also take two meals a day at the inn. From a small pouch hanging around his neck Nosek removed a coin and made a down payment. As a child Cybula had learned how to figure out words whose meanings were hidden, but he was utterly bewildered now. It occurred to him that had Nosek not been an honest man, he could have sold Cybula as a slave. He felt completely helpless.

For the first time in his life, Cybula climbed up stairs. They were dark and Nosek had to guide him as if he were blind. He hurried ahead and opened a door, and Cybula entered a room with whitewashed walls, a wooden floor, and a window through which he could see the market below. It seemed as if he were up in the sky, near the clouds. People and horses below appeared small. In the room he saw a bed—a sack stuffed with hay on the floor—and a pillow whose torn pillowcase revealed more hay. There was a pitcher of water near the wall, and an earthen vessel near the bed. Nosek told Cybula to use it whenever he needed to relieve himself. Cybula's head was reeling. He felt the room swaying and the walls spinning. Nosek conducted himself like a man accustomed to travel. He took a swig from the water pitcher, sat himself down on a bench, and untied Krol Rudy's bags. He took out handfuls of coins, gold chains, brooches, bracelets, rings. For each item he had a name.

During his years of looting and killing, Krol Rudy had amassed a fortune, but had never made any use of it. Nosek had been the only kniez who never looted or raped. He wandered about with these Poles because he could not find a place to settle. He learned a great deal during those years. Among the woyaks, who kept changing with the years, he always found someone like himself whom he could befriend. He had no craving whatever for jewelry. He knew that the other kniezes had their own hidden bags of loot.

As Nosek counted the coins, examining each item separately, he wondered exactly what he could get for this treasure. Was there a set price for everything? He knew what he and Krol Rudy wanted to acquire—healthy horses, several mares, a stallion to mate with them, a carriage, swords, spears, knives, daggers, royal garments, perhaps a crown. Krol Rudy had also quietly instructed Nosek to bring him a young slave girl. Lying with Laska did not satisfy him lately. He craved a young wench who would submit to all his desires, dance for him, drink with him, tell him stories about demons and witches. Nosek had promised not to reveal this to Cybula. Nosek also had to buy plenty of seed for the camp, not only wheat and corn, but barley, oats, millet, beans. But could he actually purchase these things? Nosek was not as clever in trade as Cybula believed him to be, but he knew there were always swindlers and thieves. So the day was spent counting and reckoning. Nosek also explained that in distant cities there were men who could keep accounts and inscribe words with quills on parchment, or with chalk on boards.

In the evening the innkeeper came to announce that a meal had been prepared for the guests. In their room he lit the wick of a small clay lamp filled with seed oil. He carried a candle in a candlestick to light their way down. Cybula had never seen a candlestick, though in camp they sometimes used wax candles with wicks braided from sheep wool. The innkeeper now led Cybula and Nosek into a large chamber where they saw a long table with benches along both sides. Guests were already seated at the table and maids served them food in large wooden bowls. The guests were all men. How could it be otherwise? Women did not travel, because they did not ride horses. When Cybula and Nosek appeared in their long zupans, there was a moment's hush, then the din returned.

The guests made room at the table for the new arrivals. Everyone asked who they were and where they came from. Nosek responded to all their questions, while Cybula listened in silence. When they heard that the two came from a tribe of former Lesniks who had recently become Poles, they were astonished. They asked Nosek where this camp was located, and he could only point out the direction with his finger and add that it was beyond the mountains. They all spoke at once. When the maids came in carrying dishes of meat, the guests pinched them, even strained to grab hold of a breast, and the wenches laughed.

When the guests wanted to know why the two men undertook their long journey, Nosek told them that he had goods to sell and wanted to buy horses, weapons, a carriage, seeds. A new Polish kingdom had been created at the foot of the mountains. The talk soon shifted to trade. Every man was eager to grab a bargain, raise his worth, enlarge his fortune, become powerful and rich.

(4)

Cybula had promised Yagoda that his journey would last no more than four months, but the moon changed five times and the two emissaries were still in Miasto. Snow now covered the town and an epidemic was spreading. Children died by the score. Nosek, after he bought five horses, was paying for their feed while the carriage he had ordered was being readied. It was no trifle to make an axle, wheels, seats, a trestle. Wheelmakers and smiths toiled from sunrise to sunset, but still their work was not finished. Since few guests stayed at the inn in winter, Cybula and Nosek were often alone. The cook prepared their meals and the maids waited only on them. The innkeeper gave them two quilts stuffed with down.

Cybula was growing accustomed to living in town, and it often struck him as unbelievable that he had once been a hunter and cave dweller. Still, he missed Yagoda. He often awoke during the night, lay still for a long time, and thought about her. Did she still love him? Had she found someone new? In his thoughts he spoke to Yagoda, told her how much he longed for her, and promised to return to her, bearing gifts, with renewed love, as soon as his tasks were accomplished. He swore that never again would he leave her. But could she hear his promises? Sometimes he suspected that she no longer loved him, that she lay in the arms of another. At such moments so much sorrow overcame him that he thought of putting an end to his life. A number of times he told Nosek that he could wait no longer and he was ready to return alone to the camp. But Nosek dissuaded him: Cybula would freeze to death on the unknown way, he would be devoured by wolves.

One of the maids, Gloska, began to pursue Cybula. When Nosek was away at the smith's or the wheelmaker's, Gloska stealthily came to Cybula, took him to an upstairs room, and gave herself to him. Sometimes she submitted to him behind the stove, standing up. The other maids also teased him. And as if that was not enough, Nosek purchased a concubine named Kosoka. He pretended to want her for himself, but Cybula was well aware that Nosek felt no lust for women. He finally admitted he had bought her for Krol Rudy.

Kosoka said that she came from a remote region—from a tribe known as Tatars. Many tribes lived in that region—Kalmucks, Cossacks, and others with unpronounceable names. A woyak had captured her when she was still a child and she had lost her virginity. The woyak rode with her over the steppes; he stole, looted, sometimes murdered. He stole a horse, was caught, and finally hanged—while Kosoka was forced to stand by and watch. She was sold to another man, who sold her again. By the time she was fourteen, she had had many men. Twice she became pregnant, and twice she miscarried. She bore one infant, which she threw into the garbage pit. Kosoka had slanted eyes—black and fiery—white teeth, and shining black hair. She spoke Russian, Polish, Tatar, the languages of those who roamed the steppes and taigas and tundra. Some of her captors taught her to speak their own language. In all of them Kosoka could intone incantations, invoke devils, babuks, demons, imps. She came from a region where they ate horsemeat and milked mares. The men bought their wives with sheep. She boasted that by witchcraft she could stop a cow from giving milk, hens from laying eggs. She could make bees abandon their beehive, she could make a rooster stand still as if glued to the ground. She could close up a woman's womb, cause men to lose their vigor. Nosek had bought her from a pockmarked old woman with a blind eye and a lump on her forehead as large as a goose egg. The

truth is that Kosoka herself helped to arrange the sale. She
took twelve coins for herself and gave only six to the old
woman.

Kosoka was a born storyteller and remembered everything
she learned from the old Tatar men in the evenings as they
sang by the fire. Nosek had no patience with her small talk,
but Cybula liked to ask her questions and listen to her
rambling answers. She sang mournful tunes which resembled
the yodeling of the Lesnik shepherds in the mountains. She
told him stories of men with curved swords and women
whose faces were veiled. Kosoka's father was an old man who
had a long white beard and two wives, one old and the other
young. When Kosoka was six, because of some sin that the
young wife, Kosoka's mother, had committed, Kosoka's father
chopped off her head.

Cybula became quite attached to Kosoka and her stories,
even though he suspected that they were not all true. But
Cybula decided that even if she was lying, he loved to hear
and to be with her. When he asked for Nosek's permission,
Nosek said, "Do with her what you like, but don't make her
pregnant, because then she would lose all value to Krol
Rudy." Cybula told Nosek that he had taught himself to spill
his seed on her belly and between her breasts. All the while
Cybula lay with her, Kosoka went on chattering. In the heat
of passion, she sometimes cried out and said that soon she
would die. She wanted her soul to fly to the end of the world,
where darkness covered the earth and her mother's spirit
awaited her. At other times, her lust caused her to sing
whining songs which she herself did not understand. She liked
to tell how the woyak—the one who was hanged—used to
whip her. When she said or did something to annoy him, he

beat her with his stick. Later he licked the blood off her body. He told her that he had eaten the flesh of his enemy and had killed his own brother. Kosoka could read in the palm of a man's hand what his destiny would bring. She foresaw Cybula's end, but would not tell him what it was. She told him things about his dead wife, Yasna, and about Kora and Yagoda which she could not have known on her own.

After long delays and after the artisan who worked on Nosek's carriage had broken every promise, it became clear that the carriage would not be ready before spring. They had to leave. Nosek decided to spend three days buying as many goods as the horses could carry and then return to the camp. They had come with three horses, and now they had seven. Nosek traded Krol Rudy's silver and gold to a goldsmith for seeds, horses, hammers, nails, pitchforks to rake and pile hay, and shears to shear sheep. Nosek was planning to raise sheep as well as cattle. Requiring no effort at all, meadows surrounding the camp grew lush grasses and leaves. Horses, oxen, cows, sheep could graze and grow strong during the summer months. Only hay—their winter feed—would have to be provided.

The innkeeper, Dworak, and his wife, Pociecha, had often said that the tradesmen and craftsmen of Miasto swindled Nosek, sold their merchandise at the highest value and bought his at the lowest. Now that Cybula and Nosek were planning to leave, the innkeeper promised to secure from the tradesmen the goods for which high payments had already been made. Cybula and Nosek would come back for these goods and the carriage in the spring. Dworak seemed to be an honest man, but some gossip told Nosek that he, too, was dishonest. After Miasto, Cybula could see that the

few Lesniks who stayed behind in the mountains refusing
to join the Poles were right. He resolved to join them as soon
as he could.

(5)

Several days before Nosek and Cybula planned to leave
Miasto and return to their camp, Nosek gave Cybula two gold
coins to buy gifts. For Laska Nosek had bought a gold
bracelet. Cybula could not decide what gift to buy Yagoda,
and he settled, finally, on shoes. He never forgot how
beautiful Laska had looked in her shoes when she came to see
him off. But to have shoes made for Yagoda required the
measurements of her feet. Cybula knew only that Yagoda's
feet were small, smaller than her mother's or Laska's or
those of his dead wife, Yasna. Several times he had passed
the huts where the shoemakers worked, and he now made
up his mind to enter. It was a cold, dreary day. The sun was
about to set in the west, throwing a reddish light on the snow
through a gap in the clouds.

A small shoemaker sat on a low bench in the room, cutting
a sole out of a piece of hide. He was short and dark-skinned,
a type seldom seen in Miasto. His eyes were black, as was his
beard. He wore a sheepskin hat. He could not have been a
Pole, nor did he resemble one of the Lesniks. He might have
come from Kosoka's land. He was so absorbed in his work that
he did not look up and see Cybula. Suddenly he started, put
down the hide and the knife, stretched out his hands, and
began to wash and rub them in the snow outside his door. He
wiped them on some rag skin and stood facing the wall. What
was he doing? Could he be urinating, Cybula wondered. But

no, he stood for some time with his head bowed and murmured to himself. From time to time he rocked backward and forward. After a while he raised his hand, made a fist, and clapped the left side of his chest. Cybula looked on with amazement. Cybula decided he must be a sorcerer or a madman. The little shoemaker stood before the wall for a long time. Then he bowed down low and took a few steps backward. Only then did he raise his eyes and see Cybula, but he still continued to murmur. Cybula said, "What are you doing? To whom are you speaking? I want to order a pair of shoes for a girl."

The man mumbled a while longer. Then he said, "Where is the girl? I must measure her feet. Besides, night will soon fall. Come back with her, pan, tomorrow morning."

The man spoke the language, but it sounded strange. The words came out clipped; his voice was not the voice of the Miasto people. He added, "Soon I will close my door."

No one had ever addressed Cybula as pan. He asked, "How did you know I was a pan?"

"Ah, we know, we know. You live at the inn with the other pan, the one who bought horses and ordered a carriage. People think Miasto is big, but where I come from it would be thought of as very small. The merchants here are not honest. You two were cheated. But don't tell them that I told you. They will kill me immediately, those ruffians. They are evil people—thieves, robbers, murderers. They serve idols, not the true God. They carve a piece of wood or a stone, then bow to it and worship it. It is a lifeless idol, not a living God."

"Who are you? What is your name? Do you come from Miasto?" Cybula asked.

"No. My name is Ben Dosa and I am a Jew."

"What is a Jew?" Cybula asked.

"A son of the people whom God chose above all others, and to whom he gave the land of Israel. But our forefathers sinned, and they were driven out of the land."

He said all this without stopping, using words which Cybula did not understand. He had already learned from his talks with Kosoka that those who came from foreign regions spoke a mixed-up tongue and scrambled words.

"What is the name of the place you come from?"

"Ah, pan, you would not know it. It is a city and it is called Sura."

"Where is it?"

"Far far away. The land is called Babylon. It is never as cold as it is here. And there is no snow, only rain."

"Why did you come here?"

"I did not come by my own will. There I was a merchant, not a shoemaker. I boarded a ship intending to go to Sidon, but bandits took all my possessions and sold me to Canaanites who sailed the seas. I labored heavily for them, and they forced pig meat on me, which I am not permitted to eat. I worked for them for many weeks and months until I became ill. When a slave falls ill and can no longer work, the Canaanites throw him into the sea. This is how all idol worshippers behave. They are beasts. I thought my end was near, but God the Creator of all things took pity on me and I recovered. And so they dragged me from place to place, until we reached the region where the Vistula flows into the sea. There I was sold to men who spoke Polish; I was handed from master to master until I was brought to Miasto to become a shoemaker. My master takes the money I earn and gives me bread, sometimes a radish, an onion, a cucumber. I cannot eat the meat he gives me because it is unclean."

"What does that mean, unclean?" Cybula asked.

"It means that the animal was slaughtered against God's will. We call it *trayf* or *n'velah*."

"Who is this God?" Cybula asked.

"The creator of heaven and earth, as well as of man and all the animals," Ben Dosa said.

"Where is he?" Cybula asked.

"He's in heaven, on earth, in the depths of the sea, in the heart of all good men, on the mountaintops, deep in the valleys."

"Was he on that ship where they made you eat pig meat?"

"He is everywhere. Come back tomorrow with the girl."

"The girl is not here."

"Where is she?"

"Back in the camp, in the mountains."

"How can I make shoes for her if I don't know the size of her feet?"

"She has small feet, the smallest in the camp."

"What is she—a child?"

"No, an adult."

"I cannot make the shoes you ask for. What one man calls small another calls large. I have to take measurements, otherwise the shoes will come out too loose or too tight. I will have taken your coins and given you nothing. I would be cheating you."

"Well, then come with me to our camp and take the measurements there," Cybula said.

The man sat up excitedly. "Do you really mean this, pan?"

Cybula thought for a moment. "Yes, really. We have many animal skins, but we have no shoemaker. Our women make shoes for themselves from the skins of animals, but their crude work cannot compare with the shoes made here in town. We need a shoemaker. We can give you a hut and provide you with food, and if you wish, you can take one of our sisters or daughters to be your wife."

"Ah, I am not permitted to eat your meat, and I am not permitted to take for a wife a woman who worships idols. Besides, I left a wife and children back in Sura."

"I see. But they are there and you are here," Cybula said.

"Yes, but God is everywhere," Ben Dosa said. "He sits in heaven on his throne of glory and sees all that happens here on earth. He knows even what thoughts a man has deep in his heart. Flesh and blood can be deceived, but not God, who is eternal and lives forever." A while later he added, "Come tomorrow, pan. Perhaps I'll go with you to the mountains, if they let me free. This town is full of evil men. Perhaps God has sent you to me."

5

The Mutiny of the Woyaks

THERE was frost on the ground, but the sky had cleared and the sun was shining as Cybula and Nosek made the return journey to their camp, with seven horses laden with goods Nosek had bought—most importantly a supply of seeds and a stock of weapons. They were also bringing back a man, Ben Dosa, and a woman, Kosoka. Nosek let himself be persuaded to take the shoemaker along, this man who was also a tailor and furrier. He even claimed to be well versed in the art of writing on parchment. He carried a scroll around his neck, with letters and words he wrote. As a young boy he had learned many skills, including mathematics. Although he mixed words of his own language into the Miasto Polish, he could more or less make himself understood. In his home-land Ben Dosa had been a kupiec. Now he spoke not only Polish but even some Niemcy language, the language of the

Germans. He said he had learned it while a captive, before he was sold to the Poles.

The camp could use a man like Ben Dosa. He showed Nosek how the traders cheated him at Miasto, and taught him how to avoid being cheated again. True, he frequently mentioned the nation that was exiled for its sins, the temple which wicked men destroyed, the God whose name he was forbidden to utter, and other strange things. But what was this to anyone? They bought him and his cobbler's tools for two gulden, not much more than the cost of a horse.

Because the snow had hardened and the road was slippery, the four travelers preferred to walk. As Ben Dosa took cautious steps on the frozen ground, he praised God and enumerated his good deeds. When he ate a bit of food, a piece of bread, an apple, he blessed God before and after eating. Does he really not see what I see, Cybula wondered. Perhaps he pretends not to see.

Temporary and perilous though men's lives were, the mountains, valleys, and waterfalls were radiant on this fine day with permanence and certainty. The mountain snow sparkled in the sun. Here and there a melting trickle of water twisted down the rocky slopes. Under the snow the pines and firs shone green with their freshness. The breezes which blew from the woods brought the smells of spring into this winter day. Most of the birds had flown to warmer lands, but a few remained in the wintry blueness, flying on outstretched wings, bobbing up and down in the heights. In Miasto the snow was soiled with trampled refuse and mud. But in the mountains the snow spread out as pure as it fell.

For a while Cybula felt hopeful that a world as splendid as this could not be cursed. But soon something within him whispered that bad news awaited them in the camp. What could it be? Had Yagoda left him for someone new? Had the other kniezes incited Krol Rudy against him, plotting to behead him when he arrived? Cybula could no longer keep these dark thoughts to himself. He blurted out to Nosek, "I'm afraid to return home. Sometimes I wish I could go straight to the mountains, back to the cave."

Nosek looked at him, astonished. "What are you thinking about? They know in the camp that a journey like ours takes time."

"Something has happened there."

Ben Dosa suddenly joined in: "Do what Jacob did."

"Who is Jacob? And what did he do?" Cybula asked.

"Jacob is the father of all the Jews. When Jacob left his uncle Laban with his wives, his concubines, his twelve tribes, afraid that his brother Esau might attack him, he divided his family into two groups, so that if one was attacked the other could save itself."

Ben Dosa used so many foreign words and unfamiliar terms that Cybula could not grasp what he meant. He snapped at Ben Dosa, "Please use clear language, not the babbling of the Niemcies!"

"This is not babbling. It is the holy tongue in which the Torah was written."

"I still don't know what you are saying."

"Let us not all arrive together," Ben Dosa said. "If you have enemies in the camp, don't let them destroy everyone at one stroke."

"Not bad advice," Nosek said. "If you agree, Cybula, I'll ride ahead with two horses while you remain behind. Although I cannot believe that someone means to harm us."

"We have plenty of time to make our plans."

As Cybula uttered these words, he guessed what had gone wrong in the camp. The winter wheat was not sown, it was eaten instead. And if the summer wheat was not sown on time, there would be no fields this year. Cybula decided to say nothing. Why reveal his suspicions when they might turn out to be false? Cybula wanted to tell Ben Dosa to mind his business, but restrained himself. After all, Ben Dosa's advice was good. Cybula regretted that he had blurted out his worries, and yet at the same time he felt somewhat eased. From time to time he threw a glance at Kosoka. Alone with him she was a talker, a chatterer, but she held her tongue when Nosek was present. She regarded Ben Dosa with a sort of anxious curiosity.

Ben Dosa carried his tools in a sack on his back. Several times Cybula urged him to let the horses carry them, but Ben Dosa refused, saying the sack was not heavy. No matter what one said or asked of him, he answered with sayings from a holy book. He sometimes made Cybula wonder. He had lost his home, his family, was exiled in a foreign land, was never able to eat enough because so many goods were forbidden, unclean. Yet despite this, his face expressed peace and assurance, and his gaze was gentle and keen. Who knows? Cybula thought. He might be a sorcerer, or even a stargazer.

The horses' uphill climb in winter, with Kosoka and Ben Dosa and the heavy loads, was difficult. It took much longer to go uphill than downhill. Both men and animals left tracks behind them in the snow, inviting robbers and murderers to follow. Yet no harm came to the travelers. They were now close to their destination and could easily enter the camp that night, but Cybula and Nosek preferred to spend the night in the woods and wait for daybreak.

Early the next morning the first hint of trouble was revealed. Cybula came upon the field and saw that it was neither plowed nor sown. Then he caught sight of Kora. She seemed to be waiting, as if expecting his return. He looked at her and stopped in his tracks. Her skin was sallow, her cheeks hollow; she looked haggard, emaciated, prematurely old. She was barefoot. When she saw him she cried out, clasped her hands to her head, and began howling like an animal. Cybula stood and gaped. Before he managed to utter a word, Kora clapped her hands together and shrieked, "They are here, they have come back! My heart did not deceive me!"

She approached Cybula in a kind of dance, then began to bend and kneel as if seized with some pain in her belly. Cybula, Nosek, Ben Dosa, and Kosoka all watched her with amazement. Even the horses shook their heads from side to side and glanced backward. Nosek and Ben Dosa tightened their grip on the reins. Cybula asked Kora, his voice mocking, "What happened? Did the sky fall?"

"Krol Rudy lost his mind. The woyaks had another blood-bath. They killed your mother-in-law, Mala. They raped and killed her."

"Raped old Mala?"

"Yes. Raped, then stabbed her. Can someone tell in the dark who is young and who is old? Some of the woyaks wanted to leave. They rose up against Krol Rudy. They did not allow us to sow the fields; they seized the wheat and wanted to brew spirits from it. They tried to kill Krol Rudy, but Kniez Kulak was loyal and killed several of them. When

our people in the mountains heard this, they came down and
fought the woyaks. Yagoda and I ran to the woods and hid,
otherwise we, too, would have been killed. They would have
killed you, too, if you were here. In the darkness it was impossible to know who was killing whom. Suddenly the rains came
and the floods. Then the frosts—and it was no longer possible
to sow. Only twenty or so woyaks remained in the camp, and
they called themselves pans and kniezes. They took all the
land for themselves, and we became their slaves. The few of
our Lesnik men who survived are forced to chop down trees
in the forests so that the woyaks will have more land. We
were all forced to build huts for them. Someone said that you,
Kniez Nosek, stole Krol Rudy's gold and that you were not
coming back. Yagoda cries day and night."

"Where is Yagoda?" Cybula asked.

"She is not in the camp."

"Where is she?"

Kora did not answer.

"What happened to her? Tell me!" Cybula shouted.

Kora began to look to her left and her right, behind her,
as if to make sure that no one was listening. Then she said
in a low voice, "Yagoda is hiding."

"Why?"

"Krol Rudy wants her. He is always drunk. He slaps
Laska's face, although she is the mother of his child. He
shouts that if you do not return, he will have her head cut
off."

"When did Laska deliver her child? What did she have?"
Cybula asked.

"A red-haired boy. His eyes are yours, but the hair is Krol

Rudy's. At first, when he heard it was a boy, he hopped and danced and distributed drinks and pretzels to everyone. The mother named the boy Ptashek, and Krol Rudy calls him Ptashek Rudy. Then the fights and the mutiny began, and Krol Rudy became completely unsettled. He struck his own kniezes. He ordered the young women seized and given to him as wives. Six woyaks guard him day and night. When he remembered Yagoda, he wanted her to take your daughter's place. That is why Yagoda ran and hid."

"Where is she hiding?"

"I cannot tell you."

"Where is she? These people here are my friends, you can trust them."

"I'll whisper the place in your ear. Bend down."

Cybula lowered his head, and Kora began to hiss and spit until his ear was wet with her saliva. He could barely catch a word in the torrent that poured from her mouth. She mentioned a rock, a tree, and added that she, Kora, brought Yagoda her food.

"We will all be killed if we stay here!" Nosek snapped.

"What should we do, then?" Cybula asked.

"We should turn back."

"Masters, kniezes, don't leave us," Kora began to wail. "They'll kill us all. They have all gone mad. Yagoda is sick, she doesn't speak, she doesn't eat. No sooner do I put a morsel of food to her mouth than she spits it out. All day long she asks, 'Where is he? Where is he?' A curse is upon us, a dismal curse. Our own Lesniks have gone mad. Ah, the wrath of the gods is upon us! We did not sacrifice to Baba Yaga this year, and this is her revenge. Some say that new woyaks are coming and will slaughter us all. We have no more men to protect us. Those in the mountains treated us like enemies and even killed each other. So few of us are left now."

"We brought back seeds with us," Cybula said.

Ben Dosa, who had stood silent until that moment, now spoke up. "May I say something, kniezes?" he asked.

"Yes, you may speak," Cybula answered.

"Worthy kniezes, you are my masters and I am your slave. But I belong to a nation that does not permit its people to become enslaved. Even if one of us is sold into bondage, he serves six years and in the seventh must be set free. We are God's slaves, not slaves to other slaves. I have heard and understood what was said here, and I would like to offer some advice."

"What is your advice? Be brief!" Cybula interrupted.

"My lords, neither you nor I nor the horses have the strength to undertake the long journey back to town. We have escaped many dangers and this is proof that God Almighty wants us to live not die."

"What is your advice. Be brief!" Cybula interrupted.

"My advice is that one of you go to your krol and tell him we have arrived with seeds, with horses, with gifts, and that no one has robbed him of his gold. I suggest that you, Pan Nosek, speak to the krol, because you speak his language best. I can accompany Pan Nosek as his servant. Should the krol fly into a rage, one of us will run and inform you, Pan Cybula. If we both do not return, then you'll know that you must flee. Yet I know that we will not be harmed."

"How do you know?" Cybula asked.

"It is said in the Mishnah that when one of our great

masters prayed and the words flowed from his mouth smoothly, he knew that his prayers were accepted in heaven. I prayed to God for all of us while we traveled together. Since the words flowed from my mouth smoothly and rapidly, I know that your krol will receive us with favor."

"What do you think, Nosek?" Cybula asked.

"He could be right," Nosek answered, but he added, "If Krol Rudy is truly mad, the devil knows what will please him!"

"If you are afraid to go to him, I'll gladly take your place," Cybula said. "My daughter is his wife, and I don't believe he'd harm his father-in-law."

"Don't go to him, Cybula!" Kora shrieked. "He tried to kill your daughter even when she was nine months pregnant. He is always drunk and yells so loudly that his voice carries all over the camp! He has a house full of women, but he comes to them only to curse and abuse them. At night you can hear him howling and grunting and whipping their bare flesh with his whip. Your daughter . . ."

"Enough!" Cybula shouted. "I want to hear no more! Where is Yagoda?"

"Do you want me to take you to her?"

"Yes. If we are meant to die, then let us die together," Cybula said.

"Do you want to go now?" Kora asked.

"Soon."

"My god! My husband! Son-in-law, father, master, redeemer!" Kora was once again sobbing. "I thought the ravens had plucked out your sweet eyes, and here, suddenly . . ." Kora tottered and swayed while she moaned. But now they heard a great noise and realized at once that it was no longer possible for Nosek to see Krol Rudy in advance. The matter was no longer in their hands.

(2)

Someone had evidently seen the newcomers and run to inform the camp. There was loud shouting and cheering, and crowds of people came running from every direction. Women wept, children shouted, old men shook their walking sticks and waved their arms. When Krol Rudy arrived, he was surrounded by kniezes and woyaks. He wore a long zupan, a fox-skin hat with tails dangling on both sides of his face, and at his hips hung two swords. His right hand held a dagger. He seemed to have aged during these last months and his red beard was streaked with gray. Among the kniezes Cybula recognized only Kulak. No sooner did the krol see Nosek and Cybula—before they had time to kneel before him and greet him—than he began to wave his dagger and shout. His voice had changed; it was hoarse now, sometimes shrill. His nose had a strange red color and was crisscrossed with blue veins. It was hard to understand what Krol Rudy said, as he cursed, threatened, gesticulated wildly. Nosek bowed his head, waiting for the royal wrath to subside, then he spoke in a loud and clear voice:

"Our king, forgive us for tarrying longer than you had ordered. Our journey was an arduous one, both the journey out and the return home. Several objects we wanted to purchase for you could not be readied in time and we waited days, even weeks. But all obstacles were finally overcome, and now we are here, ready again to serve you faithfully."

He had apparently prepared his speech beforehand. Krol Rudy fixed on him a pair of bloodshot eyes under disheveled red eyebrows. "Where were you? I was sure you were devoured by wolves or hidden in some cave with the other rebels. And who is this?" Krol Rudy pointed to Cybula with the tip of his dagger.

"My krol, don't you recognize him? This is Kniez Cybula," Nosek answered. "He is the one who made peace with you and came down from the mountains with his Lesniks."

"Cybula, huh? And who is the dark one with the sack on his back, a prisoner?"

"He is no prisoner, Krol, he is a shoemaker who sews shoes for men and women. He is also a furrier and has other skills as well. Kniez Cybula brought him here to work for you."

"From what do you make shoes—from snow?" Krol Rudy asked and chuckled at his own wit. Out of his throat burst a roar and a whinny which seemed hardly to be human. Kulak, known in the camp for imitating his master, parroting his speech, aping his mannerisms and quirks, immediately began to bellow with a voice which issued out of his immense belly and sounded like some giant hiccup.

Ben Dosa, his hand clutching the white horse's bridle, approached Krol Rudy, bowed down low, and said, "Allow me, krol, to offer you a benediction. When we encounter a king we say: 'Praised be God who granted a part of his honor to flesh and blood.' It is true, king, that my wanderings took me to a town where I became a shoemaker. But in my home, Sura, which is in the land of Babylon, I was a merchant. Wicked men kidnapped me, carried me over the great sea to distant lands, and sold me as a slave. Your kniezes, Pan

Cybula and Pan Nosek, were kind to me. They treated me
not as a prisoner but as a friend."

"Huh? We need shoes," Krol Rudy spoke both to Ben
Dosa and to the others. "But shoes are made of leather and
leather is made from animal skins and animals must be killed
before they can be skinned. Is this not true, Kulak?"

"Yes, my krol, true," Kulak thundered.

"But there are few of us men left now," Krol Rudy continued. "And women cannot hunt or shoot. We Poles brought
seeds and plows to this region. We wanted to give the Lesniks
the best fruits of the earth. But those whom we wanted to
help fought us, shed our blood and the blood of innocent
women and children, and caused so much mischief that we
could not sow the fields this fall."

"My king, we have brought with us seeds of wheat, corn,
barley, and oats," Cybula said. "We can sow them early in the
spring, and if we have a good harvest, all is not lost."

"No, not lost. What is your name?"

"Cybula."

"Is it you, Laska's father?"

"Yes, my king."

"What is the matter with me?" Krol Rudy slapped himself on the forehead. "We have had such calamities here that
I would not recognize my own father. You *are* my father!
Why are you standing there like a stranger? Come here and
let me kiss you, Father-in-law. Your daughter bore me a son,
my Ptashek Rudy is your grandson. Forgive me for being so
confused. We've had such mishaps here that it is a miracle
from the gods that I am still alive. My own brothers betrayed
me and became my sworn enemies. They tried to set my house

on fire and burn me alive. If it were not for my true and loyal friend Kulak, I would have long ago descended to the dark hollows of the earth. Because of all this, my thoughts became unsettled. When weeks and months went by and you, Cybula, did not return, wicked people planted the thought that you and my old friend Nosek had joined the rebels. They even made false accusations against your daughter, and I was ready to send her where I sent the others, to the devils for whom death is bread and blood is wine. But wait, who is this dark little man?"

"His name is Ben Dosa," Cybula answered.

"What an odd name! Brothers, sisters, today is a day of celebration for us. Look at the fine horses our kniezes bought for us. We have among us woyaks who want to rise above the others, to become pans, to snatch all the land for themselves. But I, Krol Rudy, will not permit it. The earth belongs to the gods, not to men! Is this not true, Kulak?"

"True, my krol."

"My father was not a pan but a poor soil tiller," Krol Rudy began. "We served a landowner, a kniez, a pan—the devil knows what he was. And when the spirit moved him he ordered my father to drop his trousers and be whipped. When I saw this, I picked up a heavy stone and smashed the man's skull. This is why I took to the road to plunder and loot. What else could a poor soil tiller do? I left behind a mother, brothers, sisters. I became a wild youth, a bandit. But I never forgot where I came from. Who is the girl with the high cheekbones and the slanted eyes? The shoemaker's daughter?"

"No, krol. She is not his daughter. She is yours."

"Bring her to me, Nosek, Bring her to my house. Hey, you shoemaker! Make her a pair of shoes. You, Kulak, give him a hut where he can live and do his work."

(3)

Nosek and Kulak took charge of the horses, the sacks of seeds, the load which the horses had carried on their backs. There were some new kniezes in the camp, former woyaks whom Krol Rudy had named to replace those he had beheaded or who had fled. The "palace" that was planned for him so many months ago had still not been constructed. One room had been added to his house—for Laska and for his other wives or concubines. Although Cybula longed to see his daughter and his newborn grandson, he postponed it for later. First he had to see Yagoda. Nosek had brought back a sack full of stale loaves of bread and rolls, and he now divided them among the hungry Lesniks—women and children, and a few old men. In the midst of the crush and the struggle to grab bits of food, Cybula picked up the satchel containing Yagoda's gifts and set off with Kora.

She led him away from the camp, back to the forest from which they had just come. All the while, as she led him to Yagoda's hiding place, Kora spoke of the misfortunes which fell upon the camp while he was away. "Dear Cybula," she said, "master, protector, it is not the same camp! So many evils and afflictions have we endured! As long as strangers raided our camp and spilled our blood, we knew that enemies were enemies. But when our own Lesniks attacked us—then nothing remained for us but death. The Poles only came together against us; they wanted to slaughter us all, to dig

one large grave and bury us in it. But the gods foiled their
plans. Many of us died of terror, hunger, illness. Krol Rudy,
our great protector, completely lost his mind. Today he spoke
with some sense, but most of the time he rants and raves. In
the midst of all our trouble he remembered Yagoda, and now
he wants her as well."

"Where is she?"

"Here in the forest. I found an old oak, not the one that
is a god, but another. It was hollowed out by lightning.
Yagoda came to me weeping and begging, 'Mother, I want
to be no one's but Cybula's. If he is dead, I want to be with
him in the hollows of the earth.' I bring her food, and she
sets traps and catches what she can. Small as she is, she is
nimble and strong. She scampers up the trees like a squirrel.
Perhaps Krol Rudy has forgotten her by now, the old goat,
but at any time he may remember again. Oh, Cybulla, my
love, what will become of us?"

"It will not end well," Cybula said.

"Why do you say this?"

"We have no men. Any day may see the coming of a new
enemy."

"Then what should we do?"

"We should be ready for death."

"My own life means nothing to me. I have lived enough—
too much. But I grieve for you and Yagoda. She is so young,
and has not even borne a child. Why don't you make her
conceive?"

"What for? I spill my seed on her thigh."

"Why are you doing this? You sin against the gods!"

"I do it because we are doomed. I saw this immediately
after the first massacre."

"You can predict things long before they happen. But a young girl is like a tree. It wants to bear fruit, and does not know that tomorrow someone may cut it down or that a windstorm may blow it over. I would like to have a child of your seed, Cybula. I am too old to have children, but I can love stronger than a young woman. Even Yagoda does not love you as much as I do. But I know men desire younger women."

"Are you jealous of your own daughter?" Cybula asked.

"As long as we share you, I am satisfied."

"Where is the oak?" Cybula asked.

"We will be there soon. Let me carry your bag, your arm must be free to receive Yagoda."

Cybula gave the bag to Kora. They stood and faced one another with the silence that comes from great lust. Kora asked, "You found others to take our place, huh?"

Cybula finally answered, "A girl who cooked at the inn."

"Was she better than us?" Kora asked.

"No one could be better. Don't tell your daughter."

"Was she young?"

"Younger than you but older than Yagoda."

"We remained faithful to you. The woyaks chased me, but I fled from them. I did not know that I could run so fast. One woyak threw his spear at me and it missed me by a hair. Our former neighbors threw themselves at me, but I tore myself out of their arms." Kora had suddenly changed her tone. "How much time have we left to live?"

"Not long."

"What should we do, then?"

"Serve Shmiercz, the god of death."

"How do we serve him?"

"By drinking the juices of life," Cybula said, puzzled at his own words. A thought like this had never occurred to him before. It was as if some unseen spirit spoke through his mouth. Kora bent down to kiss his feet. "You are not a man, you are a god."

"No, Kora, only a man."

"No, you are a god. I want you to kill me."

"Why, Kora?"

"I want to offer myself as a sacrifice to you."

"No, Kora, I need you now."

"When will you do it?"

"When enemies surround us."

"Then it will be too late."

"No, Kora. It will not be too late."

"You will accept my sacrifice?"

"Yes, Kora."

"My daughter also?"

"Yes."

"Kill me first. Swear to me you will do this. Make a sign in my flesh with your sharp knife."

"Later."

"No, now." Kora fell on her knees before him. Cybula's satchel dropped from her hand. Cybula picked it up and took out a knife he had bought at Miasto. His hands were trembling, and he could hear his teeth chatter. "Where shall I engrave the sign?" he asked. And Kora answered, "In my left breast."

6

Ben Dosa, the Teacher

BECAUSE Krol Rudy was almost always drunk or sick, power had fallen to several kniezes, especially Kulak, who led the woyaks loyal to their krol. Kulak had charge of the armed woyaks who watched Krol Rudy's hut day and night, changing guard every so often. He also had charge of all the arms, although he had seldom fought with weapons. If he needed to kill, he used his bare fists. Or else he threw his massive weight at his victim, crushing or suffocating him.

Another kniez, Czapek (or Piesek, as he was nicknamed in the camp, because he resembled a bulldog), was the overseer of the fields, only one step below Krol Rudy. Before he joined Krol Rudy's woyaks he had served a pan in a region near the river Wieprz, where he was in charge of fields, granaries, horses, and children. Kniez Czapek was as round as a barrel. He had a broad face with wide-set eyes, and a flat nose with large nostrils. He wobbled rather than walked on his short legs. He was the oldest of the kniezes and he called the younger ones "brats." Czapek had the old Lesnik men and the women build a barn for him, and there he kept the last bit of grain remaining from the harvest. He himself often sat at the door to guard the wheat from the hungry Lesniks and the barley from drunken woyaks who wanted to brew more beer. It was rumored that Czapek had even stood up to Krol Rudy when the latter ordered that grain be used to satisfy the woyaks' craving for drink. As small and clumsy as Czapek was, he was known to be an extremely capable fighter. In wars he slashed heads with both his swords, one in his left hand and one in his right. It was also he, Czapek, who insisted that during the winter Lesnik women cut down trees and prepare the earth for new fields.

Kniez Nosek was in charge of all matters which required mental skill, such as proficiency with numbers or the ability to plan ahead. He had built a sundial, which told him the time of day by the shadows it cast over the markings on its face. Nosek's talents for measuring, weighing, allotting provisions or pelts so that everyone had the proper share were widely known. He also became the camp's judge. People often said that Nosek was able to keep a cool head because he had no interest in women, and because there were no young men in the camp who appealed to him.

Kniez Cybula shared some of Nosek's burdensome duties and acted as intermediary between Krol Rudy and the Lesniks. It was Cybula who spoke for the Lesniks and brought their grievances to Krol Rudy's attention. Cybula was no longer the sole hunter in the camp. In order to survive until the sowing in spring and the harvest in late summer, the camp needed meat. What little was caught in the traps that the women and old men had set up would not suffice to feed them.

The gods were merciful that winter. The snows and frosts were not as severe as during the winter before. Often the days were sunny and mild. The animals in the woods multiplied rapidly. A day did not go by when Cybula did not shoot at least one stag or doe, and most days he shot several. Even the woyaks, who were inept hunters, were able to kill some animals with their spears. The number of Lesniks who remained in the mountains steadily dropped, until they became merely a handful. The fear that they might descend on the camp and begin killing anew now seemed remote, at least until the summer, since most of their women had died of cold and hunger or in childbirth.

The many stories that Cybula told about Miasto seemed to have awakened the Lesniks from a deep sleep. Renewed hope prevailed in the camp. They saw the horses with their fine saddles, bridles, and reins that Nosek and Cybula had brought back, as well as the copper coins, tin knives and spoons, hammers, saws, and other implements. In Czapek's barn they could see wooden plows, scythes, sickles, hoes, spades, and even a plow with an iron blade. Nosek told them that when the winter was over, the ice melted and the mud dry, a *britska*, or large carriage, built in Miasto, would arrive, filled with tools for building tables, benches, stools, and other furniture. He told them about the spindles for spinning flax and the looms for weaving cloth from wool or flax. Merely to hear about the town gladdened their hearts. If it could spring up so near, without their knowledge, why not here?

Even though Cybula described the hardships of life in Miasto—the crowded streets, the dirt and filth, the noise and smells—his words could not dampen their desire to see it all for themselves. Every day they made Czapek open the barn doors and display the treasures the kniezes had brought back.

The dark-skinned shoemaker, Ben Dosa, aroused the camp's interest as much as the treasures. He had lived in faraway places and seen towns even bigger than Miasto. They questioned him constantly. Where did he come from? Who were his parents? How did he learn the strange language of the Niemcies, the people on the seashore? Ben Dosa answered them all willingly. His parents were Jews, whose God had given them the Torah on Mount Sinai, and then exiled them for their sins. He was always prepared to let them return if they repented, to send his Messiah to them, to bring them back to Jerusalem, to rebuild his temple. Though Ben Dosa uttered such strange words, it was nevertheless a pleasure to listen to him. He patted the children on their heads, wished their mothers happiness and health. Again and again he insisted there was only one God, who created the world in five days: the sun and the moon and the stars, the mountains, rivers, fish, the flies and worms. Then God created man on the sixth day and gave him the greatest gift of all—the freedom to choose between good and evil. Ben Dosa worked and spoke at the same time. One could hear him day and night. His fingers moved nimbly and swiftly. From his lips—half hidden behind a black mustache—words poured out which astounded and comforted, fired the imagination, awakened the mind.

Even persons of rank like Cybula, Nosek, and Czapek came to order shoes and to chat with the shoemaker, who was full of so much wisdom. Cybula brought Laska, his daughter, his wife Yagoda, and her mother Kora to see Ben Dosa, who now worked in a small hut. One day Krol Rudy ordered him to come to his house and sew boots for himself and his wives. While Ben Dosa took measurements, Krol Rudy questioned him about his country, his family, his God. He asked, "Are you a man or a god?"

"A man, my krol—flesh and blood. There is only one God, and all men are his children."

"Where are the other gods?" Krol Rudy asked.

"There are no other gods," Ben Dosa said.

"What about Baba Yaga?"

"There is no Baba Yaga."

"Did you fly as high as the mountains and see this for yourself?"

"No, this is what our prophets taught us."

"Where are the prophets?"

"They are no longer alive. Our generation is not worthy of having prophets."

"Where did you hear all these things?"

"From the Torah."

"What is that?"

"The words of God written down on parchment."

"What is parchment?"

"It is made of animal skins."

"You are telling lies, you made up these stories yourself. But if you make me a good pair of boots, I'll give you some bread."

"Thank you, krol."

"You can also find yourself a wife here."

"Thank you, krol, but I already have a wife."

"Where?"

"In Babylon, in the town of Sura."

"Where is Babylon?"

"Far away, in the East, across the sea."

"And your reach goes so far that you can possess a woman across the sea?" Krol Rudy winked and broke into uproarious laughter.

(2)

Ben Dosa obtained permission from Nosek and Cybula to teach the camp children to read and to write. He opened a *cheder* in his own hut. Using wooden beams, he constructed several long tables, then attached narrow benches to them. The children came to him willingly. Their mothers also came along whenever they were not needed in the forests. Cybula and Nosek both wanted to learn the art of reading and writing, and they, too, became Ben Dosa's pupils. First he taught the children to say a prayer in the holy tongue: "I thank thee, living and eternal God, for returning my soul to me in your mercy and your great faith." Ben Dosa instructed the children to go outside and rub their little hands in the snow. Then he pronounced the unfamiliar words slowly, in a clear voice, and the children repeated after him. Then he translated them into the Polish tongue of the Lesniks. He translated the word "soul" as *ducha*, a small ghost or spirit. They asked, Where does the soul reside? In the nose? Head? Stomach? What does it look like? Ben Dosa explained that the soul could not be seen, it had no form or color, but it was the power which gave man life. Even when the soul departed, when man slept, it left behind it something called *nefesh*, and this nefesh existed not only in man but in animals also.

A while later Ben Dosa carried out a board on which he had written the letters of the alphabet. Ben Dosa touched each letter with a pointer and called it by its name: aleph, beth, gimel, daleth, he, waw, zayin . . . and so on, until taw. He hung the board on a nail on the wall and asked both adults and children to name the letters and identify them. Cybula tried to remember each letter, but they all looked the same to him. I will never be able to tell them apart, he thought, even if I see them a thousand times. And he saw with amazement how several children named and identified all the letters correctly. Cybula felt proud that it was he who had brought this man to the camp, but he was disheartened to see children absorbing the man's lessons faster than he. "Ah, their heads are still fresh," Cybula consoled himself. A child was like fresh fruit just picked off the tree, or a radish recently dug out of the ground. Later the head filled up with thoughts, worries, cravings. It was strange: Nosek was not a young man, but he could easily identify the letters and name them all correctly. Cybula glanced at him with admiration. Nosek smiled, nodded his head, and winked. Ben Dosa held a sliver of chalk between his fingers and with rapid strokes drew letters on a sheet of oak bark. He placed the letters in such a way that they formed words, in his own language and also in the language of the Poles and the Lesniks. He wrote from right to left the names of Krol Rudy, Cybula, Nosek, Kora, Yagoda, and he added his own name.

After a while Ben Dosa dismissed the children, telling

them to run home or play outside. To the adults who remained Ben Dosa said, "It is important to know these letters. With these letters God created heaven and earth." Cybula wanted to ask, "And how did God do it—with a piece of chalk?" But he was ashamed to voice his question aloud. Nosek asked, "About which god are you speaking? The god of your country?"

"God is the God of all lands, all words," Ben Dosa answered. "Without His word the world would return to darkness and desolation."

"Darkness is caused by our own Baba Yaga when she is angry at us," an old Lesnik called out.

"Baba Yaga cannot make light and she cannot make darkness," Ben Dosa answered. "The true God is everyone's—yours, mine. The false gods are deaf and blind. They have eyes which cannot see, ears which do not hear. They have feet, but they cannot run."

"Can your god run?" asked another Lesnik.

Ben Dosa considered the question. "He has no need to run. He is everywhere. The whole world is full of his presence."

When Cybula was outside again he felt dazed. His head was reeling. He felt that a new time had begun for himself and for everyone in the camp. He glanced at the children. One of them picked up a stick and carved in the snow a letter similar to those Ben Dosa had drawn with chalk. Cybula asked him, "What is this?" And the child answered, "Aleph."

Nosek took the stick from the child's hand and traced another letter in the snow.

"What is this?" Cybula asked. And Nosek answered, "Beth."

"I must learn these things, even if they cost my life," Cybula decided. He returned to Ben Dosa's hut and asked him to recite the alphabet once more, from the beginning. The men studied the letters together, and Cybula learned to name and eventually to identify them. Only a few of the letters confused him. Nun looked to him like a gimel and daleth like a resh. Ben Dosa showed him how these pairs differed; then he said, "Letters are like faces. From a distance they may look alike, but when we take a closer look, we see that each is different."

He gave Cybula the chalk and told him to copy the letters from the aleph–beth board. When Cybula held the chalk in his fingers, his hand began to tremble. He caught his breath, but at last copied all twenty-two letters correctly. Although it was cold in the hut, Cybula felt warm. From time to time spots whirled in front of his eyes. He felt as if the camp had become a town and he had become a learned man. He embraced Ben Dosa and kissed his forehead. He said, "If I were the krol, I would make you my closest kniez. The truth is that you should be our krol."

"I don't want to be a krol," Ben Dosa answered. "A king lives his life and dies. But God lives forever and his mercy is forever. It is said, 'God is good to his creatures, and his mercy is cast upon his creation.' "

Cybula thought a moment and said, "But how can this be? We kill his creatures and eat them. The wolf devours the sheep. We humans kill the wolf. God is not always good to his creatures."

"He is good to them," Ben Dosa said. "We humans do not always understand God's goodness."

"Why does your god let small children become ill and

die? Why did he let the woyaks attack and slaughter our people?"

"God need not reveal all his secrets to us."

"I must go. I'll return tomorrow with my daughter Laska —the krolowa—my wife Yagoda, her mother Kora, and others who want to learn to read and write."

"Yes, kniez. Come, all of you."

"Meanwhile, I'll send you some food. Why don't you eat with us when we bring home our catch?"

"This, kniez, I cannot do," Ben Dosa said after some hesitation.

"Why not? You are one of us now."

"I am not permitted to eat the flesh of an unclean animal."

"Which animals are unclean?"

"We may not eat pigs."

"Why not? If you wash the pig's flesh, it would be as clean as a sheep's."

Ben Dosa wanted to tell Cybula that only animals which chewed their cud and whose hooves were split were considered clean, but he could not find the words he needed in the Polish tongue. He said, "You, kniez, may. But I may not."

"Why is that so?" Cybula asked again.

"Because I am a son of the people of Israel. God gave us the Torah on Mount Sinai and offered it to other nations as well, to the sons of Esau and Ishmael, but they did not accept it. Yet men like you, descendants of Noah, must obey seven of God's commandments."

"What commandments?" Cybula asked. And Ben Dosa answered, "You may not lie with your mother or sister or daughter."

Cybula was silent.

(3)

Laska lived with her child in a room which was often
crowded with Krol Rudy's visiting women. When Cybula
finally pushed through the guards surrounding the krol's
house, preparing to spend a few moments alone with his
daughter, Laska cried out to him, "Father, save me. I've
fallen into the hands of a madman!"

The room smelled of smoke, sweat, decaying food, and
excrement. The skins on which Laska lay with her newborn
son stank. From the adjoining room, which was Krol Rudy's,
came sounds resembling an animal's grunts. Laska told her
father that because her husband feared that his enemies might
be lurking, he no longer went outside to relieve himself.
Krol Rudy made Kniez Kulak sleep at his side to protect
him from sudden attack.

Laska's son, Ptashek, cried incessantly. Laska pushed her
breast into his little mouth, but Cybula showed her that the
boy spat out more than he swallowed. Cybula remembered
how well his former wife, Yasna, had raised children. Never
had he known the pain and helplessness he felt when he
visited Laska, his only daughter.

Yagoda, having grown accustomed to her hiding place
in the oak, refused to return to the camp. The women there
mocked her, because they knew Cybula was husband both to
her and to her mother. They called her a fool, a barren field,
and wondered why she did not conceive when so many men
pursued her as dogs pursue a bitch. Only there, in the oak's
hollow, did Yagoda find peace.

Sometimes she lay for hours, covered with pelts, thinking of nothing, listening to the wind, to the cawing of the crows, to the chirping of the birds, who for some reason did not migrate that winter. As she lay in the darkness, she imagined she could hear the oak's roots sucking the juices which would cause leaves, buds, blossoms to sprout and grow. Brooks gurgled under the snow. In the thicket of molding leaves and moss, tiny creatures swarmed, creatures that—like Yagoda—silently, longingly awaited spring. Yagoda never grew tired of waiting for Cybula.

The hollow in the oak was narrow, even for Yagoda. But with her bare fingers, like a mole, she dug out the earth between its roots and cleared a small space for herself and her husband. She lined it with leaves, grasses, pelts. So small was the space that their bodies always touched. Cybula's lips touched Yagoda's ear. Cold as it was outside, together they were warm. Heat flowed from his body to hers, and from her body to his. When Cybula returned from Miasto he had confessed to Yagoda that there, in the distant town, he had lain with another. Yagoda also knew that he frequently visited her mother. But she was never resentful. First, how could she, an insignificant creature, resent a god? Second, Kora was her mother, as dear to her as her own life.

To Yagoda Cybula bared all his secrets, his plans for the camp, his opinions of every woman and man. At other times he spoke to her about gods. Had there really been a time when nothing existed—no sky, no earth, no mountains, no streams? Would everything one day come to an end? He repeated to her Ben Dosa's words about the Jews who existed somewhere in the East. For them there was but one god, who had chosen them; they built a golden temple for him. But later, when they sinned against him, he destroyed it and sent them into exile.

"What did they do?" Yagoda asked.

"They stole, killed, lay with their mothers and daughters."

"Is this bad?"

"So he says."

"Whatever *you* do is good."

"He believes that our gods are deaf and blind and that only his god can see and speak," Cybula said.

"Is this true?"

"How can it be true? There are no gods." Yet Yagoda also knew the gods as though they did exist. Sometimes he said the world was an evil place and death the greatest gift, yet he also promised to take Yagoda over the mountains and live there with her in a house surrounded with fields, gardens, lakes, and streams. He would tell her a story, confessing later that he made it up, about a krol as tall as a pine, with a beard that reached to his navel, with the horns of a deer, and with one eye in his forehead. This krol could fly like a bird, speak with trees, rocks, pigs, dogs, oxen. He flew up to heaven and married a goddess, also named Yagoda, who bore him thousands and thousands of children, who turned into stars.

Once when he told her a story about a god, Yagoda asked him, "What is a god?" And Cybula answered, "*Wszystko*—everything."

"Everything?"

"The oak, Krol Rudy, Nosek, Ben Dosa, I, you, your hair, your breasts, your thoughts, your dreams at night."

"How can this be?" Yagoda asked.

"This is how it is."

Suddenly Cybula began to sing a song Yagoda had never heard before. He half sang, half spoke the words. What he said aroused both laughter and fear in her. He said that Everything was a man and Always was a woman. Everything and Always were man and wife.

"Have they any children?"

"Yes, we are their children."

"Oh, this frightens me," Yagoda said.

"Why should it frighten you?"

"Is Kora not my mother?"

"Yes, she is your mother."

"And who was Kostek?"

"Your father."

"Where is he now?"

"Everything swallowed him up."

"Is Everything an animal?"

"Everything is everything."

"Who told you this—Ben Dosa?"

"No, I thought of it myself. Sometimes when I lie awake at night, strange thoughts come to me. Where did everything come from? What was there before I was born? And what will there be after I'm gone? It occurred to me that Everything is Always, and that they are like man and wife."

"Like us?"

"Yes, like us."

"Cybula, I wish that it was always night and that you were always with me," Yagoda said.

Kosoka was among those who came to hear Ben Dosa's morning lesson. After Krol Rudy had thrown her out, for reasons she did not understand, no one in the camp would take her in and she wandered about aimlessly. She lived in an abandoned, half-burned hut, and made a bed from the straw left in the fields. She lit a fire on the ground between two branches and roasted her daily catch in it. This day Ben Dosa's lesson was about the sacrifices that were offered at the temple in Jerusalem. He said there were burnt offerings that were completely consumed on the altar, after the priests had taken the meat for themselves. There were also offerings of thanks, in the form of the finest crops or a pair of turtle-doves. One boy named Wilk asked, "Why don't we have any of those things here?"

Ben Dosa's black eyes sparkled. "My child, everything can be had, if only we will it. Here we have a camp where men live almost like beasts, going barefoot. But some weeks' travel from here a town has been built, with houses, shops, and workshops where craftsmen can practice their crafts. If we all wish it, we, too, can build such a town in our camp. We have all that we need: trees, fruit, fertile soil. We can build houses, streets, shops, and spin flax, weave cloth, tan leather. If we will it, we can raise herds of sheep, shear their wool, make woolen garments."

Ben Dosa addressed his remarks to Wilk, but he glanced at Cybula and Nosek as he continued: "The women here complain bitterly: We do not have enough men! But the Book of Proverbs, which King Solomon wrote—he was the wisest of all men—tells us that the woman of valor spun and wove flax and wool and was dressed in fine garments. Her husband sat with the elders at the city gates while she traded with merchants or sewed rugs. She even had time to learn new things and help the poor. It is said she was so diligent that she did not extinguish the light in her house all night long."

"Teach us what we must do!" a woman called out. She looked like a young girl, but she was already pregnant.

"You will first have to undergo the pains of childbirth. Then you will look after your child and nourish it, both its body and its spirit. It is said that the greatest virtue the woman of valor possessed was her fear of God. When a man ceases to fear God, he becomes lower than the beast, which has no free will."

An elderly woman called to Ben Dosa, "Where is she, this woman of valor? Let her come here and teach us!"

Ben Dosa smiled. "She has not been among the living for a long time. Her body has turned to dust, but her soul is with the righteous women in paradise."

"Where is that, in Miasto?"

"In heaven."

The people assembled in Ben Dosa's hut were silent. Cybula whispered in Nosek's ear and Nosek shook his head. Cybula said, "Ben Dosa, after you teach us the letters today, come to my hut. Nosek and I want to speak with you."

"Yes, Kniez Cybula."

Ben Dosa took out his chalk and began teaching the letters again. The brightest pupil among them was Wilk, twelve years old, who could recite the alphabet and write his name. His father had been killed during the mutiny, and the woyak had raped his mother, Basha, and also blinded her in her left eye. Wilk had blue eyes and golden hair, and when he smiled, dimples appeared in his cheeks. The other boys teased him and gave him girls' names. The women, however, had a spe-

cial liking for this half-orphan and showered him with kisses.
Wilk was a skillful hunter and often went out with his bow
and arrows. Once he caught a young deer. He climbed up
trees in search of beehives, and when he found them, he
brought honey to his mother and to others in the camp. During Ben Dosa's lesson, Cybula noticed that Nosek often
looked at the boy, often followed his movements with his
eyes. When Ben Dosa praised Wilk, Nosek smiled. Cybula
could not recall ever having seen Nosek smile.

When the lessons were over and the pupils had gone, Ben
Dosa's door opened and Kosoka stood before him, barefoot,
half naked, with only a pelt to cover her hips and breasts.

"Welcome, Kosoka," he said.

Kosoka held a basket made of braided twine and approached the bench on which Ben Dosa sat. "I brought something for you." She lifted the small hide which covered her
basket and Ben Dosa saw a dead rabbit. He stood up.

"Kosoka, I cannot eat this. It is not permitted, it is unclean."

Kosoka then asked, "What shall I do with it?"

"Whatever you like. You can eat it yourself."

"You said God forbids it."

"It is forbidden only to Jews. You are not a Jew and therefore you may eat it."

Kosoka said, "I want to be what you are, a Jew."

"You a Jew? Why?"

"I want to go to heaven when I die." And Kosoka pointed
upward with her finger.

Ben Dosa smiled. "You will not die so soon. You are still
young."

"The young also die. Before long I will be dead."

"Is that why you want to become a Jew?"

"Yes."

"How did you come to this belief?" Ben Dosa asked.

"It is what you taught us."

"A Jew must truly believe in God, not in what some man teaches. Today I teach you one thing, tomorrow another may teach you something different. You must think these things out for yourself and begin to believe that the one true God is the God who created the heavens and the earth, not some idol made of stone. Do you believe in one God?"

"Yes."

"Our kniez Cybula told me that he does not want me to teach this belief to the camp. He wants to remain an idol worshipper, and he wants the others left as they are. If he should hear that you want to become a Jew, he may punish us both. This is the first thing you must know. The second is that since our temple in Jerusalem was destroyed, we have been dispersed among the nations, disgraced, threatened, and made to live like lambs among the wolves. Whoever becomes a Jew takes a heavy burden upon himself. We have two hundred and forty-eight commandments which we must observe, and three hundred and sixty-five transgressions which we must avoid. Are you willing to assume such a burden?"

"Yes." A long silence followed. Then Kosoka said, "I want to be a sacrifice to your god."

"A sacrifice? What do you mean by a sacrifice?"

"You told us about the sacrifices in the temple, the ones whose blood was sprinkled on the altar."

"Those were animals, not human beings."

"I want to give you my blood."

Ben Dosa was so bewildered by her words that he remained
speechless. He looked at Kosoka with astonishment. In the
years since he was captured on a ship bound for Sidon, he
had encountered a variety of savage men. He had witnessed
fights among the sailors in which they broke each other's
bones. He had seen violence, homosexuality, idolatry, aber-
rations of many kinds. But what Kosoka proposed to him
was entirely new. He had an urge to reproach her, but something restrained him. How could a creature come to such
thoughts, he wondered. Perhaps her ancestors were a people
of madness.

Ben Dosa need not have been astonished. Human sacrifices were offered by idol worshippers throughout the ages.
Fathers and mothers willingly gave their children to the
fires of Molech. Men delivered their daughters and wives into
prostitution, as gift offerings to the priests and false prophets
of Baal and Ashtoreth. It was all recorded in the Torah and
in other holy books: the sins of the generation of the Flood,
the evil deeds of Sodom, of those who wounded their faces
and tore chunks out of their flesh when they mourned a death
in their family. About the generation of the Flood it was
written that even their animals had been mated with those of
other species. Ben Dosa said, "My girl, the Master of the
Universe does not ask for any sacrifices. Be honest and do
good. Nothing more is needed."

"What shall I do?" Kosoka asked.

"Marry a man and be a faithful wife."

"I want to be your wife," Kosoka said.

Ben Dosa shuddered. "I have a wife and children."

"There in Babylon, not here."

7

The Power of Kora

CYBULA had many worries about the camp and also about his own position. Yet there was now no danger from Krol Rudy: he no longer wanted Yagoda for himself, and he told Nosek that Cybula could live with Yagoda or whomever he pleased, no harm would come to him. The real danger came from the younger woyaks, who wanted to overthrow Krol Rudy, Kulak, and Nosek and take over themselves. Cybula knew that he, a Lesnik, was despised by these woyaks.

There was also the problem that Yagoda no longer wanted to live in the camp. Neither Kora nor Cybula could dissuade her from what she had chosen to do. She had become increasingly silent. When Cybula came to her, she kissed and fondled him, but it was difficult to make her speak. If he asked her a question, she answered in a low murmur. Her voice had become hoarse and she coughed at night. Although she still caught small animals for herself, and Cybula and Kora often shared their catch with her, Yagoda was growing thin. When Cybula held her in his arms, he could feel her bony ribs. Her body exuded a strange warmth at night, which Cybula at first believed was the heat of passion. She clung to him and covered him with kisses, but the heat of her flesh and the heat of her breath had begun to make him afraid.

In the camp he had encountered many fevers and illnesses, premature deaths, and even forms of madness. He believed that Krol Rudy was already mad. For years he had noticed that some Lesniks were able to withstand cruel adversities, afflictions, hunger, and shame, while others, oppressed by some slight quarrel or insult, fell into melancholy and soon died. There were men in the camp who, although covered with blisters, boils, ulcers, and scabs, were able to live their lives to the end, while others, because of a minor ache, were soon carried out and buried. Yes, he knew of men who had died from insults, treachery, shame, and mockery, broken hearts, unrequited love, angry words, or of longing for a lost friend or relative.

That night in Kora's hut Cybula was suddenly awakened. Kora was sitting up, mumbling softly to herself. Cybula asked, "Why are you hissing there like a witch? Are you conjuring up demons?"

"Cybula, I can no longer bear it! While you sleep, I lie awake. That daughter of mine will bring me to an early grave!"

"What is it that you want?"

"Don't let her die, Cybula! She is all I have left."

Cybula put on his hide pants and a pair of sandals that Ben

Dosa had made for him. Kora asked, "Where are you going? It is still dark outside."

Cybula did not answer.

"Don't go roaming in the dark. The goddess Zla waits there for you."

"How do you know? Do you see her?"

"Listen to the barking dogs. They see her."

"Nonsense, there is no goddess Zla."

Cybula left the hut to go to Yagoda. A cold wind blew outside, but he could already smell the scents of approaching spring. Soon the summer wheat would have to be sown. He longed to go to the field, to gaze at it again in the moonlight. But what was there to be seen in a patch of earth still covered with snow? Although he was a kniez, he knew he carried no weight in the camp. A score of ruffians ruled it with no laws since Krol Rudy had lost his power. It was as if they held him captive. Cybula continued to walk along the path which led to Yagoda's oak.

Suddenly he saw a man walking toward him—a woyak. By the light of the stars Cybula recognized the man as Lis. He was one of the woyaks who, although not possessing the title of kniez, ruled over the Lesniks with a strong hand. It was he, Lis, who forced the women to chop down trees in the forest. It was he who together with two other woyaks, Drevnik and Ptak, divided the camp's lands among themselves and gave themselves the title of pan. They wanted to make the Lesniks their slaves. Cybula had heard that Lis and his accomplices were plotting to murder Krol Rudy, Kulak, Nosek, and perhaps himself, Cybula. Lis shouted, "*Kto tam?*"—"Who's there?"

"It is I, Cybula."

"Cybula, huh? And why do you creep there in the dark like a mouse?"

Some restraint in Cybula broke. "I am not your servant. I need not answer to you."

"You are our enemy, a spy, a stinking Lesnik!"

"I am a kniez, while you are nothing but a—"

Before Cybula could finish his sentence, Lis's fist struck him squarely in the face. Cybula threw himself at Lis, but the pan was taller, stronger, younger than he was. Lis hit Cybula with both his fists, striking him in the face and head, kicking him with his foot, until Cybula fell to the ground. Kicking him again as he lay there, Lis shouted, "If you open your swinish snout once more, I'll squash you like a worm!"

For the first time in Cybula's life, someone had struck him. So many Lesniks had been killed, maimed, stabbed, injured —yet he, Cybula, had always escaped unharmed. He always felt that a godly hand protected him, although he refused to believe that gods existed. But now what he had feared for many years had finally happened. He lay in the mud like a beaten dog. He tried to rise, but all his strength had left him. As he lay on the ground, he could feel lumps swelling on his forehead, his nose, the back of his head. "I am covered with blood," he said to himself. He was overcome by a humiliation that could never be wiped out except by the blood of his assailant. Cybula understood now that the Lesniks in the mountains had been right: there could never be peace between the Lesniks and the Poles.

Somehow Cybula managed to stand up. He could not go to the oak where Yagoda lived. He could also not show himself to Kora without washing the blood and the mud off his wounds. He began to drag himself toward his hut. There he had his sword and his spear. He thought of waiting for Lis in Lis's hut, attacking him and killing him, but quickly abandoned this plan. Even if he overcame Lis, who was stronger, the other woyaks, when they learned what he had done, would torture and castrate him, perhaps even behead him—as they had done to others who dared to challenge them. His revenge, when it came, would have to come as a surprise.

It was still long before daybreak, and he had managed to reach his hut. Piles of untrampled snow lay near his door, and Cybula used it to wash his face. He melted some snow in his hands and drank the water. He entered his hut and almost immediately his knees buckled under him and he fell on his bed. His head ached, and he could no longer think. He fell into a deep sleep. When he awakened, it was still nighttime. When he moved his body, he felt a sharp pain, but his sleep had apparently restored some of his strength. He heard Kora's footsteps outside. "Cybula, where are you?" she cried. He wanted to answer, but his upper lip was swollen and his tongue refused to obey him. Kora cried, "Why didn't you return to me? Did something happen?"

Cybula knew he could not hide the truth from her. He said, "I was attacked, I was beaten."

Kora clapped her hands together. "Who? Where? Oh, sacred gods!"

Cybula barely recognized his own voice, which sounded heavy and dull. Kora began to shout, wail, sigh. Cybula silenced her. "Be quiet! I don't want the camp to see me in my shame."

"My heart told me that evil would strike you. As soon as you left my bed, I knew that Zla was waiting for you."

Kora bent over him. Whenever she touched a wound or a swelling, a muffled cry escaped from Cybula's lips. She left the hut and returned carrying snow in both her arms. Gently she washed and rubbed his aching body. She hovered over him, choking back her sighs and laments. Scalding tears dropped from her eyes and landed on his face. He had warned her to make no noise and she restrained the wails that threatened to break out of her throat. "Woe is me! Who did this to you?"

"Lis."

"Wait!" Kora ran out of the hut.

Cybula lay still. Had Kora gone to Lis's hut to seek revenge? If so, she was as good as lost. Lis would kill her on the spot. But Cybula had no strength to run after her and stop her. Soon dawn would break and the woyaks would come for him as well. "I must put an end to my life!" he warned himself. He carried in his sack a potion he had prepared from poisonous berries. He had promised himself that should a new woyak bloodbath break out, he would take his own life. But as the weeks and months passed, the potion had weakened and evaporated. Now, despairing of his life, Cybula called to Shmiercz, the spirit of death, to come and take him. A moment later he dozed off and began to dream.

It was summertime, and he was running across a green swamp trying to kill some creature that lived in the murky waters. The water rose and covered his ankles, reaching almost up to his knees. But the creature—a crayfish, a snake, a turtle—swam on, playfully teasing and challenging him to follow. A kind of wheeze, a snort, a guffaw, issued from its throat, as if it was mocking Cybula for his clumsiness and helplessness. Cybula shivered and opened his eyes. Kora was back in the hut, and when she saw Cybula awake she said, "The act is done."

"What! Is Lis dead?"

"I crushed his head with a rock. He cried out once, and no more."

Cybula said nothing. He should have felt joy, but he felt nothing but astonishment at the events of recent days and the speed with which they had happened. Kora said, "I went to his hut and heard him tossing and turning on his bed, bellowing like an ox. I ran in with the stone and crushed his head with one blow."

"Perhaps he is still alive," Cybula murmured.

"His brain oozed between my fingers," Kora answered.

Cybula lay still, with confused thoughts in his head. He was not asleep, but neither was he awake. It was as though something had petrified inside him. Kora's action had come too quickly to satisfy his thirst for revenge. He even felt a kind of pity for the coarse giant who had so easily overpowered him. Soon the sun would rise and with it would come a new bloodbath, a massacre.

"Kora, we must flee."

"Not without Yagoda!"

"Yes."

Slowly and painfully Cybula sat up. Kora said, "I'll gather a few things," and left the hut. Holding on to his bed, Cybula stood up. In the darkness he found his sword, his spear, his bow with the arrows. He put them into his sack and added a roasted rabbit. "These things are all I possess in this world," he said to himself. Around his shoulders he wrapped the skin of a bear he had caught in the mountains. The sky outside was red and the east had begun to glow. Kora was taking longer than was necessary to gather a few articles for herself. My life is as good as over, Cybula thought. Well, what is meant to happen will happen. Kora returned carrying a large pack wrapped in a straw mat.

"Come, we are taking Yagoda with us," she said.

He followed her on limp legs and with a resignation he would never have believed possible. All fear had abandoned him. He no longer cared if they caught him, quartered him, tore off his flesh. Kora took his arm and together they walked in silence. He, Cybula, had brought misfortune upon everyone. The woyaks might even take their revenge on Laska, he thought. Daylight was growing stronger. He remembered that the Lesniks in the mountains had called him a traitor. He had escaped from one danger only to be caught in another, but he no longer feared death. I could have avoided all this, it occurred to him, if I had stayed with Kora in bed. From time to time he glanced back to see if they were being followed. But no, everyone still slept. When Cybula and Kora reached the oak, they found Yagoda waiting for them, barefoot and shivering.

Kora called out to her, "Why are you outside?"

"I couldn't remain inside. Everything is wet."

"Never mind. Come, we are fleeing, running for our lives. See what they've done to him." Kora pointed her finger at Cybula.

Yagoda looked at Cybula and said, "Who did this?"

"The one who struck Cybula has already descended into the valley of the dead," Kora answered.

They walked in silence until suddenly, from behind a

clump of bushes and trees a distance away, they heard women's voices raised in song and froze in their tracks. All three knew what the singing meant. A woyak was leading a small group of women into the forest to chop down trees and prepare new ground for sowing. He had ordered the women to sing, and they complied with a funeral song, a slow, mournful tune which they sang when they buried or·burned the dead. Cybula drew in his breath. Kora put her finger to her mouth for silence. Cybula knew of the work that the women were forced to perform, but had never witnessed it at first hand. Their singing on this cold winter morning made Cybula shiver. It caused him to forget his own troubles. Their tired voices belonged to those with neither hopes nor dreams, the singing of orphans, widows, slaves. To Cybula it seemed that these women were marching to their own graves. The singing grew fainter and more distant.

A thought came to Cybula, so simple that he wondered why it had not come to him sooner. "Kora, there is no reason for you and Yagoda to flee."

"What are you saying?"

"When they see me and my wounded body, they will know that I had a hand in the killing of Lis. But they will never suspect a woman, you or Yagoda. Why should you run away with me? It would be better if you stayed here."

"What are you planning to do?"

"I'll wait until my wounds heal, and then I'll return."

Yagoda broke her silence. "Cybula, don't leave me behind!"

"No, no, no. But your mother . . ."

Kora interrupted him. "What are you trying to say, Cybula? That I did wrong by killing Lis?"

"No, Kora. But we must free ourselves of the whole band

of woyaks, or else put an end to our own lives. While they live, we cannot survive."

"What do you propose we do?"

"I'll go to our people in the mountains and ask for their help."

"When they see you, they'll tear you limb from limb. When they came here, slaughtering their own wives and children, they were looking for you. It was your head they wanted. Besides, they are too few now, hungry and ill. They will not come to our aid. They will attack you and Yagoda like wolves. And I will remain all alone. No, Cybula. If we are destined to die, then let it be by your own sweet hand."

"Yes, Cybula. Kill us now," Yagoda said.

Cybula glanced at the handle of his sword. He was too tired, defeated, and disgraced to do away with himself or those he loved. Even death demanded strength. He heard himself say, "Before we die, let us eat." And his own words made him laugh.

(2)

It was Kora's decision, not his: the women alone would free themselves. It was not necessary to go begging to the Lesniks in the mountains. If she, Kora, could kill Lis, then sixty able-bodied women could bring down seventeen or eighteen woyaks. Cybula was amazed at Kora's vehemence and at her solution to the problem.

They did not venture far into the mountains, but instead found a cave where they could spend the night. The clouds thickened, an icy wind blew, snow arrived, whirling and falling in great heaps, so there was no danger that the woyaks would come out and search for them. Cybula had used the cave long ago, when he was a hunter. Ready shelters were essential when one hunted in the mountains, especially in winter. They had walked throughout the day, reaching their cave toward evening. Cybula feared that Yagoda could not endure the rigors of the journey, but the vigor of youth still throbbed within her. She clambered up the rocks with greater speed than he could muster. Being with them seemed to have brought her back to life. She said she had never been happier than in these days she spent with Cybula and her *matka,* her mother, in the cave.

When they reached the cave, Cybula was astonished to discover half-decaying pelts he had used many years ago and stacks of wood, as well as stones he had once used to build an oven. He rubbed one piece of wood with another and a fire was lit. This cave extended farther than the others and led downward through narrow winding passages, so narrow that one had to crawl through them. At its bottom flowed a river, and they could hear the sound of the rushing water. Cybula realized it was easy here to put an end to one's life: one had only to throw oneself into the cold current below.

Sitting by the warm fire, eating the meat which they had brought with them, Kora discussed her plans. She would return to the camp, not in daylight, but long after dark, after the woyaks had fallen drunk into their beds. She would speak to those women who were strong and dependable, especially those wives of woyaks who hated their husbands, and together they would plot their massacre. Whoever among them had courage and daring would take up a knife, an ax, whatever she had at hand, steal into the woyak's hut, and slay him while he slept. They would make sure that the woyaks all died on the same night, so that the plot could not be discovered in advance.

Kora knew the camp's women. She knew their natures and their fears. She did not need all sixty of them to help her rid the camp of eighteen woyaks. She would choose the ablest, the strongest, perhaps the youngest—those she could trust. When Kora discussed the details of her plan, she could not keep from laughing. She said, "Those woyaks will have a quick death, they will never know who did them in. In the morning we women shall rule the camp. We shall wear the swords, carry the spears. We shall never cut trees again! You, Cybula, will be our krol. Yagoda will be your krolowa, and I shall be the krolowa's mother. Why didn't we plan our revenge earlier—it is all so easy!"

Yagoda, who until that moment had been depressed and sullen, suddenly brightened up. "You, Mother, be the krolowa. I shall be your maid."

Cybula listened and from time to time he smiled, but he remained silent. He knew that in life what appeared to be easy often proved in the end to be difficult, if not altogether impossible. The gods did not grant women the courage and skill to mount resistance, rise in revolt, conclude a pact, fight a war. They were better at talk, not action. They could not be entrusted with secrets. One of them was sure to blab about the plot, and a bloodbath would follow. Even if the plot was not discovered, some women were sure to lose their nerve at the last moment. Cybula had other reservations. Several women carried the woyaks' offspring. His own daughter, Laska, was the krolowa and had borne Krol Rudy's child. Would Laska stab her husband and make her child an orphan? And what would become of Nosek if all the Poles were murdered? Although he hated the woyaks' oppression, it seemed to him wrong to slay unarmed men sleeping in their beds. And he had one final objection: he had sworn his loyalty to Krol Rudy.

After some time he said, "If you women win your victory, why make a man your krol? You, Kora, should rule the camp."

"I don't want to rule. I want to wash your feet, and afterward to drink the water," Kora answered.

"Oh, Mother, the things you say!"

"It is the truth."

Yagoda had begun to yawn and soon was fast asleep. After carrying her to a pelt near the fire and covering her, Kora sat up with Cybula. From time to time she threw Cybula a glance whose meaning he knew. What she had done for him that morning and was planning for the future aroused in her a passion for him. Despite the beating he had received from Lis and his weariness from their journey, a desire for her was kindled in him also. At the same time, they both needed to rest. A film covered his eyes, and his arms and legs hung limply from his body. They lay down and Kora embraced him. Heat streamed from her face, her breasts, her belly. Even her hands were hot. Cybula closed his eyes and immediately sank into a deep sleep. Hours later, someone awakened him; it was Kora. She licked his ear and bit his earlobe. Through the cave's opening he saw that it was still night, but he had awakened refreshed. An extraordinary heat flowed from Kora's body to his. She whispered, "Cybula, my god, come to me!" And almost like an animal, she attacked him.

(3)

The next morning he heard a howling, a whistling, a
hissing. A windstorm blew from the mountains, bringing with
it a mixture of snow and hail. Kora was already up. She had
added wood to the fire and was busy roasting a chunk of meat.
Cybula had intended to hunt, but it was now impossible. The
cave was fragrant with the smells of meat, blood, and smoke.
The light of the fire fell on the bare calves of Kora's legs, on
her arms, her face. Cybula was reminded of the woman of
valor, of whom Ben Dosa had spoken. Kora had often called
him a god, but to Cybula it seemed that she herself possessed
the powers of a goddess. Although she had given herself to
him during the night, he awakened with renewed desire for
her body. Yagoda was still sleeping. Cybula called to Kora to
come and lie beside him, but she refused. "Not now, my lord
and master. There is much that needs to be done today. I
must preserve my strength."

"What can you do in this storm?"

"First, I must fill your precious stomach with food. Then
I'll be on my way."

"In this blizzard? How? Your road will take you to the
hollows of the earth."

"Whatever the gods have ordained, so shall it be. If they
take me, you still have my daughter."

Cybula sat up. "What will you do in the camp? The woyaks
will tear you limb from limb."

"Either they will kill me, or I'll kill them. There is no
middle ground. Give me your sword."

"Kora, I don't want you to die. I need you."

"Don't worry, my love. The stars are with me."

"How can you be sure?"

"Baba Yaga came to me, but it was not in a dream. She revealed herself to me. You fell asleep with your head between my breasts. I was getting ready to lift your sweet head, to cling to you and go to sleep, when suddenly I saw her. She had a fearful face, disheveled hair—as black as a crow—with the eyes and claws of a hawk. She said to me, 'Go, my girl, and clean them out. Spill the blood of your enemies.' "

"She spoke a human language?"

"As you speak to me and I to you."

"You must have dreamed it."

"No, Cybula. I was awake when I saw her. I saw her mortar, her pestle. Her hair bristled, as if thorns grew out of her head. When she spoke, her tongue spewed flames. Her eyes blazed, like lightning. Cybula, I must borrow your sword."

"Wait. You're not going yet."

"I'm going."

Suddenly Yagoda sat up. She was still asleep. "Mother, don't go!"

"What is this?" Kora asked. "The chicks are wiser than the hen?"

"Matka, I dreamed that you lay dying and vultures pecked out your eyes," Yagoda said.

"A deception, a trick, brought on by some babuk or demon!"

Cybula argued with Kora, but she refused to yield. She picked up his sword, removed it from its sheath, then rapidly and forcefully waved it back and forth as if slashing off her enemies' heads. At the same time she spoke. "You, Cybula, know the truth. When those murderers came upon us, they plunged us into darkness. How many times have I made up my mind to make peace with them? But I cannot. They have destroyed us forever. We thought they brought us the blessing of bread, but they afflicted us instead with curses and hatred. They preyed on us like the wolves, waiting for a chance to annihilate us."

"You lay with them, not I," Cybula said, bewildered by his own words.

"Those woyaks have already paid their price." Kora had said what she wanted to say.

Cybula went outside to relieve himself. He lifted a clump of ice from the branch of a tree and chewed on it. He would have liked to wash himself with the freshly fallen snow. He returned to the cave and said, "Kora, you will never get there."

"Wait. The day has just begun."

They sat by the fire and bit off chunks of half-roasted meat. He licked the clump of ice he had brought into the cave. Kora was silent and Cybula began to think about Shmiercz, the god of death. Everyone tried to draw away from him, but instead they only drew closer. If everything was God, as Cybula believed, then death was also a part of God. If everything had life in it, as Cybula also believed, then there was life even in death. But how could that be? Cybula decided to ask Ben Dosa. That Jew, born in a distant land, had an answer for every question. But who knew whether Ben Dosa was still alive? Cybula was sure that when the woyaks found Lis dead, they would begin a new round of killing, and Ben Dosa would be the first victim.

Cybula had heard from the camp's women that Kosoka
loitered near Ben Dosa's hut and brought him gifts, which he
refused. In Miasto, where Cybula lay with her, he was not
overly fond of Kosoka. She chattered too much; her body had
an odor which other women did not have. Her breasts were
hard as rocks, the nipples longer and stiffer than other
women's. The bone under her belly, where hair grew, protruded too much. But when he had seen how quickly she
learned to read the letters and write with chalk on bark, a
desire for her awoke in him. "If Ben Dosa is dead and I am
alive," Cybula decided, "I'll take her and make her my
servant."

Cybula had long known that bad seed gives rise to bad
seedlings. Because of one six-fingered great-grandfather, there
were twelve Lesniks in the camp who had six fingers on their
hands. What was true of the body was also true of the spirit.
The seed of murderers, drunkards, idlers, and fools produced
their like. At night when he lay with Kora, Cybula often
revealed his innermost thoughts, his masculine desires. He
was not even ashamed to admit to her that he sometimes felt
lust for Laska, his own daughter. Ben Dosa told him of a
king in that distant land who had a thousand wives and
concubines. Jacob, the father of the tribe to which Ben Dosa
belonged, had four wives, two of them sisters. A whole nation
descended from this man's loins, as numerous as the sands of
the sea and the stars in the heavens. Kora always agreed with
Cybula and mocked women who begrudged their man his
other loves. She argued, "Does a man sin against the gods
when he tastes more than one dish?"

While the windstorm howled outside, and Kora prepared
to risk her life at the camp, Cybula wanted to remain sitting

by the fire and daydream. What was there to do on such a day?
He stood on the brink of disaster, but in his mind he conjured
up all the pleasures of life: young women, nights of passion,
a palace, a carriage, servants, horses. The children who ran
about playing were now all his. With the woyaks killed, he
was fathering a new generation. All the women in the camp
were now his concubines or wives and bore his children. He
had become a patriarch, the father of a new kingdom of the
fields. He even lay with his own daughters and tried out his
daughters-in-law before they married his sons. Now great
stretches of forestland had been cleared, and the camp was
surrounded with fields, gardens, orchards. The camp had
become a town, like Miasto, with tall buildings, a high tower,
workshops . . .

He fell asleep, and when he opened his eyes, the wind had
died down. The air that streamed into the cave was ice cold.
By the light of the fire Cybula saw that Kora was wearing his
sword. She had covered her bare arms and legs with skins.
Yagoda sat by the fire and roasted a rabbit she had brought
from her former burrow.

Kora was ready to return to the camp. He stared at her,
and she smiled at him through the shadows that fell on her
face. He asked, "Are you really going?"

"Yes, I am really going."

"Why must it be today?"

"Because the sky is covered with clouds and at night the
moon will not shine."

"Even if you don't die of the cold, the woyaks will surely
kill you."

"No, my krol. The gods are with me."

PART TWO

8

Krol Cybula

THE cold and harrowing winter, one long night strewn with nightmares, was over. After spring came, Cybula wondered how they had endured the bitter cold. The sun now shone brightly and warmed the camp as well as the large plot of land that had been planted with summer wheat. The women's revolution, led by Kora, had succeeded and the camp was at last free of the woyaks. Kora and her followers had slaughtered ten of them. The women stole into the woyak huts one night and slashed off their heads with swords, or smashed them with the stones they used for grinding wheat. Kora had agreed to spare Krol Rudy and Nosek, who were not oppressors, and because she knew Cybula did not want Laska made a widow and Ptashek an orphan. Krol Rudy himself lay ill and half-crazed. With ten woyaks dead, the four woyaks who had been injured but not killed by the women gave up the fight when they realized their power was broken.

They took to the road to loot and kill elsewhere when they recovered from their injuries. Kulak and Czapek luckily escaped death by not going to their beds that night; they had caroused all night and drunk themselves into a stupor and, while the massacre proceeded, snored away on the floor of the barn. When they were sober enough to understand what had happened, they joined forces with Nosek and Cybula.

Women now dominated the camp, because few males were left—apart from children, old men, and a remnant of Lesniks whom Cybula had persuaded to come down from the mountains. The women crowned Cybula against his will. It was foolish, he said, to be krol of an assembly of women, children, and old men. He asked the women to choose a queen from among themselves, or else wait until Krol Rudy died and appoint Laska queen. But the women placed a pumpkin on his head, lit several wax candles, and declared Cybula krol.

Kora, Laska, Nosek, Kulak, Czapek, Ben Dosa, and one of the returning Lesniks became Cybula's kniezes. The next morning the entire camp went barefoot to the fields to plow. Kernels of wheat had apparently been left in the fields after the last harvest, because here and there green shoots had already sprouted. The women wanted to chase Krol Rudy from his cabin. Cybula persuaded them to let the former krol remain.

Cybula was well aware that the camp's true ruler was no one else but Kora. Since he considered their newly established kingdom little more than a game, he thought, Why not let the children play? He even suspected that Kora had a queer passion for the bodies of women as well as for the bodies of men. Ben Dosa reminded him that Miasto was surrounded by a wall, and Cybula then and there decided that their camp would have a wall, too. The region was rich in rocks which could be used for construction. With every rock they cleared and every tree they cut, they would gain another plot of land for fields. Nosek, who was able to count, multiply, and divide, calculated that for the camp to construct a wall which no enemies could destroy would require many years.

Ben Dosa argued that the work should begin immediately, without delay, and that one of the most important things was digging wells. Isaac, the son of Abraham, had a special passion for digging wells. He also told them the history of Beersheba. This little shoemaker with the dark face, the dark beard, the sparkling black eyes, spoke not only of God, heaven, and Jerusalem but also of matters they could all understand. He argued, for example, that what was done in Miasto could be done in the camp as well, and even the camp could become a town. Almost everything needed was available here: land for fields, pasture for cattle and sheep, gardens for vegetables, orchards for fruits, while the rivers teemed with fish and the forests with animals and birds. They could trade in food and goods, but to become a true city the camp would need money. To trade goods there had to be measures in gold, silver, tin, or copper. They would have to put prices on all merchandise. The people of Miasto, and those of the surrounding estates, needed meat, skins, wool, flax, honey, wheat, timber. Not far from Miasto tree trunks were bound together and made into rafts, then sent down the Vistula, which flowed into the sea. Merchants from lands where many people lived and many languages were spoken paid for the timber with articles of iron, copper, glass, and brass, as well as woven carpets and clothes, and even beautifully fashioned jewelry. Ben Dosa said that in those cities there were men who practiced every craft: tailors, shoemakers, blacksmiths, carpenters, furriers, bricklayers, spinners, weavers, carvers, dyers, tanners, braiders, polishers, and so on. The Mishnah listed thirty-nine crafts which could not be practiced on the holy day of rest. One of them was writing. Yes, in Babylonia, in the land of Israel, in Egypt, Syria, and in many other lands, there were scribes who copied words on parchment. It was necessary to study God's commandments day and night, so that believers could keep away from sin. He suggested that when the boys of the camp reached a certain age, they be sent to craftsmen in Miasto to learn their trades. He also suggested that tradesmen from other towns be brought to the camp. The unmarried men could find wives among the camp's women, settle down, raise families. Thus would the camp increase its size, while the danger of being attacked would lessen.

The camp never grew tired of hearing Ben Dosa speak. Even the children, who did not always understand, came to listen. The women had only one thing to say: What a pity it was that he refused to marry one of them—he could father a whole generation of clever children! But Ben Dosa abstained from women. He permitted no woman to befriend him. He often reminded them that, in the distant land of Babylon, he had a wife and children. And even if he were free, he could never marry a woman who did not with all her heart and with full understanding embrace the Jewish faith.

Of all the divine laws which Ben Dosa explained to them, the one about circumcision seemed to the Lesniks strangest. Why cut the flesh of a boy only eight days old? Why shorten a part of a boy's body when everyone knew it must grow with

the years? Whenever Ben Dosa mentioned this commandment, the people laughed, and even the children snickered.

(2)

During the long interval that stretched between the sowing
and the reaping, Kora began to prepare for Cybula's public
marriage to her daughter, Yagoda. The days were sunny and
warm. The forest teemed with animals that, foraging for food,
often came so near the camp that women and old men could
shoot them with bows and arrows. Other animals fell into
their traps. Early one morning Cybula shot three deer. The
boys of the camp vied with each other hunting birds, field
mice, squirrels, rabbits, hares. They went to the stream with
their nets and caught fish.

The women of the camp often mocked the meek and
helpless Yagoda. They took her for a fool. When they met
together, she was the chief subject of their gossip. What did
Cybula see in her? Why did he lust for her? She was small
and scrawny, she had neither breasts nor buttocks, her arms
and legs were thin, her bosom flat. She was most likely
barren or else long ago she would have borne his child. She
was not by nature a big talker. Some of the women suspected
that Yagoda was deaf. When they asked her a question, they
often got no answer. If Yagoda became the krolowa, some
women said, the camp would be disgraced. But still they
prepared for the approaching wedding. Girls and women
gathered in a meadow where cows, goats, and sheep grazed,
and danced the dances of days gone by: a water dance, a
quarrel dance, a babuk dance, a goat dance, the dance of the

dying bird, and the Baba Yaga dance, which in former times was performed when they offered the goddess a sacrifice.

Dancing with one another, without men, held little pleasure for the women. Some women swept the old Lesnik men into the circle, where they barely managed to stay on their feet. One girl, in high spirits, danced with a he-goat, whom she dragged into the circle by its horns. Cybula came out for one round of dancing, but he danced with no one but Kora. For a while the old entertainer awoke in Cybula, and once again he told jokes, and mimicked the fools and ne'er-do-wells who had long ago descended into the hollows of the earth. He even tried to turn somersaults, and the camp roared with laughter. Several women laughed so hard that their laughter turned into crying.

Krol Rudy no longer left his hut in the daytime, but when Laska came out to join the merrymakers, she danced with both her stepmother and her father. Yagoda, for whose wedding the camp was preparing, hid in her hut and refused to come out. Someone in the camp likened her to a field mouse. When she left her hut to go to the forest to pick mushrooms, she hurried by so quickly that she did not stop when people called her name. In the forest she looked for spots where there were no other women. And yet, at the same time, she showed herself to be a skillful huntress. The women finally agreed that the only thing alluring in Yagoda was the shape of her mouth. Her face was small, her cheeks sunken, her neck as thin as a bird's, but in her full lips and in her chin lay a hidden lust.

Because of Cybula's wedding, Ben Dosa was laden with work. All the camp's women had ordered shoes. He spent many long hours taking measurements of women's feet, while at the same time murmuring prayers to help him withstand temptation. Some of the women lifted their skirts above their bare knees, revealing their thighs and even their bellies. Often they said to him, "Don't be a fool, Ben Dosa. Come lie in my arms." And Ben Dosa would murmur, "Forgive me, but God forbids it."

"What god? The gods also carouse and play."

"Only idols and demons do. The God of Israel is holy."

Ben Dosa no longer worked in the hut in which he lived and taught reading and writing. He had built a small workshop for himself nearby, and planned to build a shop where he could sell articles from Miasto, and buy pelts, honey, pig's hair, and wool. While he cut skins and scraped wooden heels, Ben Dosa studied the Torah, rocked back and forth, and prayed to his invisible God. How could he make these heathens understand God's existence, God who cared for every person, every gnat, every leaf on a tree? Their fate was to live out their lives in darkness. Yet was it their fault that they had never heard of God? Ben Dosa felt that the person most capable of understanding his thinking was Cybula. But Cybula was completely immersed in everyday tasks and always succumbed to the females who kissed him, caressed him, tickled him. Nosek's thoughts, on the other hand, revolved around food, tools, horses. There was a rumor that Nosek liked men better than women. Well then, where could he learn that his conduct was sinful?

It was strange, but in Kosoka—a half-breed of Tatars—a spark of godliness stirred. She never ceased to ask Ben Dosa about God, the angels, the Torah, the soul. She wanted to know what a commandment was, and why something was a transgression. Simple and ignorant as she was, her thoughts sometimes astonished him. Although she was not Jewish, she refused to eat the flesh of a pig or to do any work on the Sabbath. Although Ben Dosa tried to dissuade her from embracing the Jewish faith, she strove with all her strength to be like a daughter of Israel. When she revealed her desire to become his wife, it aroused a suspicion that she wanted to become a Jew only to win him as a husband. Yet after all, it is said that sometimes even from a sin a good must come.

(3)

It was Nosek's idea that the camp should build a house for Cybula. Many of the trees which the women chopped down lay in piles in the forest. It was not necessary to trim them, Nosek said, or to shape them in square blocks. They could be heaped one on the other as they were, and tied together with leather ropes. The camp possessed axes now, and saws, planes, hammers, nails. The woyaks who were killed left behind the horses which Cybula and Nosek had bought in Miasto. Those horses could now be used to carry lumber. When Nosek finished speaking, the women-filled camp became eager to show how well and quickly they could work. When the building began, Ben Dosa, Nosek, Kora, Czapek, and Kulak worked side by side with the others. They dug up clay and cut wood. Laska left her child with an old woman, Mila, and came to lend a hand. Kosoka also wanted to participate, but the women pushed her away. Ben Dosa immediately came to her defense, saying, "What have you against her? What evil has she done to you? The Torah teaches us to love the stranger in our midst. When King Solomon was building the temple in Jerusalem, King Hiram sent him spruce trees and craftsmen from the city of Tyre. They were heathens who helped build a temple for the Almighty, and the Almighty looked upon their work with favor."

"She is not human," one woman shouted. "Her eyes are slanted!"

"Slanting eyes are as good as eyes which do not slant. We are all descendants of Adam and Eve."

"Speak to us in the language of humans, so that we can understand you!" an old Lesnik called out.

"Whose language am I speaking—oxen's?"

Not only adults but children lent a hand to the building. Yagoda's hands were too small and delicate for most of the work, so Kora gave her a bucket of water and told her to circulate and dole it out to the builders who needed it. Cybula constructed a ladder, and together with Nosek and Czapek, he put up a roof. Later they intended to construct an oven, but meanwhile they left an opening for the chimney. The workers themselves were impressed with what they had accomplished. Both Ben Dosa and Nosek exhibited a marked talent for construction. They knew exactly where to place a door and where to cut a window. They laid a heavy foundation so that the house would not sink in the mud or sway in the wind. The women sang while they worked, and some of them shamelessly exposed their breasts. They laughed uproariously and spoke obscenities. Perhaps they have not yet tasted the fruit of the tree of knowledge, thought Ben Dosa. At the end of ten days, Cybula's house, such a one as the camp had never seen before, was completed.

Though the camp had believed itself forsaken by the gods and condemned for eternity, that spring saw hopefulness

return. The seeds in the field sprouted. Fruits ripened on the
trees. The hens laid eggs and the cows calved. Cybula's
wedding with Yagoda became a joyous and festive holiday,
with singing and dancing. There was mead to be drunk, and
with the flour from the previous year's harvest, women baked
pretzels and cakes. Fresh fish from the stream were boiled in
clay pots or roasted on hot coals. At his wedding Cybula
danced with every woman in the camp, and Kora with every
man—including Gluptas the fool. Ben Dosa's new shoes, for
those who wore them, made their feet appear slender and
sleek. Their dancing was so joyous and lively that it lifted the
spirits of even the old and the crippled. The old women who
sewed pelts for the camp had made a dress for the bride, and
when Cybula danced with Yagoda the dress billowed and
whirled around her. Some of the women clapped their hands,
some laughed, others smiled. No celebrating Lesnik could
forget their brothers and sisters who had perished at the
woyaks' murderous hands. Four Lesniks—or Gorals, as those
who had come down from the mountains were now called—
grabbed Cybula, lifted him high over their heads, and
continued their dance. Several women did likewise with
Yagoda. Hymns were sung to the gods, the goddesses, to
Cybula, Yagoda, Nosek. Some children tried to lift Ben Dosa,
but small as he was, he was too heavy for them. They kissed
him and shouted in unison: "Rabbi! Rabbi! Rabbi!" Ben
Dosa placed his hands on their heads and blessed them as
if they were Jewish children: "May God make you like Efraim
and Menashe! May you be like Sarah, Rebecca, Rachel, and
Leah." And he promised to sew shoes for them all before the
winter came.

Several women became drunk, and one of them removed

her dress and, jiggling her breasts, invited the men to come to her. One of the mountain men, a Goral, tore off his trousers. Cybula demanded that those who overexcited the camp be removed, but it was too late. A storm of emotion broke out which could no longer be contained. Men who moments ago had appeared old and frail now roared in loud voices, waved their arms, and shook their fists, grimaced and gesticulated. It was difficult to know whether it was joy that moved them or grief. Intoxicated women fell over each other, convulsed in fits of laughter and tears. Ben Dosa feared that the joyous celebration would turn into violence. One woman had already pulled his beard and spoken to him offensively. Another threw her arms around him and tried to push him down to the ground. Suddenly he heard Kosoka's voice calling him, and he saw that someone was slapping her face and pulling her by the hair. Ben Dosa ran and tore her from her attacker's hands. He spoke in Polish the words Moses uttered when he saw that a Jew had attacked another Jew: "Why wouldst thou hit thy brother?"

(4)

Cybula was still the reluctant krol and he knew Kora was gaining the upper hand. She had done so much for him that he felt he had to yield to all her wishes. The truth was that her requests would serve his own needs as well. What did she want but to give him pleasure, to increase the camp's love for him? It was as if her soul had merged with his. His masculine needs became her feminine ones. Sometimes she spoke as if she were half man and half woman, like the spirits, babuks, bloodsuckers, about whom old women told tales by the light of the moon. In former times, when the camp could boast of many men, Cybula arranged a hunt for large animals every spring. The men went out to the forest with their bows and arrows and their spears, and they returned carrying a bear, a wild boar, a deer. A fire was built and the animals were skinned and roasted in the fire. A festive meal would follow: meat was eaten, mead drunk, men and women danced until midnight and even longer. Although Lesnik family life was firmly governed by laws, on the night of the big hunt men and women mixed with each other freely, sang together, danced together, and often couples went off into the forests to do what their hearts desired. The gods and goddesses were supposed to be benevolent during the time of the big hunt and they forgave the Lesniks what follies they committed in the darkness, under the light of the stars. Moreover, the Lesniks were all related to one another, knotted and bound by countless marriages and births, and it was not so heinous a sin when they sometimes mixed bloods.

Kora now argued that the big hunt should not be abandoned because of the shortage of men. Cybula had his bow, as did many of the older men. Bows and arrows had been left behind by Lesniks who had been killed and by woyaks who tried to hunt during the winter's great famine. Speaking in a kind of frenzy, Kora persuaded the women to try *their* hands at hunting. One need not be strong to hunt, she said. All that was needed was good eyesight and a bit of skill. Kora herself had shot some animals.

At first Cybula argued that hunting was for men, not women, since it required courage, vigor, the ability to run and jump. But Kora refused to be discouraged. A sudden attack from woyaks might force the women to put up resistance.

She had heard stories of other camps where the men were slaughtered and the women had to take over the fighting, defending themselves with swords and spears. Hadn't Ben Dosa told them of a prophetess who ruled over the people of Israel and later led them to war, and of another woman who killed their enemies' leader and thrust a hook into his forehead while he lay at her feet? In the end, Cybula agreed.

When Kora announced that a big hunt with both sexes would be led by Cybula and Nosek, the camp erupted with joy. All the women wanted to learn to shoot arrows. Even the older children began to prepare themselves for the big day. A large target figure was constructed from sticks and the people aimed their arrows and spears at it. Ben Dosa, when told about the big hunt, immediately declared it sinful. The Bible recorded the story of the mighty hunter Nimrod, whose name suggested that he came of those who were rebellious against God. Ben Dosa cautioned the children against shooting their arrows at the figure, because doing so would encourage the human urge to cruelty. But Cybula spoke harshly to Ben Dosa, reminding him that he, Cybula, was krol and only his commands would be obeyed. The camp would not take its orders from some god who dwelled in Jerusalem.

When the big hunt took place several days later, Cybula marveled at the skill shown by the women. More animals were killed in one day than the camp could eat in an entire month. Even the children's arrows hit their marks with ease. With pride, the women carried the dead animals on their backs. Children dragged behind them the small corpses of rabbits, hares, and even a fox who was not wise enough to flee from his lair. Under Cybula's direction the women pierced a large bear, as well as a wild boar, with their knives and spears. The camp was so amply provided with meat that some women wanted to make a gift of their catch to Kosoka. But Kosoka refused, saying she was now a Jewish girl and could not eat the flesh of a bear or a pig. She told the women that it was close to the time of Shevuoth, the festival which celebrated the giving of the Torah on Mount Sinai. The women shrugged their shoulders. "When does he teach you these things—at night, in bed?"

"No. He does not touch me."

"Why not? Because your eyes are slanted?"

"Because I am not completely Jewish."

"When will you be Jewish?"

"When his God wills it."

"Ben Dosa speaks with the gods?" the women asked.

"There is only one God."

The women shook their heads. "If you don't eat, you will die from hunger."

"God can bring the dead back to life," Kosoka answered.

The women looked at each other with astonishment. They had never listened to this slave before. Nosek had brought this slant-eyed monster to the camp as a gift for Krol Rudy, but Krol Rudy did not want her. A woman asked Kosoka, "Why don't you return to the land from which you came?"

And Kosoka answered, "They are all heathens in that land. Wherever Ben Dosa is, there I want to be."

(5)

Ben Dosa observed all the holy days in accord with his own calculations, figuring out the beginning of the month by the appearance of the new moon. Kora reproved him for neglecting his work on such days and complained that he would be idle for two days running, since immediately after Shevuoth came the Sabbath. Ben Dosa promised he would work without stopping to make up for lost time, and the next day he did not even take time out to eat. He worked from sunrise until just before sunset. Having recited the evening prayers in his workshop, he only then returned to his hut for the dishes Kosoka had prepared for him, food he was permitted to eat—vegetables, fruits, a fish roasted on coals. The woman has a sacred soul, he thought. She strove to do good deeds and wished to follow the laws of his people. He had promised her that if she remained steadfast in her desire to embrace the Jewish faith, he would make her a Jew.

Kosoka had even tried to persuade him that they should flee from the camp. "We will never be set free as long as we are here," she argued. "We are their slaves." She wanted to steal away at night and meet him on the road to Miasto, but he would not agree.

"I will never be able to take on the true faith," Kosoka argued.

"As it is destined to be, so shall it be," he replied, and she had burst out crying.

Ben Dosa now finished his eating, fell upon the bed exhausted from his work, and immediately went into a deep sleep. He had barely remembered to recite the proper benediction. His dreams often brought him more grief than his wakeful hours. He found himself aboard the Canaanite ship on which he had been kidnapped. He again lived through his captors' savagery, as they whipped him and mocked him. Evil demons also invaded his dreams, and he awoke from these visions bathed in perspiration and sexually aroused. He felt a weight resting against his legs and touched a face, a head, hair. Ben Dosa was terrified. Was it Lilith who had possessed him in the night? Or Shibta? Naama? "Who is this?" he cried out. And he heard her answer, "It is I, Kosoka."

Ben Dosa sprang up, and a hoarse moan broke from his throat. "What have you done?"

"I am Ruth, your servant," she answered.

Ben Dosa shivered. Before the festival of Shevuoth he had told her the story of Boaz and Ruth. And now Kosoka had gone even further than Ruth had when she lay at the feet of Boaz, her redeemer. He stood up and the perspiration poured from his body. "Filth! Defilement!"

"Redeem me, my Boaz," Kosoka murmured. "Forgive me for uncovering thine feet, my lord."

He raised his fist to strike her, but then withdrew it. His body was shaking and he could hear the chattering of his teeth. This Tatar girl whom he had intended to bring into the Jewish fold had caused him to sin. He remembered the sentence in the Gemara: He who takes an Aramite will be set upon by zealots. Hot tears streamed from his eyes, scalded his cheeks. True he had erred in telling her this holy story. He shouted, "Harlot!" His throat tightened and he choked.

"I want to be your Ruth."

"You act like Orpah, not like Ruth, or like Kozbi, the daughter of Zur, who was pierced by the holy Pinchas."

"I want to be your wife!"

"Out!" He seized her by her neck and pushed her from the hut. She fell to the ground with a thud. His foot stumbled against a rock. He bumped his forehead on the doorpost. He did not know which caused him more pain, the sin or the blow. He returned to his hut, limping. "I hope I did not kill her," a voice inside him nagged. He had barely reached his bed when his knees buckled under him and he fell to the floor. "Father in heaven, take me . . ." he prayed.

Before sunrise, when Kora came out of Cybula's hut to breathe in the cool morning air and to bathe her breasts in dew (a remedy for the withering of the skin that comes with age), she saw in the distance a figure lying on the ground near Ben Dosa's hut. She approached cautiously. It was a woman lying face down, her arms and legs outstretched as if she was dead. Kora turned her over and recognized Kosoka, her face smeared with mud, her eyes closed. Kora lifted her, and she was limp and light, like a child. Could it be that Ben Dosa had thrown her out of his hut? Did someone in the camp rape her? Kora was reluctant to awaken Cybula, and half carried, half dragged the girl to the charred hut where she had lived with her husband, Kostek, and where she still kept a bed. She wet the palm of her hand in the dew and passed it over Kosoka's lips.

The girl shivered and opened two slitted eyes. Kora asked, "Did someone attack you? Were you raped?" She poured a pitcher of water on Kosoka's neck and body and rubbed her temples with the palms of her hands. The girl kept shivering. "What happened?" Kora asked. "Who did this to you?" She helped Kosoka to sit up and held her by her shoulders so that she would not slip down again. She shouted, "Who did this? Speak, answer me!"

Kosoka did not answer. Kora slapped her cheeks and pinched her nostrils, as one does to those who feel faint. A sigh and a rattle broke out of Kosoka's throat.

"Who hit you?"

"No one."

"Were you drunk, or what?"

"No."

"Why were you lying near Ben Dosa's hut?"

"I don't know."

"You do know. Come with me."

"Where? No, no."

"We all know your cunning tricks," Kora said. "Our krol Cybula and Kniez Nosek bought you in Miasto to work for us, not to frolic with Ben Dosa. Our krol married my daughter and they need someone to serve them. You will live in their hut and do what they tell you to do. The woyaks are gone and now we are the rulers. If you don't do as you are told, we will chop you in pieces and feed you to the dogs."

"Let me go."

"Come with me, or you'll die instantly," Kora said. Gripping Kosoka by the hair, she pulled her down to the floor. "I am the krolowa's mother and I can do with you as I please. Who threw you in the mud?"

"No one."

"Who?"

Holding her by the hair with one hand, Kora slapped her cheeks with the other. The girl remained silent, and as she slapped Kosoka, it occurred to Kora that she would make a fitting sacrifice to the gods.

Kosoka clung to the earth with her feet, and Kora dragged her along. The evening before, Kosoka had put on a dress made of pelts, but now it had been torn off her body. It had rained during the night and the ground was muddy. Kosoka fell into a fit of moans and muffled sobs. Doors of nearby huts began to open, and half-naked, sleepy-eyed women came out and stared.

"What has Slant-eyes done?"

"Squeals like a pig in the mud," Kora muttered.

The women looked on in disbelief and rubbed their eyes. One blurted out, "That Miasto harlot!"

"We don't want this alien scum anymore," Kora said. She had worked herself into a rage. It was once the custom of the camp that those who were to be sacrificed were offered the best of food, surrounded with tenderness, with love. But Kosoka's silence evoked in Kora an eagerness to put an end to this girl who had no relatives in the camp and whom no one wanted to take in. Someone ran to awaken Cybula, and he emerged from his hut barefoot.

"What is this?"

"I'm going to kill her!" Kora screamed. "We don't need Tatars in this camp. We are Lesniks, not Poles and not Jews."

"Kora, let her go!"

"If you want her, you can have her!" And Kora raised her foot and kicked Kosoka in the face. More doors opened. Ben Dosa emerged from his hut, also barefoot. He stood unsteadily on his feet, shaking. "What happened?" And when he saw Kosoka, he stretched out his arms and a terrible cry broke from his lips: "Sodom and Gomorrah!"

9

The Blond Stranger

THE month they now called Czerwiec was hot, but in the evening cool breezes blew in. The snow on the mountain peaks had melted. With the ice and the snow, rocks rolled down the slopes, knocking over trees, blocking trails from the valley below. There was a time long ago when the Lesniks believed that beyond the mountains lived a tribe of giant gods who had two or three heads, one eye in their foreheads, and four hands. The Lesniks knew that beyond the mountains lived the Czechs—people the same as they were, whose language even resembled their own. The Czechs worshipped other gods, and their rulers were also called krols. They had tilled the soil and eaten bread long before the Lesniks. Sometimes it happened that one of them wandered into the camp. If the stranger was not put to death, he fell ill and died. This was also the fate of Lesniks who traveled across the mountains to the Czechs: they never returned.

In the middle of summer it snowed in the mountains, sometimes it hailed, and the night air was so cold that fingers and toes froze almost instantly. Storm winds blew from the peaks. Goddesses reclined on cloud-beds and braided each other's hair, luring men to their laps, then hurling them to the depths below. In the valley, however, the days were warm. It was plain to see that the gods had showered their blessings on the fields, the gardens, as well as on the forests: there were black berries, red berries, and all kinds of mushrooms. Swarms of bees buzzed around each flower, drawing from the open calyx the juice and the fragrance which later they would turn to honey. Various weeds grew in the fields, and it was the women's daily task to pluck them out. Evil little *babas* and *dziads* were known to fertilize these weeds, together with wild mushrooms and berries that were poisonous. The women in the fields joked, gossiped, bared to one another their bellies, their breasts. The woyaks had left several women pregnant, and old hags predicted that monsters with teeth, claws, and tails would come from such unions.

Kora had nagged Cybula until he finally promised that Yagoda would be pregnant by spring. Now the girl's menstrual periods had stopped and Kora began to hang charms and amulets around her neck to ensure that the child was a boy. Although she had betrayed her husband, Kostek, both with her wanton ways and with her lustful longings for Cybula, Kora was determined to name the child Kostek, seeking thereby to appease Kostek's spirit so that harm would not come to the boy. And Kora was more determined than ever to make a sacrifice of Kosoka to Baba Yaga, to appease the gods before her grandchild was born.

(2)

A short time before the harvest, there was great tumult in the camp. A stranger suddenly appeared in their midst. He was not one of Miasto's tradesmen carrying his wares in a sack on his back but a man dressed like a kniez, a pan, even a krol. He was tall, young, erect; he had a blond beard, a long cloak, a feathered hat, and spurs on his boots. He rode a white horse on a saddle trimmed with dangling tassels. His face was thin and pale, his eyes were blue. The entire camp came out to greet him.

Ben Dosa was asleep when the stranger arrived and the loud voices awakened him. When he saw the honored guest, a tremor seized him. Could he be the Messiah? But the Messiah would come riding an ass, not a horse, and he would be a poor man, dressed in rags, not in wealth and finery. Everyone came out to welcome the stranger, who waited until they all gathered around him. He sat on his horse, tall and silent, with the patience of a king who knew that his people awaited his word.

Cybula was barefoot. Standing at the side of the horse and rider, he resembled a slave more than a krol. He asked the stranger to alight from his horse, but the man replied, "I will not dismount until you have all heard what I came to say." He pronounced the Polish tongue differently from even the people in Miasto. His voice was deep and at the same time resonant. When Cybula introduced himself as the krol, the stranger said, "May peace be with you, krol, but I come to you in the name of the Krol of all krols. He is the king of the whole world."

A man of God, Ben Dosa thought to himself, a messenger of God. He felt an urge to fall on his knees and bow to this great man, but he restrained himself. All praise and honor belonged to the creator, not to his messengers. After a while the visitor spoke: "Brother Poles, I have heard about you, about your trials and sufferings. I have come to bring you the message of God and of his only begotten son, Jesus Christ, who died on the cross to redeem us all from our sins and to bring us to the kingdom of heaven."

Ben Dosa shuddered. He wanted to shout, "Liar, traitor, messenger of Satan!" but a lump formed in his throat and he could neither swallow nor talk. Master of the Universe, I am suffocating, he thought. May my death atone for my sins. His knees shook, and he could barely keep from falling. He clutched someone by the shoulder and steadied himself. Cybula waited a moment, and then he spoke: "A guest in the house is God in the house. Dismount, sir, and come partake of what our huts have in abundance."

"Thank you, krol. I greet you in the name of our master, whose message has spread to all corners of the world, despite the wicked heathen and those who hate truth and love falsehood."

And saying these words—slowly and in a loud voice—the stranger dismounted from his horse. Inasmuch as the stranger spoke like a learned man, holding that there was but one god and dismissing the heathens with scorn, Cybula was eager to acquaint him with Ben Dosa. But Ben Dosa had vanished. He was seen running in the direction of the field, toward the forest. Cybula shouted after him to return, but Ben Dosa did not even turn his head. Standing in their midst, the stranger delivered a sermon. From what Cybula could understand of

it, the stranger—whose name was Bishop Mieczyslaw—
served the same god as did Ben Dosa. His god had also
revealed himself in the distant city of Jerusalem. His teaching was also recorded in a book. The stranger called it the
"Bible."

After the sermon, Cybula invited him to his hut. When he
mentioned that there was a man in this camp named Ben
Dosa, a shoemaker, a teacher who both read and wrote, who
was a Jew, Bishop Mieczyslaw asked, "Who is this man? The
black-bearded one who fled?"

"Yes, it is he."

"The Jews killed God. They hung him on a cross," Bishop
Mieczyslaw said. "They are cursed here on earth and they will
never inherit the kingdom of heaven."

"Can a god be killed?" Cybula asked.

"His Father in heaven sent him down to earth to redeem
the world from sin through his death," the bishop answered.

"The father wanted his son to be killed?" Cybula asked.

"God promised through his prophets that his son would
give a new Torah, but the Jews who rebelled against God
and changed money in their temple distorted the prophets'
words. They denied the miracles that Jesus Christ performed, and one of them, a liar and betrayer, pretended
to be a loyal follower of Jesus and later betrayed him for
the sum of thirty shekels and delivered him into the hands
of the heathens."

"Where are the heathens—in Jerusalem?" Cybula asked.

"Before God sent his son, all the nations worshipped idols,"
Bishop Mieczyslaw answered. "But when they saw the truth,
many of them destroyed the altars they used for human

sacrifices, expelled the whores and false prophets from their temples, and smashed their idols. One nation alone remained headstrong and rebellious—the Jews."

"Did Ben Dosa kill God?" Cybula asked.

"Not he himself. His people did."

"When did they kill God?"

"Oh, a long time ago. Several hundreds of years."

"Is Ben Dosa so old?"

"No, but he is descended from their corrupt seed."

The longer the stranger spoke, the more bewildered Cybula became. Nosek also seemed confused. Cybula blurted out: "Pan Mieczyslaw, is your Bible written in the Polish tongue?"

"No, in Latin."

"Is that the language the Niemcies speak?"

"No, the Romans."

"Is God also in Rome?"

"God is everywhere."

"Is God everything?"

"He has created everything—the heavens, the earth, the sun, the stars."

"This is what Ben Dosa also says," Nosek broke in.

Kora, who had listened in silence, asked the bishop, "Does God have a wife?"

The stranger did not answer immediately. "No. He let his holy spirit rest on Mary, Joseph's wife, and she became pregnant and bore a son, exactly as the prophet Isaiah had foretold."

"In Jerusalem?" Cybula asked.

"No, in Bethlehem."

"Where is Bethlehem?"

"In the holy land which God had given to Abraham, Isaac, and Jacob."

"Shall I send someone to look for Ben Dosa so that you may discuss with him the gods of Jerusalem?" Cybula asked.

The stranger paused before he answered.

"Ah, the Jews are a stiff-necked people; that is why God dispersed them in all the lands and banished them from his presence. Try to show them the prophecies of their own prophets, and they twist and distort the meaning of the words."

"Ben Dosa taught our children to write with chalk, and he recites a prayer with them every morning. He says the Sabbath is a holy day," Cybula said.

"What does he teach the children? A man such as he may poison them with the utterings of his mouth. He may teach them to blaspheme against God. I would not entrust the souls of children to him."

"He tells them curious tales," Kora said.

"They may appear to be curious, but they may contain many lies. The Jews killed their own prophets. They killed the prophet Zechariah, and the prophet Jeremiah they threw into a pit," Bishop Mieczyslaw said.

"We are simple folk," Cybula said. "We can neither read nor write. When the woyaks attacked us, the gods were not with us and most of our people died. Later the woyaks began to kill one another, until it happened that I became krol. Now we are a small band of women, children, and old men. Any day new enemies may come to wipe out what remains of us. That is why we live with hope only. Why, Bishop Mieczyslaw, did you come to us?"

"I have come to teach you to serve the true God, to teach you the way of love."

"Of love?"

"You will learn to love one another, and even to love your enemies."

"We tried to make peace with our enemies because they had given us seeds and taught us to plow and to sow," Cybula said. "But they used our crops to make intoxicating beverages. They broke into our huts and tents and attacked our women and children. Their former king, Krol Rudy, still lives with us. He has taken my daughter for a wife, but he no longer lies with her. He is more an animal than a man now. Kora, my wife's mother—the woman you see before you—wants to offer a sacrifice to Baba Yaga. But I don't believe that will help us."

The bishop's ears pricked up. "What sort of sacrifice?"

"A girl from the distant steppes, at the end of the world."

"Cybula, that is a secret," Kora said.

"It is a secret no more."

"Baba Yaga is not a goddess but a devil, she is Lucifer's wife," Bishop Mieczyslaw said. "And to sacrifice humans is sinful. It is what heathens do, not those who believe in God and in his son, Jesus. Those were the wicked ways of Assyria and Babylon, who served Baal and Astarte. The Jews also committed these sins. They threw their own children into Moloch's fires, sacrifices to demons, worshipped idols, practiced witchcraft, and fornicated under the trees. And when God sent his only begotten son to them, they falsified his teachings and tortured him. But he arose from the dead—his grave was found empty—because he lives and he will live forever. Amen."

"Where does he live, in Jerusalem?" Cybula asked.

"With his father, in heaven," Bishop Mieczyslaw answered.

(3)

In the evening the bishop retired early. Cybula gave him one of the huts left empty by the fleeing woyaks. Cybula had feared that Bishop Mieczyslaw would refuse to partake of their evening meals—as Ben Dosa had previously done. But the bishop explained that in the new covenant which God had concluded with the faithful he had, through the mouth of Jesus and his apostles, lifted the old prohibitions. A Christian was not required to be circumcised, he could eat the flesh of a pig, and he could light a fire on the Sabbath. These things found favor with Cybula.

"Why should men be burdened with so many difficult commandments?" he asked Kora that night in their bed. The bishop's god was far wiser than Ben Dosa's. But Kora was offended by Bishop Mieczyslaw's vehement words against human sacrifices.

"He could be a spy," she said.

"Whose spy?"

"Oh, the pans who seize all the land for themselves and make others their slaves."

"If the pans want to destroy us, they need no spies. They need only come with their soldiers and wipe us out. You know this as well as I."

"He may have come from them to make us surrender without a battle," Kora answered.

They talked together for an hour. Yagoda had been the

first to fall asleep, as always. During the feast which Cybula had ordered for the guest, they had eaten abundantly and drunk mead. Soon Cybula and Kora themselves fell into deep sleep. It was midnight when Cybula awakened. He rose and quietly walked outside, into the cool night air. The sky hovered above the camp studded with stars. As he looked, a star tore from its place and sped across the sky, leaving behind a trail of fire. As often as Cybula raised his eyes to the starry heavens, he was astonished anew. What was happening up there in the heavens? He remembered from previous years that more stars darted across the sky in late summer than at any other time. But why was that so? Cybula had heard of stargazers who could predict from the stars whether a krol would win a battle or lose it, whether an ailing man would recover or die, whether a man's wife would be faithful to him or deceive him. But how could the stars know all this beforehand? Ah, the world was filled with so many wonders, so many puzzles.

He began to walk. Crickets chirped and dew formed on the ground. From a nearby swamp arose the croaking of frogs. While Cybula was walking past Ben Dosa's hut, he saw a dim light shining within and stood listening. He heard a voice. Was Ben Dosa speaking to himself? No, he was saying a prayer to his god. But how could he pray to a god he had killed? Cybula opened the door and saw Ben Dosa with a long robe wrapped around his body, his hair sprinkled with ashes as one who mourned a death. When Ben Dosa saw Cybula, he fell silent. Cybula asked, "To whom were you speaking, to yourself or to your god?"

Ben Dosa hesitated. He put his finger to his lips, a sign

that he was not permitted to speak until he had concluded his prayer. But Cybula did not understand his signal. He called out, "Have you lost your tongue?"

"No, my krol. I am praying to God."

"In the middle of the night? Perhaps your god is asleep and you will wake him up," Cybula said.

"No, my krol. It is said, God neither dozes nor sleeps. He watches over Israel."

"Who is this Israel?"

"The father of the Jews was named Jacob, but God renamed him Israel, and all his children and grandchildren carry this name."

"Does Jacob still live?"

"In heaven, not on earth."

"Is he God's son, whom the Jews killed?" Cybula asked.

Ben Dosa was startled. "No, no. He whom the Jews are supposed to have killed was named Joshua, not Jacob. The Greek scribes wrote the name as Jesus and the name Christ is a Greek word for Messiah. But Joshua was not the Messiah. The Jews did not kill him, the Romans did, the same Romans who destroyed our temple."

"The bishop who came to us today said that the Jews killed Jesus."

"It is not true, my krol. How can a god be killed? And if he was God's son, why would God allow his son to be killed? The truth is that Joshua was the son of a carpenter named Joseph and his wife, Miriam. When he grew into manhood he proclaimed himself God's son. The miracles he performed for his followers he performed not with God's help but with magic. He denied the Torah and its commandments.

He does not sit in paradise now, he is roasting in the fires of hell."

"Where is hell? In heaven?"

"There are seven hells," Ben Dosa said.

"Have you been there and seen them with your own eyes?"

"No, my krol. But a Jew who denies the Torah is bound to be in hell."

"The bishop says that God has given a new Torah." '

"The Torah will forever be the same Torah, just as God will forever be the same God."

Cybula raised his eyebrows. "How do you know that you are right and the bishop is wrong? Perhaps the opposite is true."

"No, my krol. The opposite is not true. They say that their Jesus is the Messiah. How can he be the Messiah, if Jews are scattered all over the world and Jerusalem lies in ruins? When the Messiah comes, God will gather the dispersed and oppressed tribes of Israel from every corner of the world and rebuild the temple, and the righteous will sit with crowns on their heads and bathe in the glow of the Shechinah."

"Who is the Shechinah?"

Ben Dosa thought for a moment. "When God is angry at the Jews the Shechinah comes, and like a good mother, she pleads on their behalf. She asks God to be patient and merciful."

"Listen to me, Ben Dosa, I wish you no evil. You have done much good for the camp. You've taught our children to read and to write. You have made shoes for us all. But now it is summertime, and the children have no patience for study. I promised you that if you wanted to journey to distant cities and search for the holy book, I'd give you silver or gold. I am prepared now to keep my promise. But you must first tell me the truth. What happened between you and Kosoka? Kora found her lying half dead near your hut. Did you strike her?"

Ben Dosa lowered his head. "My krol, I prefer not to speak of this matter."

"I am your krol and my word is the law. When I order you to speak the truth, you must."

"She has done a wicked thing. She made me impure against my will."

"While you raped her?"

"No, in my sleep."

Cybula chuckled. "How is that possible?"

Ben Dosa told Cybula his story. "And that, you believe, angered your god?"

"It is against the Torah."

"How can the Torah know what Kosoka does in the middle of the night? Tomorrow Bishop Mieczyslaw will address our camp once again. You may, if you like, come and tell him that your god is better than his. But be careful not to insult him, he is our guest. When do you wish to set out in search of your holy book, now or after the harvest?"

"Whenever my krol wishes me to go."

"Where might it be found?"

"I don't know. I've heard that in Rome there are Jews and scribes who write books."

"Where is this Rome?"

"Far far away."

"How long will your journey be?"

"I don't know. It's all in God's hands."

"By the time you return to us, we may all be dead," Cybula said. "This Bishop Mieczyslaw may be a messenger of the pans who seize all the land for themselves and make those who work it their slaves. Wait until after the harvest. I will never be anyone's slave. Better death than slavery. We all must die in any case. There is only one god and he is all there is—the god of death, Shmiercz."

"Forgive me, my krol, but the true God is the God of life."

"Not true. A man lives a few years and then he, too, is dead forever. Man lives in terror: someone may kill him, he may fall ill, his wife may deceive him, his children may die by drowning, his house may burn, he may break his leg. But the rivers and mountains and trees never worry. It is they who are God, not he who sits up in heaven and says, 'Don't eat pig, don't lie with Kosoka.' Good night."

"Good night, my krol."

Cybula left the hut, meaning to return to his house, to Yagoda and Kora, but all desire for sleep had left him. Something drew him instead to the field, and he began to walk toward it. A cool breeze blew, and Cybula inhaled deeply. He was seized by a longing to plunge into the wheat, to lie among the stalks, and to lie there forever. How good it would be, he thought, if everything remained as it is now—the summer's warmth, the silver moon, the whispering breeze. As Cybula continued to walk, he stepped over horse manure, pig droppings, cow manure, goat dung. Still, the animals were all less foul than man, who, if Ben Dosa was right, was given a brain to think, power to choose between good and evil, truth and untruth, God and Satan. "It's all made up," Cybula murmured to himself. "A pack of lies."

(4)

Was it only his imagination? Cybula thought he heard a voice singing. Yes, it was a voice, a woman's voice—raised in a long and monotonous lament, such as he heard when they buried or burned the dead. Cybula froze in his tracks. Who could be singing in the middle of the night? Was it a she-demon, or one of the dead unable to rest in her grave? Cybula did not believe in these things, but nevertheless a terror took hold of him. It seemed to him that the voice was familiar, but whose voice was it? Did it belong to one of his dead servant girls? The moon shone brightly over the camp, but Cybula could see no one. He strained his ears. There was a pleading in the voice, a suffering. All at once it became clear to Cybula that the singing came from behind a wall. Was it the pigsty? A chain and a hook locked the door from the outside. The Lesniks herded the pigs into the pigsty at night and locked them in. When Cybula opened the door, he saw Kosoka. She sat on the earthen floor, naked, surrounded by filth, tied to a roof rafter by a rope. She stared at Cybula as he stood at the door, trembling. The girl blurted out, "Krol Cybula!"

"Kosoka! What are you doing here?"

She stood up, dragging the rope behind her. Everywhere there were pigs, standing or lying on the earthen floor. Kosoka said, "Yes, krol. See what they've done to me."

"Who did this?"

"Kora."

Cybula asked, "When did Kora bring you here?"

"Ah, I don't know. The day before yesterday? I can't

remember. With the help of two other old women, she carried me here. I screamed, but they clapped their hands over my mouth. What do they want of me? I've done nothing!"

"What made you sing in the middle of the night? Had you not sung, I would never have found you here."

"I remember days of long long ago. Krol, I don't want to live. Please, be kind to me, kill me."

"No, no, no. Wait, I'll untie you. I didn't know Kora was so cruel. Wait!"

Cybula tried to free Kosoka, but the hide rope had been tied in many knots. The stench in the sty nearly overwhelmed him. He felt nauseated. Slime covered his arms and his legs. He became enraged at Kora. "I'll kill her! I'll whip her until she is dead!" he vowed. "Who were the other two women? What are their names?" he asked.

"I don't know. I don't remember. They beat me, blackened my eye. I couldn't see. Where is Ben Dosa?"

After some effort, Cybula succeeded in untying the rope. The sun was beginning to rise. The pigs tried to escape through the open door, but Cybula pushed them back with his foot. The crimson light of dawn fell on the sty, and Kosoka and the pigs looked as if they were spattered with blood. Fear filled Cybula's heart. What an ugly death, he thought. To be trampled to death by pigs. Quickly he left the sty with Kosoka, locking the door behind him with the hook. "Come with me to the stream. We both need to wash the dirt from our bodies."

His anger drove Cybula to the stream with speed. The dawn arose clear and bright. Birds sang, twittered, trilled. Flowers which had closed their petals for the night now opened again, and their fragrance mingled in Cybula's nos-

trils with the smell of his own body. Cybula remembered he
had often witnessed cruelty in Kora. When she slaughtered
a hen, a duck, a rabbit, she did it with a fury, as if the creature had harmed her and she was taking revenge. During
their nightly talks she often urged him to kill his enemies.
Cybula considered this chatter of hers as a ruse to arouse
both him and herself. There is no telling what a man and a
woman may say to one another in the heat of passion. But
now he knew Kora was in truth a bloodthirsty animal.

Cybula reached the mountain stream and plunged into
the water. The stream had its source in glacial snows, and
so its water was ice cold. Cybula caught his breath. But he
quickly began to swim, splash, rub his body. Kosoka did the
same. Cybula had left his loincloth in the pigsty and he was,
like Kosoka, stark naked. He caught a glimpse of Kosoka's
wet body: it was lean, dark, her breasts were small, the nipples erect. Cold water often cools passion, but Cybula nevertheless felt desire for Kosoka. He emerged from the water to
warm himself in the sun and signaled Kosoka to join him.
But she remained in the water, repeatedly immersing herself, apparently to wash out her hair. Occasionally she left
her head submerged in the water for some time, as if she were
trying to drown herself. But then quickly she surfaced again.
The sun rose in the sky, its heat warming Cybula's body.

Kosoka still splashed in the rushing waters, and Cybula
suddenly realized that he should not have left his loincloth at
the pigsty. It would be recognized as belonging to him. Without it, he need never reveal that it was he who had freed
Kosoka from her imprisonment. Cybula was well aware that
the women in the camp—perhaps the men, too—craved

sacrifices. As soon as their own beating stopped, the beaten always turned to beating others. Kosoka was now climbing out of the water—scrubbed, slim, and agile as a doe. Although he had made up his mind to let her escape, Cybula now signaled to her to come to him. Kosoka stood motionless, looking at him. After a while Cybula approached her and said, "Come with me behind that clump of trees."

Kosoka hesitated. "No, krol, I cannot go with you."

"Why not?"

"Because I want to be Ben Dosa's wife."

"Ben Dosa doesn't want you. He threw you out of his hut," Cybula said.

"He wants to wait until I am a Jew. Therefore . . ."

"Come with me. Ben Dosa is going out into the world to look for some holy tablets. He may never return. He may find his wife and children and go to that city of his, Jerusalem."

"Wherever he goes I will go, wherever he lodges I will lodge, his God is my God," Kosoka answered, repeating word for word Ruth's answer to Naomi. Cybula remained standing, half angry, half ashamed. No woman had ever refused his advances. He blurted out, "Ben Dosa doesn't want you. He has a wife."

"He will take me as his concubine."

"Ah, you are a fool! I have already lain with you, you are not a virgin. I have also saved your life."

"For this God will reward you. But as for me, I am already as good as Ben Dosa's."

"You belong to no one but me. I bought you in Miasto and you're mine."

"You bought my body, not my soul."

In the midst of his predicament, Cybula wanted to laugh. The girl parroted Ben Dosa's every thought and every word.

"I want your body, not your soul. Don't be a fool—I am the krol; every woman in the camp belongs to me."

"The krol who rules over all krols is God in heaven," Kosoka said.

She began to run along the river, on the path leading to the mountains. Cybula stood and watched the receding figure with bewilderment. She scrambled on her hands and knees like a wild animal. He did not want to chase after her. In any case, he would never have caught her.

Well, this is what happens when you act kindly to slaves, Cybula thought. I should have left her to die in the pigsty! Soon Cybula's anger turned against Ben Dosa. You buy a little shoemaker for a few coins, and immediately he becomes a teacher. Such a man could certainly have killed God or his son: the thought flashed through his brain. He stood and waited as if he believed that Kosoka might return to him. But she had already vanished into the woods where the stream twisted between bushes and trees.

(5)

Cybula should have hurried back to the camp. He had promised Bishop Mieczyslaw to eat the morning meal with him, and to gather the camp together so that the bishop could speak about his god. But Cybula was ashamed to be seen in the camp stark naked, particularly in the presence of a learned man who dressed in such finery.

What do they want of me with their silly beliefs? Cybula

thought. A band of Jews quarreled about some god in Jerusalem, and this bishop comes here to denounce them. Let them both go to the devil, the bishop and Ben Dosa! We are burdened with enough cares without them. As Cybula began to retrace his steps, he heard the sound of horse hoofs. He saw Nosek on a brown horse and Laska on a white one riding along the trail. Kora had often told Cybula that his daughter loved Nosek, but he had taken it to be mere women's gossip. It was common knowledge that Nosek liked men, not women, and that he had dealings with that handsome boy Wilk. Moreover, Laska had a child that was not yet weaned. A fatherly shame overcame Cybula, and a fear that the couple might see him. He quickly hid himself in the bushes. It was strange, but he had often thought that if Krol Rudy died, he would like to give his daughter to Nosek. Nevertheless Laska's conduct irked him, all the more so because she was hiding from him what the entire camp suspected. Cybula crouched down low, trying to avoid being seen by the two riders. His heart thumped and a bitter fluid filled his mouth. This was indeed a cursed day, he thought. It seemed that he had roamed about for many hours, but it was still daybreak.

The two riders reached the stream. They talked and apparently joked with each other, because Laska was laughing. They dismounted from their horses and tied the animals to nearby trees. Nosek threw off his loincloth from his hips, and after a while Laska removed her clothing. For the first time since she had married Krol Rudy, Cybula saw his daughter undressed. Her breasts had grown large, swollen, the nipples red. A tremor shook Cybula's body. But why? Did he expect his daughter to look unlike other women?

For a long time the two stood by the stream, as if hesitating whether or not to enter the water. Cybula expected them to kiss, embrace, fondle each other. He wished that they would, and at the same time felt ashamed. Then Nosek threw himself into the water and was followed by Laska. Cybula's palate was dry. He felt disgraced, as if he had seen something he should not have seen. He amused himself with women whenever he wanted, and moments ago he had tried to seduce Ben Dosa's woman. "But why do they hide the truth from me?" Cybula asked himself. He remembered Ben Dosa's discourse on the two spirits which belonged to each man, a good one and an evil one. When Cybula said he had never seen the two spirits, Ben Dosa answered that they lived deep within each man, deep in his heart. Yes, within each man a battle raged. There were many men in the camp he could have killed had he not suppressed his anger. Had he carried his sword this morning, he would surely have slain Kosoka for denying him her body. For an instant he imagined himself shooting an arrow into Nosek's head, even into Laska's.

"Well, I must go home. A party of men must be out looking for me," Cybula told himself. Suddenly a playful thought came to him. Why not take Nosek's loincloth? Nosek and Laska had swum far from where he stood, beyond the point where the stream bent sharply to the left. There was no time for reflection, he would have to do it quickly. With the speed and agility of a young man, Cybula ran to the spot where the two had left their clothing, grabbed Nosek's waistcloth, and sped off toward the camp. He continued to run for a long time, feeling light, nimble, as if he had truly become young once again. Finally he stopped to rest and to put on Nosek's loincloth, which he found a trifle tight. When he pictured to himself Nosek searching for his garment, incredulous that it could have disappeared, Cybula wanted to laugh. "He will probably think some ghost stole it away." His gloom lifted. Even if his own loincloth was found in the pigsty, they would not know to whom it belonged.

He saw Kora and halted. Yes, Kora had come out to look for him, exactly as she had that night when the woyak Lis attacked him. He regretted that he had freed Kosoka; it would cause Kora much grief and anger. But how could he have acted otherwise?

Cybula called Kora's name and waved his arm at her. Kora shouted, "Where do you spend the nights? I open my eyes and you are not there! Yagoda was also worried about you. I am beginning to think you are a sorcerer, or maybe a monster!"

"Yes, Kora, that is what I am, but keep it a secret."

"What sort of loincloth is this?" Kora asked. "It is not the one I gave you."

"Yes, that is true."

"Where is your loincloth?"

"I threw it away, into a heap of garbage," Cybula answered.

"Why? It was a gift from me. And whose is this?"

"Nosek's."

"Are you joking again?"

"No, it is the truth."

"Have you spent the night with Nosek?"

"Yes. He has sent Wilk away and he has taken up with me."

"I beg you, Cybula, speak to me honestly."

"I left the hut at daybreak and I saw Nosek and my

daughter, Laska, riding together on two horses. I followed them to the stream and I saw them bathing there. I crawled to the place where they left their clothes, and I took Nosek's waistcloth," Cybula answered.

"Did you see him entering her?"

"That I did not see."

"Did they embrace, kiss?"

"No."

"I always told you she loved him. What was your purpose in swapping your loincloth for his?"

"No purpose, but I did not say we swapped."

"My mark is on yours. He will know that you followed him."

"I did not swap loincloths. I took his, and I threw mine away."

"Every time you leave my bed at night, something happens to you. Wilk is waiting for you in the camp. You were supposed to eat with the bishop and to call a gathering afterward. Instead, you go tracking down your daughter's footprints! I told you long ago to put an end to Krol Rudy. Why should she languish with that boor if she loves Nosek?"

"Kora, if my daughter wishes to consort with Nosek, I will not forbid it. But there is no reason to kill a man for that."

"What? And how many men and women did *he* kill? More than the hairs in his red beard."

"As long as I am krol, there will be no killing of an innocent man."

Kora looked at him, astonished. "I don't understand you."

"I don't want to kill anyone. I will also not permit a

sacrifice in this camp. Remember my words, Kora, and do nothing without my knowledge."

Cybula ordered the camp to assemble, and Bishop Mieczyslaw addressed the gathering that morning. He wore a long zupan, his blond hair reaching his shoulders. With his strong and loud voice, he pronounced each word slowly and clearly. He unrolled a scroll and read to the assembled people the story of Mary. How she was betrothed to Joseph, how the holy spirit caused her to conceive, how the angel warned Joseph to flee to Egypt with his wife and his son. He told about John the Baptist, who preached in the desert, telling the Jews to repent because the kingdom of heaven was at hand. He preached that you were to love not only your friend but also your enemy. When the bishop told about the Jews who persecuted Jesus and handed him to the Romans to be crucified, a tumult arose in the camp. Someone shouted, "Ben Dosa is a Jew. He is the one who killed God!"

Cybula broke in. "This happened a long time ago. Ben Dosa was not yet born then. Isn't that true, Bishop Mieczyslaw?"

The bishop waited before he answered. "Yes, he himself did not kill God. But the Jews have remained a stiff-necked people. They don't want to know the truth."

"Where is Ben Dosa? Why is he not here today?" someone shouted.

"He hides in his hut like an ostrich," an old Lesnik answered.

The bishop resumed his sermon. He told the story of Jesus,

reading it from his unraveled scroll. From time to time he looked up at the gathering and added a few words of his own.

"Bring Jesus to us and to our camp," another woman shouted. "Let him be our god!"

"I have brought Jesus to you!" Bishop Mieczyslaw answered. "Not his body, but his spirit. Let us all kneel before him and serve him!"

The bishop fell on his knees, and the entire camp followed suit. Even Kora and Cybula knelt on the ground. Then the bishop began to sing. The words were in an unfamiliar language, but the melody was pleasant and soon everyone sang along. Bishop Mieczyslaw made the sign of the cross with his hand, and his listeners tried to imitate him. The bishop addressed them in the Polish tongue: "All of you gathered here—men, women, children—have undertaken this day to adore God in his son and in the holy spirit. From this day on, you are no longer heathens, you are faithful Christians. God will erase and forgive all your sins. From this day on, Jesus is your shepherd, and you are his sheep. Those who serve idols will, like the Jews, burn in the fires of hell. But your souls, my brothers and sisters, will fly to heaven and repose under God's wing. May you all be blessed from this day and forever in the name of God, his son Jesus Christ, and the Holy Spirit. Amen."

"*Tak, tak, tak* [yes, yes, yes]!" voices rang out.

"Come here tomorrow at the same hour and I will sprinkle your heads with the holy water."

"*Tak, tak, tak!*"

Some women were weeping loudly, others wiped their eyes. Suddenly Laska cried out, "Holy man, take me to Jesus Christ!"

"You are with him, my daughter. His spirit hovers over your head!" the bishop answered, a tremor in his voice.

"I want to be with him in heaven!"

"Laska, be quiet!" Cybula called to her.

"My daughter, the way to heaven leads through faith and love," the bishop said. "Our Lord said, Call no man on earth your father, because only God in heaven is your father."

"I am your father, you have none other, not in heaven and not here on earth!" Cybula said.

"You, krol, are her father in body, but her true father is her spiritual father."

The camp was silent. All at once a shrill squawking was heard, like the cawing of a crow. But it was not a crow, it was an old woman, Paskuda, the witch. She was small as a child, hunchbacked, and she had only a few tufts of white fuzz on her bare scalp. Her tiny face was as yellow as wax, wrinkled like a cabbage leaf. She hobbled, always leaning on a stick for support. She stretched out a crooked finger, tipped by an overgrown and sharp nail, and pointed to Cybula.

"Holy man," Paskuda half wheezed, half shrieked, "a father does not commonly sell his daughter to enemies, but Cybula sold his to a murderer and now to Nosek, and the two of them ride horses in the woods. Children died because of these sins, and so great was our hunger that their own mothers ate . . ." Paskuda fell into a fit of crying. She tottered and almost fell to the ground, but one of the Gorals caught her and held her up.

"Bishop Mieczyslaw," Cybula said, "this old woman has lost her mind. She is a witch, she drinks her own urine."

"What she says is the truth!" called out the Lesnik who held Paskuda. "Cybula is a *zdrajca*, a traitor. He made a pact with the murderers. He became their kniez, and condemned the rest of us to die. He went to a place where smoks and demons live, and with Krol Rudy's booty he bought this Jew who killed God, and a bitch who was raised by wolves and howls like one of them."

"Pipe down, you old man! You gorged yourself on their bread with your rotten teeth and you asked for more!" a woman interrupted him. "You are angry because Cybula is our krol and our god, and because we'd give our lives for him. While from you we flee because you stink like a corpse . . ."

"Monster! Freak! Bitch!"

"Leper! Scarecrow!"

Everyone began to shout all at once, to wave fists, stamp feet. Young children cried, older ones attacked each other, imitating the adults. But then a frightful shout was heard: "Look! Over there!"

The entire camp froze. Every eye turned in the same direction to see Kulak carrying Krol Rudy on his back. The krol was barefoot, his naked body clad in a zupan. Tufts of red hair protruded from his long ears and from his flat nose— swollen, red, with the blue veins that come with drink. Many believed Krol Rudy dead. Others swore he had become a werewolf, who was tied to his bed at night to prevent him from devouring his subjects. Krol Rudy had apparently awakened from his long hibernation. Several in the crowd again fell to their knees, followed almost immediately by the rest of the camp. Only the bishop, Cybula, Nosek, and Kora remained standing. Krol Rudy was still among the living!

"*Niech zye krol*—Long live the krol!" someone shouted. And the whole camp repeated, "*Niech zye!*"

"*Niech zye Polska!*" Krol Rudy answered. And Cybula,

in the midst of the uproar, suddenly found it odd that this savage, Krol Rudy, was his daughter's husband and his own son-in-law. At that moment his life seemed a mockery. He nodded his head at the former king, his son-in-law, who had awakened from the throes of death. He could scarcely believe that a man could carry Krol Rudy's body and not collapse under its weight. But Kulak stood firm, his massive feet rooted to the ground.

"Greetings to you, Krol Cybula, father of my beloved Laska," he shouted. "Greetings to you, worthy guest, whoever you are! I have been ill for a long time; therefore, I was forced to turn over my crown to my beloved father-in-law, Cybula, who is younger than I am, wiser, a mighty hunter, a leader who is beloved by all—mostly by our women. But I have not forgotten the people of this camp. After all, it was I who brought you the blessing of the fields. This good deed no one can take away from me. Now I hear that one of our people, one who speaks our language, has arrived to bring us tidings of a new god. We Poles have our own gods, but we are ready to serve another if he can help us, and . . ."

Krol Rudy fell silent. He had forgotten what it was he wanted to say. Then he shouted, "Kulak, let me down! I want to stand on my own feet! I don't want to ride on your back as if you were a horse." Kulak squatted on the ground and two men came to help Krol Rudy. Some of the Lesniks who had been kneeling arose and gathered around Bishop Mieczyslaw, who began to tell them the story of the ten virgins who went out to meet their grooms, carrying their lanterns. Five of the virgins, who were clever, remembered to fill their lanterns with oil. The five who did not were left alone sleeping in the dark when the grooms arrived in the middle of the night. Krol Rudy wobbled unsteadily on his feet, forcing Kulak to prop him up, but when he heard the bishop he slapped his knee and roared with laughter. "And the bridegroom was left with only five virgins, ha? Well, it's better than nothing!"

10

❧

The Altar of Sacrifice

DURING the middle of the night, when Kosoka entered his hut, Ben Dosa fell silent. He had assumed that she had already fled to Miasto, but here she was, standing on the threshold of his hut. She was thinner and she had the pallor of one recently arisen from a sickbed. Hot tears filled Ben Dosa's eyes, and he swallowed the lump that lodged in his throat and said, "Blessed be God who brings the dead to life."

"I wasn't dead. It was worse."

"What do you mean?" Ben Dosa asked.

"Ah, Kora dragged me off to Swiniarka, the pig woman. They put me in the pigsty, tied me to a beam, and left me in that filth without food. They wanted to sacrifice me to Baba Yaga. I prayed to the God of Israel and he saved me."

"How?"

"Cybula opened the door and untied me. He took me to

the stream and I washed myself. He wanted to lie with me, but I told him I belong to you."

The blood drained from Ben Dosa's face. "You belong to God, not to me."

"You are my god."

Ben Dosa was speechless. He wanted to tell her that her words were blasphemy, but he did not know how to express this. He also did not want to cause her more pain. He asked, "Where have you been all this time? I prayed for you."

"I fled to the forest. If Kora and Swiniarka catch me here, they will tear me limb from limb. But they are all asleep. I yearned for you, my teacher. I've come to beg you to forgive me for what I've done. I wanted to be like Ruth."

"The ancients were closer to God than we are," Ben Dosa said. "Moreover, the stories we are told about them are full of mysteries. From Ruth, for example, King David descended, and she must have been pure and righteous to be worthy of such honor. Ruth only lay at Boaz's feet, while you, my daughter, committed a grave transgression."

"Yes, I know. That is why I came to beg you to forgive me."

"I forgive you. Why are you still standing at the door?" Ben Dosa hesitated to ask her in, but her life was in danger and saving a life preceded all other laws. Kosoka had sensed Ben Dosa's hesitation and said to him, "If you wish, master, I'll go away."

"Where will you go? They will try to kill you. Come inside and shut the door."

While Kosoka had been gone, Ben Dosa had had a chance to think over the Law. Had she been Jewish, her transgression would have been much graver, but these laws did not pertain to women who were not Jews. If she was truly and properly to convert and become a pious Jewish girl, then he would be permitted to marry her. Ben Dosa had even begun to regret that he had sent her away in anger. He pointed to a small bench and motioned to Kosoka to sit down. "You are not sick, God forbid, are you? You look weary."

"No, I am not ill."

"What did you eat while you were away?"

"Ah, in the forest there is always food to be found."

"I thought about you often. Your intention was good. You wanted to be kind to me, as Ruth was to Boaz. But you did not have a Naomi to guide you. I fell into a rage, and anger causes men to blunder."

"Did Cybula give you the money to go and look for Jews in other lands that keep Torah?" Kosoka asked.

"No, not yet. He put it off until after the harvest. But there are evil doings going on in the camp. They are again preparing for a human sacrifice. This Cybula is a clever man, he is also compassionate, but they draw him into their mire. One of those who believe in the man called Jesus Christ has come to the camp and completely turned their heads. He has lured them into the web of false belief."

"Let us flee together," Kosoka whispered.

"I gave my word to Cybula to remain until the harvest. But you, my daughter, run, hide. Should they catch you, God forbid, they may . . ."

"They will not catch me. When will you start out to search in other lands for your people?"

"Cybula promised to let me go immediately after the harvest."

"I'll go with you."

Ben Dosa considered her words for some time. "So be it.

But you must promise that, while you are not properly converted, you will do nothing wrong."

"I promise."

"Since your life is endangered in this camp, you should flee from it without any hesitation," Ben Dosa said.

"I want to go with you."

"If they see us leaving together, they may drag you back, God forbid," Ben Dosa said.

"I'll wait for you on the road that leads to Miasto."

"How will you know when I will be there? I am in their hands."

"I'll come to you every night."

Dawn was breaking by the time Kosoka left the hut. Ben Dosa did not openly promise it, but she could understand from his words that he intended to marry her when they reached a Jewish settlement where she could obtain the learning she needed in order to follow a righteous path. It was too late for Ben Dosa to return to his wife and his children. He had lost his hope that the Almighty would carry him back home, despite the verse that reads, "God's salvation will come in the blinking of an eye." His wife had insisted that he never confront her with a rival. What would she say to one like Kosoka—conceived, born, and raised in uncleanliness, a child of generations of savage idolaters?

"Father in heaven, I'm caught in a net, but I am in your sacred hands!" Ben Dosa cried out.

(2)

The last day of the harvest signaled the beginning of a great celebration, to last for three days and three nights, and end with the casting of lots for the sacrifice. Kora was the priestess who would offer the sacrifice, sprinkle the blood on the altar, burn the flesh. She had never spoken to Cybula of Kosoka—neither of her imprisonment in the pigsty nor of her release by someone unknown. Inasmuch as she kept a secret from him, Cybula decided not to forewarn her that he knew of her schemes. He would show her at the last moment who in this camp was the krol.

The first day of the feast was hotter than anyone in the camp could remember. On most mornings cool breezes blew from the mountains, but on this day the air was stifling and still.

Cybula was awakened by shouts—the shouts not of one man but of a mob, like those he had heard on the night when the woyaks had attacked the camp. Several children flew by him and he tried to stop them, but they scurried away. One girl turned and shouted back to him, but Cybula did not catch her words. The pans attacked, it's a new bloodbath, he thought. Then he realized that these were not the sounds of a massacre. He heard peals of laughter, cheers, applause, as if the camp had started festivities in his absence. All of a sudden he saw Ben Dosa staggering, stark naked, his head and feet bloodied, half his beard gone. He shouted some unintelligible words at Cybula, speaking in his native tongue. He ran up to him, almost threw him to the ground, letting out a terrifying howl. With all his strength Cybula pushed Ben Dosa off and shouted, "What happened? Who did this to you?"

"Ko-so-ka!"

And Ben Dosa began gasping for air. Blood frothed out of his mouth, and several of his front teeth fell to the ground. Cybula bent over him, shivering, and asked, "Kosoka attacked you?"

"They captured her!" And Ben Dosa spat out a lump of congealed blood.

In a flash Cybula understood. Kora had captured Kosoka and had dragged her to the sacrificial altar as an offering to the gods. When Ben Dosa had come to her aid, he was himself attacked. As Cybula helped Ben Dosa to his feet, his heart filled with sorrow and rage. This was Kora's doing. He began to stride toward the din and clamor. "I'll kill her!" Cybula said to himself. "It will be Kora's death or mine." He considered going to the hut for his sword, but thought they might kill Kosoka before he got there. He continued to pull Ben Dosa after him. As the two men reached the edge of the forest, the shouting grew louder and louder. When the camp saw them approaching, the noise instantly died down. Cybula began to wave his arms and to shout, "Wait! Wait! Wait!"

Someone ran toward him; it was Kora. She hugged him in her arms and shouted, "Cybula, don't do it! Don't interrupt our celebration!"

He shoved her aside, and Kora stumbled and fell. "You filthy monster!"

In the center of the crowd Cybula caught a glimpse of the pile of stones which served as an altar. In a depression between the stones, as if entombed, sat Kosoka. She was naked, her hands bound behind her back, her face bruised and swollen. Someone had cut or torn off her hair. For a moment she seemed to Cybula to be dead. Her eyes were closed; they looked like two slanting slits in her face. Near her, on a stone, lay an ax.

It is too late, Cybula thought. Now the silent crowd came back to life. They shouted at him, cursed him, threatened him. Several Lesniks came up behind him and tried to pull him away from the altar, but Cybula gave them a powerful kick and they fell to the ground. He heard someone call him traitor. Two Lesniks were holding Ben Dosa, and fists were raised. Many in the crowd held stones in their hands, and Cybula was well aware of the danger that faced him. He was a hairbreadth away from being stoned, from dying along with Kosoka. Her round head nodded and a moan escaped from her lips. He turned around to face the crowd and roared, "Kill me, too! Murderers, fools, madmen!"

"Cybula, don't interfere with our holiday," Kora wailed again.

"Baba Yaga wants a sacrifice!" a woman shouted.

"Let us sacrifice her! Baba Yaga yearns for her!"

Cybula moved with a strength and a boldness which surprised him. He flung down the stones which imprisoned Kosoka and kicked over the bucket that was meant for her blood. He seized the ax and waved it at those who tried to pull him away from the altar. An old woman rushed up to Kosoka and tried to revive her. Cybula shouted to the crowd, "Baba Yaga, huh? Where was Baba Yaga when the woyaks came to butcher you? And what do you want from Ben Dosa? He made shoes for us. He taught our children to read and to write."

"He killed God!" someone shouted.

"God cannot be killed!" Cybula shouted back. "The bishop himself said that whatever happened happened long long ago."

Ben Dosa coughed, whined, spat blood. Cybula caught a glimpse of two naked women behind him with flowers over their breasts, trying to help Kosoka off the altar. Naked men roamed about as well. Again he spoke to the crowd: "You

want blood, that's what you want. When you are not yourselves slaughtered, you want to slaughter others."

"Cybula, you yourself promised me to cut off her head,"
Kora called out.

"I promised, huh? You lie with me on the pelts and babble
foolish things. Why must you kill, when death comes in any
case? A few years from today our bodies will rot in the earth.
Worms will eat us, or else we'll turn to dust."

"Our duchas will live."

"They will be as dead as our bodies. No spirit has ever come
back to tell us what happens down there in the hollows of the
earth. There is only one god, his name is Shmiercz, the god of
death. He takes everyone to himself and he needs no sacrifices
from you."

"*Pravda, pravda, pravda*—True!" voices shouted.

"He is the god over all gods. When he comes, all worries
cease, all sorrows, all pain. We can kill ourselves, but we have
no right to take the lives of others. Do you understand?"

"*Tak, tak, tak!*"

"If you want me to be your krol, leave the two strangers
alone."

"We want you, we want you!" the camp shouted as one.
"Only you! No one else!"

"Cybula is our god!" a woman shouted.

"*Tak! Tak! Tak!*"

"*Niech zye Cybula!*"

"*Niech zye bag krol*—Long live our god the krol!"

All at once people began to fall on their knees. Several
men hesitated, but then they, too, knelt down. Kosoka lay on
the ground, bleeding, and only Ben Dosa remained standing.

Someone tried to force him to kneel, but Ben Dosa, in a hoarse voice, cried out, "I kneel only before God, not man!" And he raised two blood-covered arms to bear witness to the truth of his words.

(3)

Yagoda had fallen asleep. Through the window, rain trickled into the room. Although their roof was new, water dripped down from the ceiling, collecting in a bucket Cybula had placed near the bed. He himself had worked on the roof, plugging up the cracks with clay, but the rain had apparently washed the clay out. After the extreme heat of the day, the air suddenly turned cold. Cybula looked at Yagoda and covered her with a pelt, so that she would not be chilled and begin to cough. He covered himself as well. His hands and feet were cold and he warmed them against Yagoda's belly, her breasts. Yagoda slept soundly and did not awaken. Cybula lay half dozing, half daydreaming. The contradictions in his own conduct baffled him. He had spoken of killing Kora, yet he risked his life to save a Tatar girl who wanted to embrace Ben Dosa's faith. He had wanted to wipe out the whole camp, and yet he fretted over sheaves of wheat which the rain would cause to rot. In the end Shmiercz would take them all into his dark abode deep under the earth. And yet another god, a god of life, would see to it that the entire species did not disappear.

Cybula fell asleep and dreamed that he was pursuing a large animal, larger than a bear. On its back rode yet another animal. While Cybula fired his arrows at his prey, the other tore and bit chunks of its flesh and fur. Every now and then the creature looked back at Cybula, laughing at him, spitting venom and froth. Cybula could hear himself saying to Ben Dosa: "You like to speak to us of your merciful God. What has this animal done to suffer so cruel a death? Was it because it did not keep the Sabbath?" In his dream Cybula laughed, and this laughter woke him.

The rain had intensified, coming down in sheets. Lightning flashed, and Cybula saw that the bucket of rainwater had overflowed to the floor. The roof had sprung another leak, and water dripped from the ceiling in yet another corner. Cybula rose and went in search of a bucket; he thought he heard the front door open. "It was only the wind," he said to himself. Cybula opened the door to the front room and saw in the darkness the form of a man, perhaps a woman. Suddenly he heard his own voice asking, "Who is it?"

"Father, it is I."

"Laska, why did you come in the middle of the night?"

Laska moved closer to him. "Tatele, a terrible thing happened."

"What?"

"Krol Rudy, my husband, is dead."

For a moment Cybula said nothing. "When did this happen?"

"Just now. Kulak woke me up."

"Yes, yes."

"I went to him, but he was no longer breathing."

"Was he ill?" Cybula asked.

"No, Father. He ate and drank with Kulak last night. He died in his sleep."

"A good way to die, the best way," Cybula murmured.

Again lightning flashed and Cybula saw that Laska was entirely naked, soaking wet, her hair dripping water. A fatherly embarrassment came over him. "Why did you come in the pouring rain, and with no clothes even to keep you dry?"

"To whom would I go if not to you? What shall I do now? Shall I come to reap tomorrow?"

"We'll reap without you—if there is any reaping. This rain is not likely to end soon."

"Father, what will become of me?"

"What will become of you? We will bury him, or burn his body, and there will be one more widow in the camp. You and Nosek are on friendly terms, aren't you?"

"Father, what are you saying!"

"I know everything."

"Father, he doesn't want me."

"You two ride horses together."

"He is teaching me to ride, but he doesn't want me. He told me openly he needs no woman."

"If he doesn't, he is lucky."

"I need a man."

Cybula could scarcely believe his ears. He had never heard a daughter address her father in this manner before. A new generation had arisen, a generation laden with impudence. He wanted to scold her, to send her away, but he restrained himself. He said, "You know what kind of men we have in the camp—barking dogs who have no teeth to bite with. If you want one of them, whoever it is, I am sure he will oblige you."

"Father, this is not the time for your jokes."

There was more lightning, followed by thunder. Cybula

said, "Daughter, there will be no reaping, not tomorrow and perhaps not the day after. There can also be no burial in this deluge. I envy your husband, he knew when to die. All that awaits us here is a long famine, a long and difficult ordeal."

"We can return to hunting."

"No, Daughter, we cannot. We have destroyed a sizable part of our forest, we have driven off the animals. We no longer have tents to take along on a hunt. Instead, we have houses with chimneys and floors. And worst of all, we have no men. Until our boys grow up, famine can wipe out the camp. Wait, I'll bring something for you to put on."

"I am not cold."

"*I* am cold."

Cybula opened the door to the living quarters and went in. Yagoda slept on, unaware of the visitor in the next room. He left with two pelts, one for Laska and one for himself. He put a straw mat on the floor for Laska to sit on, and he sat down next to her. "Where did you leave Ptashek?"

"With old Malenka. I nursed him before I left."

"Why do you nurse him still? It is time he was weaned."

"Ptashek likes my milk. If I give him other food he spits it out."

"In my time women used to smear their nipples with coal soot," Cybula said. "It nauseated the little infants, and thus they were weaned. I remember when my mother did it to my sister Milutka."

"I tried it, too. Nothing helps. He has teeth and he bites the nipple until I cry out with pain. And what will I do with the milk? My breasts are full."

"Once he stops sucking, your milk will dry up."

Father and daughter sat still for a long time. The lightning had stopped, but the rain kept falling in torrents. Suddenly Laska said, "Tatele, I need a man."

Something broke inside Cybula. With tears in his eyes, he embraced her warmly. "Oh, my daughter!"

II

The New Krol

ONE morning, after the harvest had ended, Cybula sat with Nosek, trying to determine how the wheat should be distributed. They had to decide how much should be stored for sowing the following year and whether more ground should be cleared of trees and shrubs to extend the cultivated fields. Cybula also had a quiet talk with Nosek concerning his daughter, saying that Laska was too young a woman to remain a widow. Nosek frankly confessed that the opposite sex held no attraction for him, but said that he would marry Laska if that was what she and her father wanted. But to father her children? That was unlikely. In jest Cybula said he hoped Laska would have at least one other child, so that Ptashek would be provided with a brother or sister. Nosek wisely answered, "We can try," and Cybula doubted that the marriage would take place.

Suddenly loud voices were heard, and the sound of horses'

hooves. Cybula and Nosek went out; before them stood nearly thirty riders, in flaxen coats, leather boots, fur hats, wearing swords on their hips and carrying spears. At their head, on a white horse with an ornamented saddle, rode a man with a long mustache and a hat from which a feather dangled. His coat was richly embroidered with red and white threads. There were spurs on his boots. Two riders sounded the trumpets and shouted, *"Nabok, nabok!"* meaning that pedestrians should move aside and make way for the riders. The pan in charge had apparently asked the onlookers for their krol, because when Cybula and Nosek appeared at the door they heard voices shouting, "There he is! Here is our krol!"

The pan with the long mustache was short and broad-shouldered, with a pockmarked face. He stopped his horse and in a hoarse voice asked, "This is your krol—barefoot?"

Cybula, recovering his composure, replied, "We are a small and poor camp. We had one shoemaker, and he has left us."

"What is your name, krol?"

"Cybula."

"Cybula, eh? And why not Radish or Garlic?"

The riders all burst into laughter. Several horses seemed frightened by the noise and made a move as if to bolt, but the riders held them back. Cybula answered, "This is what my father named me."

"Your father, eh? You know, Cybula, that you are no longer their krol, or even a sub-krol. From this day on I am your krol, your pan, your leader." The rider on the white horse turned toward the camp. "I know that you call yourselves Lesniks, but from now on, all who live on this land and speak the Polish tongue will be known as Poles. We do not come to you as enemies but as brothers, we are of one family. I was told that you have no young men, that your camp is composed of women, children, and old men. But my boys here are strong and daring fighters, and what others want they want as well: vodka and women. *Pravda?*"

"*Pravda! Pravda!*" the riders shouted in unison.

"I was told that you began to construct a wall around your camp. Even a frog could leap over your wall. You deceive yourselves if you think you can resist us. Our swords are sharp and our spears are aimed straight at your navels. We will give you bread, clothing, shoes, but in return we demand full loyalty and complete obedience. Should anyone raise a hand against us, we will chop off that hand. Should anyone speak against us, we will tear his or her tongue out. Is this clear?"

No one answered.

"Is this clear, Cybula?"

"Yes, clear."

"The wall that you began to build you will take down. No wall should separate one Pole from another. I myself and the boys here wish to have houses to live in, food in abundance, enough honey, barley, and fruit to brew mead and other spirits. All this you will provide for us in full. We do not wish to rape your women, but women were created to serve men's needs and all of us here have plenty of needs. *Pravda,* boys?"

"*Pravda! Pravda!*"

"My name is Krol Yodla, and that is how you will address me. I will receive anyone who comes to seek my favor, but you will come on your knees, and with your heads bowed. So shall it be with the men, and so also with the women. The two men behind me are my kniezes, Kniez Woll and Kniez Niedzwiedz. They will convey my orders to you. You may also choose an elder from among yourselves, a *starszy*, who will speak for you. If you wish, you may choose your Cybula, but he will have to put on shoes and not walk barefoot like a beggar."

"I do not wish to be a starszy," Cybula said. His throat was so dry that he could barely pronounce the words.

"You do not wish, eh? No one asked what your wishes are. From now on, you are the starszy of this camp. Who is this long skinny one standing at your side?" Krol Yodla pointed his finger at Nosek.

"My name is Nosek."

"Nosek? And why not Nos?"

"That is my name."

"From now on your name will be Nos. Are you one of the Lesniks?"

"No, Krol Yodla. I am a Pole. I came here with Krol Rudy, who has recently died."

"I was informed of everything. With me there can be no secrets. Even before a man begins to think evil of me, I know it, and I order my boys to chop off his head. An enemy without a head—that we can tolerate; *pravda,* boys?"

"Pravda! Pravda!"

"We Poles have many enemies; some are hidden and others are known to us. We have rid ourselves of most of them, but not all. We want to become one large nation, to speak one language, to live in one land. But our enemies want us splintered, divided into small camps, speaking many tongues and serving many foreign gods, so that the Russians, the Germans, the Czechs may rip us apart, enslave us, exact tolls from us, rape our women. But they will never triumph. Much blood may be shed, but in the end the victory shall be ours. Many of our heroes may be rotting in the earth, but their names and deeds will live forever. Do you have a wife, Starszy Cybula?"

"Yes, Krol Yodla."

"What is her name?"

"Yagoda."

"Yagoda, eh? Cybula and Yagoda. A pungent onion and a sweet berry. That should be easy to remember. *Pravda*, boys?"

"*Pravda, pravda!*"

(2)

Cybula had expected that Krol Yodla would immediately take over his, Cybula's, house, or the house occupied by Laska. But the day was nearly over and Krol Yodla was nowhere to be seen. Kora came to tell him that the krol and his riders had settled in the huts which remained unoccupied after the woyaks were gone. Several of the new woyaks moved into the hut where Ben Dosa had lived. Others occupied cabins used for storing wheat, some moved into the horse stables, and still others into the workshop where Czapek kept plows, scythes, sickles, and other valuables that had been bought in Miasto. Although the day was sunny and warm, few of the camp's people ventured outside their huts. Even the children did not come out to play. All thoughts of resistance had evaporated. None of the women, and certainly none of the old men, could stand up to these young armed riders. Inasmuch as Krol Yodla had assured them that he came as a friend, not a foe, the girls and the younger widows began to wash and primp themselves, to comb their hair, and to put on the dresses they had worn for Cybula's wedding with Yagoda, as well as the shoes Ben Dosa had sewn for them.

After Krol Yodla rode off with his men toward the field, Nosek returned with Cybula to his house, and the two men spoke in low voices for a long time. Laska came in, bringing with her bad news: Ptashek was ill. His little face was hot to the touch, he refused to suck her breast, and he barely opened his eyes. Cybula, who, among other things, was also the camp doctor, said that he could not know, on this the first day, what ailed the boy. Ptashek might have caught the measles, smallpox, or scarlet fever. Laska left her father and Nosek and returned to her house, weeping.

Both the men and the women walked about in a stubborn, heavy silence. There was no knowing what nightfall would bring. The sun went down wreathed in crimson, leaving behind it flaming clouds. The birds, as always, settled on the branches of the few remaining trees, as well as on roofs and chimneys. The crickets chirped, the frogs croaked. Stars kept dashing across the heavens, becoming lost or extinguished behind the mountain peaks. In the evening Yagoda roasted on coals the side of a young deer which Cybula had shot earlier with his bow. Then husband and wife sat and ate their meal in silence. The evening before, Kora had brought her daughter a pot of cooked berries, and Cybula and Yagoda added them now to their evening meal. Yagoda's lips and cheeks were stained with the black juice, and she looked more than ever like a young girl.

Since Cybula had foiled Kora's plan to sacrifice Kosoka, silent tension and unspoken anger separated the former lovers. Kora no longer came to lie in the bed he shared with Yagoda, and when she spoke to him her eyes remained downcast. She was not alone; others in the camp were resentful. When Krol Yodla and his riders appeared, several old hags predicted that these invaders would wreak Baba Yaga's revenge.

On most summer evenings the camp's people had no reason to light their torches. They could eat by the light of the fire they built for cooking their meal. Cybula, however, often lit a wick in a small bowl that was filled with seed oil. He had learned from Ben Dosa, and later from Nosek, to convert the alphabet letters to numbers. Aleph was 1, beth —2, gimel—3, yodh—10, kaph—20, and so on until kuf, which was 100. When he wanted to write the number 11, Cybula wrote a yodh followed by an aleph, and 12 was a yodh followed by a beth. It was not easy for him to learn all these numbers, but he finally handled them easily. He could use some of the letters to sign his name and to write some words, even whole sentences, in the Polish tongue. No letters existed for several soft sounds in his language, but Ben Dosa had shown him that he needed only to put a small mark over the zayin, the tzadik, or the shin—and they, too, would become soft. Sometimes Cybula spent long hours writing the letters on a block of wood or carving them in bark. For Cybula, who had charge of an entire camp's accounts, these scribblings were exceedingly useful.

That evening Cybula had no accounts to occupy him, but still he sat and carved some words in bark. Yagoda asked him what he planned to do, now that he was no longer krol, and Cybula snapped, "I was not born a krol, you know."

"For me you will always be my krol and my god," Yagoda said.

Cybula busied himself a while longer with his writings, and then he turned out the light and lay in his bed beside his wife. Now that Kora was gone, Yagoda no longer dropped off to sleep so quickly. Yagoda had grown more excited at night. She was saying playfully, "When I have our child, you will suck my breasts every night."

"If I am still alive at that time."

"Why should you not be? You are not so old," Yagoda said.

"Our new krol will put an end to my life."

"Why? He said he came to us as our brother."

"Brothers sometimes kill each other," Cybula said. And he reminded Yagoda of Cain and Abel, of whom they had learned from Ben Dosa.

Ben Dosa was gone, and he would probably never return. But he was not forgotten, Everyone in the camp repeated the same sentiment: his body had vanished but his ducha, or soul, had remained behind. The children often spoke of him. After weeks of idleness, after they had helped the grownups to gather fruit and dig up roots, they felt the need for study, they longed to read and to write, to listen to stories again. Whenever they played, one of the older children would become their Ben Dosa, teaching them the alphabet, reciting "I thank thee, O Lord," inventing all sorts of miracles for them.

That night Cybula and Yagoda made love several times. Speaking of the child in Yagoda's belly, Cybula asked her whether she already felt the being that lived inside her, and Yagoda answered, "It is still too early. Later it will start to kick. What shall we name it? I know! Let's call it Cybula."

"And why not Radish?" Cybula said, repeating Krol Yodla's joke.

At that moment someone opened the door, which Cybula had forgotten to lock. Startled, he sat up in bed. "Who is it?" he called out.

A man's voice answered, "Don't shout. Don't be frightened. My name is Paletz. It used to be Shliwka. I used to be a woyak here in the camp, but I left with the others some time ago. Now I came back with Krol Yodla. Do you remember me?"

"Certainly, Shliwka."

"I also remember you," Yagoda said.

"Yes, I am Shliwka. There were six of us, but along the way we quarreled and fought. Two of us were killed, and the others vanished—the devil knows where. I roamed the countryside alone, until I joined Krol Yodla's riders. I was always skilled with horses, if you remember."

"Yes, yes. Why did you come to us in the middle of the night?"

"Stay where you are! Don't stand up! If you do—I'll slip a knife into your belly. I'll also kill your wife, that fool, Yagoda. I know all about you. Your sweetheart Kora, Yagoda's mother, killed my best friend, Lis. Keep quiet, Yagoda. If you make a sound, you'll die!"

"What do you want?" Cybula asked.

"The loot. I know that you hid Krol Rudy's booty somewhere. Before we woyaks left the camp we looked for it, but we could not find it. You were away that day. The loot belongs to Krol Rudy and his men. We, his men, fought to get it. And now that the others are gone, I am his only heir. Tell me where it is or I'll cut you to pieces."

For a moment Cybula said nothing. "Don't threaten me. If you want to kill, kill. No one dies twice, anyway."

"I don't want to kill you. I want the loot."

"Cybula, tell him everything!" Yagoda shouted. "Your life is more precious than his treasure!"

"Yes, I'll tell him," Cybula answered. "I don't need his gold. But what, Shliwka, will you do with it? The bag is heavy. Too heavy for one man to carry. If the others see you with it, they'll put an end to your life."

"That is not for you to worry about," Shliwka said. "I'll load it on my horse, and ride away tonight. I have no use for Krol Yodla and his gang of bandits and gluttons. Where is the loot?" Shliwka raised his voice.

"It is buried in the clearing behind Krol Rudy's house," Cybula said. "There are three trees there: two horse chestnuts and one linden. The booty is buried under the linden tree."

"How deep?"

"Not deep."

For a while no one spoke. Then Shliwka said, "I know your daughter lives in that house with her child. If you have deceived me, they will both be dead. Mark my words."

"I did not deceive you. If you'll dig under the linden tree you'll find your treasure. But how will you dig in the dark?"

"That is not your business. Everything is prepared, two shovels, two horses. I planned it long ago. You stay here and keep quiet. I am not alone; I have a friend, a partner. If you do anything foolish, you'll be dead—you, Yagoda, your daughter, your grandson. Also your mother-in-law, Kora, the whore."

"I will do nothing," Cybula said.

"Before I leave I want to tell you something, something that will displease you, but it's true," Shliwka said. "Let me speak to you man to man. We woyaks always liked you, and you were not a stranger to us. Your daughter was our krol's wife. You wanted peace with us. It was Kora who persuaded you to rebel."

"What is it that you want to tell me?"

"The woyaks know that Kora betrayed you all the time. She lay with you at night, but during the day she came to me and to other woyaks and she lay with us. She complained that you were too old, and that one male could not fulfill her needs."

"My matka?" Yagoda began to choke and cough.

"Be quiet, Yagoda!" Cybula's mouth filled with a bitter fluid. "You lie," he managed to say to the woyak.

"I tell you the truth. I swear by my mother's bones and by all the gods. She showed me the mark you carved on her breast. She told me you called her *kurczak*—chicken—and that you have a birthmark on your belly."

"Aha."

"I tell you all this because I like you. And I loathe her. Let me tell you more. We will not take away the entire treasure. We will leave a bit of it for you. Krol Yodla will not behave himself forever. Sooner or later he will begin to whip and to slaughter, he and his bandits. He killed his own father, you know. If you escape to Miasto with your wife and your daughter, you'll be able to start a new life. Me, I want to go far away from here. Perhaps to the river Bug, perhaps even farther. Remember my words. If I am lying to you, may my body rot before I die."

"I believe you, Shliwka, and I thank you."

"Why do you thank me?" Shliwka asked.

"Because nothing is as bitter or as sweet as truth," Cybula answered, astonished at his own words.

(3)

No sooner did Shliwka leave the house than Yagoda began to wail, "Matka is a whore! I'm not my father's child!"

She fell upon Cybula, crying, and within a moment his face was wet with her tears. Cybula said, "Your mother is a whore, but you are your father's child."

"Oh, I want to die! I want to die!"

"You will. Sooner than you think."

"I want to die with you."

"Yes, I am your god and you are god's daughter," Cybula tried to joke.

"I don't want to live!" Yagoda clung to Cybula's neck. She may appear small and frail, he thought, but her arms are uncommonly powerful.

"You are choking me," he snapped.

At that moment the door opened and Kora slipped into the room like a shadow. Yagoda was the first to recognize her mother's silhouette, and she began to scream, "Matka, you are a whore! I am not your daughter!"

"What happened to you? Whose daughter are you, then?"

Cybula pushed Yagoda away from him. He wanted to grab Kora's head and smash it against the oven stones. But instead he asked, "What are you doing here in the middle of the night?"

"Why is Yagoda shrieking like a madwoman?"

"Kora, your game is over," Cybula said, surprised at his own words. He had not expected to speak to her. Kora did not move. She stood in the darkness as if frozen. Through the four-cornered hole in the wall only the light of the stars trickled into the room. Kora asked, "What game? What is over? Have you both lost your senses?"

"Kora, you are a despicable, contemptible liar and traitor. Get out of here and never come back. If you don't leave immediately, I'll . . ."

"What have I done? Why are you attacking me like this?"

"Mother, you lay with Shliwka and with all the new enemies," Yagoda shouted in a voice Cybula had never before heard. "You deceived both my father and Cybula. I am not your daughter. Get out of here; you are a whore, filth, a piece of dirt!"

Kora shivered. "What has happened? Why Shliwka all of a sudden? Shliwka died a long time ago."

"Yagoda, be still!" Cybula ordered.

"I will not be still," Yagoda said. "Shliwka was here and he told us everything. You showed him the mark on your breast. You cavorted with him, and with others, you old bitch!"

"Shliwka is alive? He was here?"

"Yagoda, shut your mouth!" Cybula said, with warning in his voice. "No one was here, but we know everything, all your tricks, all your cunning games. You are a faithless bitch, a sly fox, a filthy pig. I should squash you as one squashes a beetle, but I don't want to contaminate my foot with your blood."

"Kill her! Squash her!" Yagoda yelled.

"Is this my daughter, whom I carried and brought into the world, or have you found someone new to take into your bed?"

"Kora, it's the truth."

"Why is she bellowing about Shliwka?" Kora asked. "I swear by the gods, I must be having a nightmare."

"You are not dreaming, Kora. You've whored with our enemies and murderers, even with those who raped and stabbed your own daughters. Your vile acts have now surfaced like oil on water. You flattered me, you told me I was the manliest man in all the world, and then you went to them complaining I was an old, weak, worn-out broom. Get out of here and don't show us your loathsome face again. There are no gods, but if they do exist, they will judge you in the end. We, Yagoda and I, will leave the camp this very day. You will never know where our remains lie buried!"

"Matka, get out of here!" Yagoda screamed.

Kora seemed to totter. "You will not leave this place until you hear what I have to say."

"Why should we listen to the hissing of a snake?"

"I may be a snake, Cybula, but I am your snake, faithful, devoted to you with my body, my soul, my every drop of blood. During the days when you were our camp's judge you used to say that one must never listen to one side alone. And now suddenly some blabberer comes to you and tells you a pack of lies, and you immediately condemn me, without hearing what I have to say. Is this right?"

"What do you have to say? And say it quickly."

"First of all, I want to say how dismal one feels when one carries, bears, suckles, raises a child who is so ready to attack its mother as this girl. I never knew her tongue was so biting, or that she knew such curses as she seems to know. I must believe that a smok or some other monster from the nether-world has settled in her throat. I will not forget this night until they put me in my grave and cover my eyes with earth.

Second, I would like to ask whether Shliwka is really alive. He has come to disgrace me, to spread lies about me, to accuse me falsely and shorten my remaining years. You, Cybula, have always claimed that the god of all the gods was Shmiercz, the god of death. Soon he will take me to himself, the same as he takes all the others. The peace of the grave is not reserved for kniezes and krols, it comes to everyone. And you, my ungrateful daughter, prepare yourself as well, because your time will also come. Is Shliwka one of the riders?"

"He came to ask where Krol Rudy's loot was hidden," Yagoda said.

"I have begged you, Yagoda, to be still. Yes, he is alive and he was here. Why? Do you miss him?" Cybula asked.

"He came here to uncover Krol Rudy's booty and at the same time to cover me with shame?" Kora asked.

"What he said was the truth," Cybula answered. "He knew things that no one but you and I would know."

"What things?"

"Enough. What sort of woman are you? A bloodsucker? A demon who flies about in the night like a bat? How many men do you need to satisfy you—a thousand?"

"I may be all that, even worse. But there is one thing I want you to know: my love for you, Cybula, is stronger than the gods, stronger than the mountains, hotter than fire, deeper than the deepest abyss. Say what you like about me—you may be speaking the truth. But if you say that I do not love you, that would be a lie."

"You love everyone."

"No one but you."

"I can no longer stay here. I never wanted to be krol, nor do I want now to be the starszy. I must do what I have long wanted to do: run away from all people. Yagoda will come with me. You have some thirty riders here to occupy you, and more will come. Kora, go away from us. I don't want to see your face and I don't want to hear your voice."

"Matka, leave us alone," Yagoda said.

"Cybula is right to chastise me, even to kill me. If he wishes it, I will put down my head on this rock for him to chop off. But you, you vermin, depraved fruit of my womb, be still or I'll..."

"Who was my father?" Yagoda broke in.

"Your father was Kostek, but you are not worthy of being his daughter, you speck of dirt. If you say another word to me, I'll tear out your hair and you'll be as bald as Kosoka."

"Kora, go!" Cybula said.

"I'm going, I'm going. If you want to leave the camp, leave now. When dawn breaks, it will be too late. Where are you going, to the mountains? I wish you luck, Cybula."

"I don't need luck."

"My life is done." And Kora went out.

(4)

As Kora left the hut, voices were heard at the entrance and Laska walked in, agitated and panting. "Father!"

"Laska!"

"Father, two robbers rode off with our booty!" Laska spoke in a loud voice, like one who has met with a calamity. "I heard their noise outside, and saw two men riding away with our treasure. I shouted at them, but they galloped away. How did they know our secret? Who are they? Everything is lost!"

"Hush, Daughter. Don't shout. We don't need Krol Rudy's

treasure. We live here, not in Miasto," Cybula said. "How is Ptashek?"

"His little head is hot. He refuses my milk. He wheezes and rattles like someone about to die. Paskuda told me to dig a little grave and put him there, in order to deceive the evil spirits and make them believe he is already dead. Now I have a real grave . . ." And Laska began to cry.

"Daughter, it's better this way. Let him die."

"Father, what are you saying?"

"We are all doomed, Laska. We are not free men, we are slaves. Death is our only escape. It is better that Ptashek's spirit should descend into the hollows of the earth than for him to grow to manhood a slave."

"What is the matter with you, Father? I cannot allow my child to die."

"He will die, anyway, Daughter. And if he lives—I don't envy him."

"Where did Kora run to in the middle of the night?" Laska asked.

"My matka is a whore," Yagoda answered.

"What?"

"Yagoda, silence! Nothing, Daughter, nothing. Kora was always a whore. I knew it, but I pretended to see nothing. Laska, we are going to the mountains." Cybula changed his voice. "I cannot remain here another day."

"Where are you going? When?"

"Now. Wherever our feet carry us. We want to be out of the camp before the sun rises."

"And what will become of me?" Laska cried out.

"Don't wail, Laska," Cybula said. "We all are lost, and we all must decide whether to flee or to stay with our new masters. They will be no better than the old ones. The others began their rule with a bloodbath, these new ones may have one a little later. Or perhaps not all at once, perhaps little by little. If you want, come with us. But you must decide this moment."

"What will become of my child? I cannot leave him and run."

"Bring him along."

"He will die on the way."

"If he dies, we will bury him."

"Father, what's happened to you?" Laska began to wail.

Cybula said, "Lower your voice, Laska, or you will awaken the camp. You don't have to come with us now. We will be in the mountains, in the same cave to which you once came to arrange peace. Do you remember? Perhaps the new murderers will not begin to murder immediately. Whenever you feel ready, come and join us. If you want to stay here, stay. You are a pretty woman, perhaps someone will lie with you. This has been woman's fate throughout the generations."

"Father . . ."

"Laska, I can no longer argue with you. Take a look inside the pit near the linden tree. Perhaps something remains of the treasure. If you find something, go to Miasto. For the jewelry, you will get all that you need there. Yagoda, we are leaving!"

"What shall I take along?" Yagoda asked.

"Take only as much as you can carry. Your knife, your bow, several pelts. Don't forget your shoes. Look, dawn is breaking. Laska, please go. They should not see you leaving our hut, they'll think you helped us escape."

Cybula took Laska in his arms and kissed her—her eyes, her mouth, her forehead, both her cheeks. Her face was warm and wet. He pressed her to his chest, and for a moment father and daughter did not move. Then Cybula said, "Go, Laska."

"Oh, Tata," and Laska went out.

Wiping her tears, Yagoda asked, "Shall I take my pantaloons?"

"Take whatever you want, but quickly!"

"Shall I take the basket?"

"Yes, if you can."

"What shall I do with the meat?"

"We'll kill fresh meat on the way."

"Shall I take the dress in which I was married?"

"No. Yes."

A crimson light was shining through the hole in the hut's wall when Cybula and Yagoda went outside. Yagoda carried all kinds of utensils, pots and knives. Despite his heavy heart, Cybula felt compelled to smile. He was also laden down with things brought back from Miasto. The two walked quickly, as quickly as their burdens permitted them. Luck was with them: both the camp and the new woyaks were fast asleep. Only the birds were up: they greeted the dawn each with its own innate song. Dew fell, and a white mist rose and curled over the freshly reaped field. Cybula had put on his zupan, and he wore his sword on his hip. On his feet were the boots Ben Dosa had sewn for him. They had leather laces which he wrapped around his calves. On his head he wore his fur hat. Although Yagoda had been crying, when she looked at Cybula she began to laugh.

"Why are you laughing, Yagoda?"

"Because today you really look like a krol."

A cool breeze blew from the mountains. Before long they were past the field. The trail meandered up to the mountains, or if taken downhill, it led to Miasto. Earlier generations had treaded these twisted paths when the Lesniks had had other camps for neighbors, and when crossing each other's borders had been forbidden and necessitated fighting. Cybula took a last glance at the field, the stables, the barn. Once he had hoped that the field and the bread it enabled them to make would ennoble man, wipe out his thirst for blood, his craving for power, his hatred of others. But this had been only a futile hope. Cybula and Yagoda reached the forest; they crossed the stream. A generation ago someone had laid an oak trunk across its banks and the trunk remained, overgrown with moss, half decayed. Cybula knew that Krol Yodla and his men could easily capture the runaways on their horses. He therefore decided to avoid the main trail and to take small, winding backpaths.

12

In the Hands of the Gods

A S he and Kosoka traveled far beyond Miasto into strange lands, Ben Dosa remembered the names of the stars mentioned in the Book of Job and the saying about the scholar Samuel: He knew the roads of the sky as well as the roads of Nahardas, his own city. He also knew that the language of the land he and Kosoka were searching for— Rome or Italia—was Latin, and he even recalled the names of Italian coins from the Mishnah and the Gemara. But this did not always help them find their way in the maze of towns and roads. One thing Ben Dosa knew for certain was that the land of Israel was in the East, since the Jews in exile always turned their face toward the East while praying.

On his pilgrimage Ben Dosa quickly discovered that Bishop Mieczyslaw and the other leaders of the new religion had amassed a great following. Jews as well as Roman and Greek

Gentiles had taken on the faith of Jesus of Nazareth. They were now called Christians. Many of the Jews who converted were expelled to Rome, where, despite their loyalty to Jesus, they were imprisoned for false interpretation of the New Testament and sometimes for denying the existence of the ancient idols worshipped by the Romans and Greeks of former times.

A day did not pass without Ben Dosa and Kosoka stumbling upon some Jewish fugitive on the road. Whenever he discovered a Jew who had become a follower of Jesus, a heated religious dispute erupted, often ending in verbal abuse and even blows. These Jews would roast in the fires of hell for their heresy. When he heard their strange tales, Ben Dosa screamed, tore his hair and his beard, quoted something in Hebrew, and slapped his head in rage and disgust. He kept referring to the false Messiah from Nazareth with degrading names. And though Kosoka could never understand what evil this man had done to deserve all these vile names, she, too, cursed the heretic, in her own Tatar language.

How strange that some of these betrayers of Israel had heard of the Mishnah, the Gemara, and the other books Ben Dosa cited in his raging debates. Some of them had come from Babylon and others had left the land of Israel, often under the most hair-raising circumstances. They all seemed to Kosoka like members of one sick and deranged family that had become embroiled in bitter arguments and hatred for which there was no cure. If Kosoka could not understand a word of these religious discords, she faithfully stood by Ben Dosa, believing that he alone knew the real truth. Ben Dosa came to realize, after years of wandering, how thoroughly Kosoka had truly embraced God and the Torah. He remembered the words of the sages: In serving one's selfish desires, one may come to the service of the Almighty.

Every so often Ben Dosa met people who believed as he did, and they fell upon one another with joy. They spoke of the Holy City, Jerusalem, which was teeming with scholars and preachers, as well as the adversaries who had brought about all the misfortunes their sages had forewarned them of.

It was a long and arduous journey. Ben Dosa and Kosoka discovered new kinds of fields, bizarre customs, clothing, shoes, weapons, and vehicles they had never seen. They learned of unheard-of illnesses as well as new healing herbs, witchcraft, salves. They passed markets where criminals were tried on the streets and hung on the spot. Whores were sold and used in the open without any shame. People were be-headed on the road for robbing, for escaping from slavery, for selling men, women, and children into bondage, for rebelling against kings and war leaders. People called healers operated on the sick, wrenched out their teeth, applied salves to their wounds, and cut matted hair off their heads.

Ben Dosa often comforted Kosoka by quoting from the Talmud: If you make an effort and find what you are looking for, this is believable. If you find it without making an effort, this is unbelievable. And so it came to pass, after many years of wandering, that Ben Dosa and Kosoka were finally ap-proaching Rome. They had come to a place near the big city where Ben Dosa acquired a book of the Mishnah written by a scribe. He had also met a man who had studied a script of the Gemara. This man had left Rome after many Jews had been arrested for mentioning in their prayers their hope for the coming of the Messiah, the son of David, and for their return to the land of Israel. The man said that some Jewish-Christian females had been hiding in caves, called catacombs, and living according to the New Testament.

In Rome, small clusters of Jews who still lived according to the Talmud were also hiding—not in caves, but in little villages where they were less harassed for religious reasons. They prayed in little huts, and a few busied themselves copying volumes of the Gemara. Ben Dosa and Kosoka arrived at one of these villages and there he told them his story: he had been kidnapped and sold as a slave. The rabbi of this group was against any effort to convert Kosoka to Judaism. Above the entrance to their little synagogue were inscribed Bilam's words about the Jews in the time of Moses: *A nation that dwells alone*. The rabbi and his small congregation looked askance at Ben Dosa. To them he seemed like an adventurer who preached strange religious customs, and they could never be sure about his sincerity and his devotion to the faith. The rabbi addressed Ben Dosa in Aramaic. No one believed that Kosoka could become a true Jewess. Again and again the rabbi refused to let Kosoka convert and asked her many questions which she was incapable of answering. Did she truly believe that there was only one God and that he had given the Torah to Moses on Mount Sinai? Did she want to marry Ben Dosa only because he pleased her as a man? Was she ready to keep all 613 commandments and never miss or neglect a single one? The rabbi scolded her and treated her with suspicion, as if she was a Christian spy. He made her wash the floors and the pews of the little synagogue. Only after long conversations and examinations was she ready to immerse herself in the ritual bath and to assume the name of Sarah, as all female converts did in honor of the first Jewess, Sarai from Ur-Casdin, whose name had been changed from Sarai to Sarah. The women of the group spoke to her in broken Hebrew and Aramaic, and in the Jewish version of Latin mixed with Greek. They employed her as a maid, a cook, a handmaiden for their children and for the women who perform ablutions in the ritual bath after menstruation. It took some time before Sarah learned how to count seven clean days after her menstruation, and how to avoid lighting a fire on the Sabbath. She carried things on the Sabbath from the Eruv, a marked border which one is not allowed to cross or beyond which one may not carry anything on the Sabbath. However, more and more, the community agreed that she was genuinely willing to do her work and to learn humility and the proper Jewish conduct.

The men of the village tried to learn the oral Torah from Ben Dosa. They also needed a teacher of the aleph-beth for their little children, one who would explain to them the laws of Moses and the holy word of the Pentateuch, as it was called in the language of the Greeks. He could help them correct mistakes that had fallen into their version of the Gemara. They all remembered the words that Rabbi Yochamin Ben Zaki had given to the invaders of Zion: Give me Yavna and its sages. Yes, they had as much trust in Kosoka as their rabbi finally had. And they were prepared to build a little hut for Ben Dosa and his bride after they were married.

It was considered appropriate for Sarah to fast on the day of her wedding, and to wash the feet of old and sick women as the start of doing good deeds. When she was given a quill and taught to sign her name on the *ketubah*, she burst out wailing and could not hold the quill in her trembling hands. No wine was allowed at the poor repast when the seven blessings were recited. To be a Jew in exile meant permanent mourning. Just the same, they put up an old silk-woven *chuppah*, or canopy, and found a shabby silk dress for the bride. They covered her face with a faded veil and provided her with an old silver ring.

Ben Dosa was dressed for the occasion in a white robe, in order never to forget that in the end every man must die and be dressed in a shroud. There was a custom among the Jews that at the beginning of the ceremony the bride be led around the bridegroom seven times, in keeping with the saying of the prophet: And the female will surround the male.

The whole wedding ceremony took place under the stars. In his speech, the rabbi mentioned the names of Ben Dosa's father, Dosa, who had been a teacher of Jewish children in the town of Sura. While the ketubah was being written, the rabbi asked the bride if she was a virgin, and this caused an outburst of laughter among those present.

It was the custom that an earthen dish be broken by the bridegroom at the end of the ceremony, to symbolize the destruction of the temple. Ben Dosa stamped on it with his right shoe, and as it shattered, it was taken as a sign that he was still young and potent. When Kosoka was handed the customary goblet of wine, it slipped out of her hand, which was considered a bad omen, that she would die in childbirth. But Ben Dosa said the Jews were not allowed to believe in such superstitions; according to the Talmud, the life and good fortune of Jews did not depend on the stars, for it is written: Astrology does not determine the fate of the nation of Israel.

(2)

Cybula and Yagoda spent the first night after their flight in the same cave in which they hid on the night Kora killed Lis. They found a pelt they had left behind, remnants of coals from the fire they had lit, bones from the meals they had eaten. The river that flowed at the bottom of the cave gurgled and splashed now as it did then.

It was pleasant to be alone once again with Yagoda. Cybula could tell her whatever came into his head: words of wisdom, foolish words. He could boast to her, invent lies, chatter about his dreams, daydreams, his exploits with women. She listened to everything, even demanded more. Sometimes she asked a question which proved to Cybula that she really understood him. Sometimes like a child she begged him, "Tell me a story." And Cybula would begin to spin a tale, inventing it as he went along.

Outside the cave it was the end of summer. But inside there was a chill which Cybula had not felt before. Yagoda snuggled close to him, trying to warm his body with her belly and breasts. But from time to time a frosty wind ran down his back. During the day, while pursuing an animal, Cybula realized that his eyesight was not what it once had been. How had this come about? When? He closed his right eye, and it was clear to him that the left eye did not see as well as the right. He made up his mind not to tell Yagoda. She was worried about his health, and complained that he ate too little. He used to eat raw flesh, from which the blood still ran, but he had suddenly acquired an aversion to blood. Ben Dosa had said that when Cain slew Abel, the God of Jerusalem told him: "Your brother's blood cries to me from the earth." Cybula now thought that he could hear the animals' blood calling out of the earth: "Why do you kill us? What harm have we done you? What if someone were to shed your blood?"

Yagoda went in search of animals and fish, while Cybula sat outside, warming himself in the sun and scribbling letters and words. He was not ill, but he was also not well. The cave did not suit him as it once had. He had grown accustomed to sleeping in a bed, not on rocks. Since meat was no longer acceptable, he longed for bread, for pretzels baked on hot stones, for the porridge which Kora sometimes cooked for him of oats and with mushrooms to enrich the taste. Something puzzled him, and he could not rest until he found the answer. He was unable to stop thinking about Kora. She had always spoken about her great love for him. She had always sought ways to please him. She had risked her life for him. At every opportunity she said that he, Cybula, was her god, and that she would not live an instant after he was gone. And at the same time, she was frolicking with a band of robbers, thieves, and murderers, disgracing herself and the memory of her murdered children. Cybula thought that until he solved this riddle he would not be able to die.

Cybula also missed Ben Dosa. Where was he now? He would probably lose his life during his journey to faraway lands. How good it would be to have him here, to listen to his tales, his parables, the wisdom he gleaned from books written by gods in faraway cities, in faraway times. And then, all at once, Cybula himself began to speak to the gods.

"God of Jerusalem, are you really here with me? Are your eyes everywhere and do they see everything? Do you know where Ben Dosa is? Is Kosoka still with him?"

Another time Cybula spoke to the god of death. "Shmiercz, god of all gods, are you really the most powerful? I will serve no one but you. As the god Sun shines on everything alike, so you bring death to everything alike. When you lay your hand on someone's head, all his cares cease: hunger, thirst, all ills, all pain. You are the ruler of the mountains and valleys, all rivers, all rocks. Whoever is in your hand knows true rest. Bestow your peace upon me, Shmiercz. I am tired of the gods of life."

It was too dark in the cave for him to write, and so, with a knife he had bought in Miasto, he tried to carve a figure out of a block of wood. It was to be the god of death. Cybula planned to carve the likeness of a skeleton, with a hole for a nose, and with teeth but no mouth. It was not an easy task, but he knew he would succeed. He had both time and patience. Yagoda slept, awakened, slept again. So it went through the day and the evening. Clearly she was troubled with something, but what it was, Cybula did not know. Whenever he asked her, she had but one answer: "It's nothing." Once she blurted out, "It's you!"

"Are you thinking about your matka?"

"Yes. No."

"Do you miss Kora?"

"No."

"Would you be angry if I killed her?"

"Why didn't you? She herself begged you to kill her."

"It is too late now. Besides, death is too good for her. If

I had killed her, she would have had peace. Death is not a punishment, Yagoda."

Although the days had already grown shorter, that day dragged on. For the evening meal Yagoda gave Cybula a chunk of fish and two apples. But Cybula ate only half of one apple. Yagoda said, "If you eat so little, you will lose your strength."

"I don't need strength."

No sooner had he uttered these words than a noise was heard outside, near the cave's opening. Cybula sprang up, agitated. Had Krol Yodla's riders come for him? By the light of the fire he recognized Kora. Yagoda cried out, "Matka!"

"Yes, it is I," Kora said. "I've come to you out of the hollows of the earth."

Cybula and Yagoda stood and stared. Kora said, "Come, help me. I've brought along a horse."

Cybula instantly felt new strength streaming into his body. He hurried to the cave's opening, and Kora motioned him to come outside. In the dim light which shone out of the cave he saw a horse tied to a tree, laden with bags and satchels. Kora herself was wrapped in fur skins. He heard her say, "I couldn't live without you."

"You miserable whore!"

"I suppose that is what I am."

And she threw herself upon Cybula, embracing him, kissing him, weeping.

"Where did you get a horse?" Cybula asked.

"I stole it."

"How is Laska?" he asked, his voice quivering.

"Ptashek recovered. Krol Yodla took Laska for himself."

"He took her for a wife?"

"He already has three others."

"Did you see her before you left?"

"They did not let me near her. She is a good-looking woman, she will do well. They always need women like her," Kora said. "I couldn't live without you." There was a change in Kora's voice. "I tried but I couldn't."

"And the field?"

"They've sown the winter wheat."

Cybula wanted to thank the gods, but restrained himself. "It will be easier to die now," he said.

"Together with me," Kora said.

He stood in the darkness and shivered, not knowing whether from the cold or from Kora's return.

"I tried to live without you," Kora started again, "but I couldn't. I thought of you day and night. I couldn't sleep. A fire burned in my hut, but I was cold. I was cold as I've never been before. I covered myself with all the pelts I had, but I was still cold. This was not the ordinary cold, it could have come only from Baba Yaga. Once I left the camp and was on my way to you, I felt warm—despite all the rain and snow."

"All those riders couldn't warm you?" Cybula asked.

"Be still, Cybula, don't be so sharp-tongued."

"Tell me about the camp."

"There is much work. Krol Yodla wants to be the krol of all krols. He meddles in everything, sticks his nose into every pot. The horse I took is not theirs but yours, from Miasto."

"How is Nosek?" Cybula asked.

"Nosek joined them. He does whatever Krol Yodla tells him to do. He lives with Wilk and his mother now. Oh, that Nosek is like a man shaped from clay. He and Piesek are now

Krol Yodla's kniezes. I proposed to Nosek that he come with me, but he said, 'Kora, I am deaf; I heard nothing.' Those were his words. He is forever counting and calculating. Krol Yodla released him from plowing the field for the winter wheat because Nosek is to devote all his time to counting and measuring and weighing. Piesek also. They are a pair of stuffed men, like birds that are stuffed and only look as if they are alive."

Yagoda came out of the cave.

Kora asked, "You no longer kiss me, eh? I am still your mother."

Yagoda did not answer. Cybula said, "You may kiss her. Whatever else she is, she is your mother."

Yagoda remained silent.

That night Cybula demanded that Kora tell him the truth, the whole truth, and Kora did as she was told. It was difficult to know whether Yagoda slept or only pretended to sleep. Kora enumerated all the men she had had since she had begun to mature. Cybula asked her to leave nothing out, and it seemed that Kora remembered every instant of passion with these soldiers, even the words that were spoken to her, and the frivolous nicknames by which she was called. At times Cybula asked, "Were you not ashamed?"

And Kora answered, "No. Not for a second."

"He spat at you, and you kissed him?"

"Yes."

"It gave you pleasure?"

"Great pleasure."

From time to time Cybula slapped her, grabbed her hair, pulled it. She said, "Pull, my god, torture me."

Once again he became young and strong. He entered her

and she shrieked, "You are the best, the strongest! Not a man but a god, a young god! Tear my flesh, stab me, break my bones, drink my blood! Kill me!"

"That is what I shall do."

"Yes, I came to you for this."

"You want to die?"

"Without you I don't want to live."

"You lie!"

"No, no, my god. Why should I? I could have stayed in the camp. They all wanted me. They swallowed me with their eyes, from the youngest rider to Krol Yodla himself. But I left them all and came to you, through rain and snow."

"You came to see your daughter."

"To see my daughter? She is not my daughter now, I am not her mother. If I saw her devoured by wolves, I would not lift a finger to help her."

"What would you do if I were to kill her?"

"You could cut her throat and I would kiss your hands. I would lick the blood off the knife."

"Don't you ever have pity for anyone?"

"I have no pity."

"You are a liar from your head to the tips of your toes. A word of truth has not yet left your swinish mouth," Cybula said.

"Ah, my sweet, how gently you speak to me. No one has spoken to me as you. Not even Ben Dosa."

"You wanted him, too?"

"Very much so. But he refused me all the time. When he tried to teach me to read and to write and he bent over me, I used to think to myself, I wonder how he is with a woman."

For a while no one spoke. Then Cybula asked, "Why did you come here?"

"I told you. To die."

"Is this the truth?"

"Without you it made no sense. I enjoyed other men as long as I could go from them to you, lie in your arms, hear you speak, kiss your feet. But when you were not there, I wanted no one. Yagoda has attached herself to you like a leech, and you let her hang from your neck and suck your blood. And yet you ran away from me. Why?"

"Because she is truthful, while you lie."

"My love for you is not a lie."

"I love her, while you I despise."

"Your words sting. How can you hate one who loves you so much? You yourself also lie. Do you believe in the hollows of the earth?"

"No."

"What becomes of us when we die?"

"Ashes and dust."

"Out of ashes a rose may grow."

"Out of your ashes nothing will grow but thorns."

"As long as *something* grows. I am tired, Cybula, very tired. Do you really want to die?"

"Yes, Kora."

"Will you kill me first?"

"If you don't run away."

"I won't run away, my sweet. I have had enough of everything, except you. When will you kill me?"

"In as many days as you have fingers on one hand."

"Five days?"

"Yes."

"And what will you do with your leech, my daughter?"

"Crush her."

"She is carrying your child in her womb. You planned to bring forth a new generation through her."

"Nothing will come of it."

Cybula and Kora lay down and soon they fell asleep. Before dawn Cybula awoke, he was not sure why. By the glow of the coals he saw Yagoda standing, a bloody ax in her hand. "Yagoda, what are you doing?"

"I have killed my matka," she answered.

Cybula said nothing. Then he asked, "Why, Yagoda?"

And Yagoda answered, "It was what she wanted herself."

That morning Cybula and Yagoda climbed up one of the high mountains. The sun was shining and the air was warm. Husband and wife were wrapped in fur skins and wearing shoes on their feet. Cybula was holding Yagoda by the hand, having told her where he would lead her. Now they walked together, neither quickly nor slowly. When they reached the summit, a yawning chasm stretched far below. They stood on the rim of the rocky ledge and looked down. There in the depths a narrow river flowed, white with froth. Cybula said, "Soon we will join your mother."

"Where is she?" Yagoda asked.

And Cybula answered, "In the hands of the gods."